Faking the Fall

Faking the Fall

JULIE CHRISTIANSON

This one's for Bill, my favorite-favorite.

Roses are red.
Violets are blue.
See you at the church.

XO

Content Awareness

More than anything, I want *Faking the Fall* to be funny, romantic, and sweet.

I also want to take care of my readers.

So while the majority of this romcom is light-hearted, and low-angst, please note this story does address the loss of loved ones in the past. (Not on the page.)

If this subject is tender for you, be gentle with your heart.

Love,
Julie

Contents

Chapter One

HADLEY

Five Years Ago

The air is crisp, but my palms are sweating, so I ignore the other contestants gathered in the square and focus on the mountains in the distance. Whatever happens today, that Blue Ridge will still be here tomorrow, because some things never change, right? Like the sun's orbit, the ocean's tide, and people's love for pumpkin spice lattes. Wait.

Unless orbits and tides *do* change.

I'm a music major. What do I know?

Still, I've never seen a crowd this big in Asheville. Not even during Oktoberfest. So I draw in a deep, cleansing breath and try not to choke on my own nerves.

"Hey, Goober." I swallow hard. "Would you pass me a turkey and provolone?" I wipe my hands down the thighs of my jeans and glance sideways at James. We're on a stone bench under a big leafy sugar maple whose yellow leaves are just starting to drop.

He meets my gaze and my stomach does a loop. Flip flop flip. Not because James is handsome and funny and loyal, although he's definitely all of those things. It's just that he's also sitting between me and my fully stocked picnic cooler.

In their email to contestants, producers warned us the auditions for *America's Hidden Talent* could last all day, and Hadley Morgan likes to be prepared.

Prepared means a picnic cooler full of sandwiches and apple slices.

James peers at me from under a swoop of black hair. Somehow his eyes are even darker than black, with a fringe of lashes so long and thick you could hang twinkle lights on them. Not that I've thought about his lashes every Christmas since we met.

"Pretty please?" I add, then I flutter my lids like a flirty cartoon character, but I'm not *actually* flirting with James. For one thing, we're just friends. *Good* friends. And yes, maybe I held out hope we could be more, but James never showed any interest.

Eventually I gave up and found Carson.

Or Carson found me.

Either way, it's been a month since Carson ended things—for the third time—and I'm here today to prove I'm not *unadventurous* and *lacking spontaneity* like he claims.

After I ace these adventurous and spontaneous auditions, Carson will probably beg to get back together. Of course, there's only so many chances one guy deserves.

Fool me once, shame on you.

Fool me *three* times, and you might be out of luck, buddy.

So I'm single now and sitting here with James of the twinkle-light eyes and the extra-long lashes. The man could have anybody he wants, and I've never been one of his *anybodies,* so I definitely shouldn't risk my heart now, right?

No.

Today's audition plans aside, I'm not *that* spontaneous or adventurous.

"Didn't you already eat a sandwich and an entire apple?" he asks, arching one dark eyebrow.

"Don't judge me, Goober." My lips twitch. "I always eat when I'm nervous." I call James "Goober" to remind myself we have no romantic future, and also because he hogs all the boxes of chocolate-covered peanuts in the residence hall vending machines.

We're both seniors at Carolina University. I'm an RA, and James has always done work study jobs on campus. We became friends when we were freshmen because—well—we both spent a lot of time at the vending machines.

And did I mention he's hilarious?

And also loyal and handsome?

"How come I'm just finding out about this?" he asks.

"Maybe you haven't been paying attention."

As the words come out, I feel my nose wrinkle, so I probably look like I'm smelling something bad. Which I'm definitely not. James smells more delicious than chocolate-covered peanuts. Just don't tell him I said that. I can't be responsible if he gets a swollen head.

I mean, the guy looks like a Calvin Klein underwear model, but he's not even a little bit arrogant. He *should* have an ego the size of the Goodyear blimp given how good-looking and good-smelling he is.

But he doesn't.

"Or maybe," he says, "you just haven't been nervous when you're around me." He pokes my nose, then the tip of his finger slides down to brush my lips. Tingles shoot straight up my nostrils. For the record, this feels as strange as it sounds.

"What was that for?" I blurt.

His eyes lock with mine. "I *do* pay attention," he says. "And you had a little something on the corner of your mouth."

Awesome.

Leave it to me to have mayonnaise smeared on my face. Luckily, James gets busy digging in the cooler, so he doesn't see me blushing. He pulls out a foil-wrapped rectangle labeled TP.

To be clear, that stands for turkey and provolone, not toilet paper.

When James hands over the sandwich, I totally ignore the warmth of his touch.

Almost totally.

You're just friends, Hadley. Don't forget.

In fact, James knows he's only here because my dad didn't want me outside alone before sunrise. This part of the city isn't necessarily unsafe, but since I've been away at school, my father tends to worry. And he's got his reasons for being protective, so I promised I'd get someone to tag along with me. Someone big and strong who could ward off muggers and marauders.

Enter James "Goober" Lincoln.

Peeling the foil off of the sandwich, I start to fan myself with the napkin underneath. James stifles a smile. "You all right, there, Hads?"

"Don't laugh." I nudge his elbow. "I'm worried about boob sweat." As soon as the words are out, my throat flames hot. Why do I say things like this to anyone, let alone Goober the Gorgeous?

"You shouldn't be nervous," he says. His eyes go soft. "They're going to love you."

I wince. "The hosts of the show hate almost everyone. It's part of their act. So I just need to survive the first round to prove I've got as much spontaneity and adventure as the next girl."

James frowns. "Carson's an idiot."

I nod and take a bite of turkey. Chew. Chew. Swallow. I wait for James to expand on his statement, perhaps saying something like, "If we were dating, I'd never break up with you, Hads. Especially not three times." But he doesn't. So instead I blurt, "I just hope I don't get pit stains before my number's called."

James darts his gaze to my armpits, and I let out a strangled "gah" over a mouthful of bread and deli meat. "Am I already pitting?"

"Relax, Hads." He lifts his focus to make eye contact. I sure do love it when he calls me that. He puts a hand on my shoulder, and his touch sends a welcome shiver up my spine. "You look fantastic," he says.

Fantastic might be an overstatement, but I did make an effort today. I'm wearing a long sweater over narrow jeans and a pair of slouchy boots. My hair is in a loose braid, and in a shade of blonde that lands somewhere between honey and wheat. But if I'm being honest, this sounds more delicious than my hair actually is.

Since my eyes are my best feature, I swiped on an extra layer of mascara hoping if my voice fails, these baby blues will pop enough for the judges to advance me.

"You sure you don't want to try out today, just for fun?" When I ask this, a crumb flies out of my mouth and almost lands on James. I can practically hear my dad saying, "This is why you shouldn't talk with your mouth full."

James ignores my flying speck and shakes his head. "I don't sing."

"Neither do a lot of people who audition." I shrug. "You could always make the blooper reel."

"Nah. I can't compete with your adventurousness and spontaneity."

"So you're just going to hang out here all day for no good reason?"

He bumps my shoulder. "I'm here for you."

"Thanks," I say, and a wave of warmth floods my insides.

Fabulous. More sweat.

"I can't even imagine standing in front of a table of judges and performing. Everyone watching. Staring. Evaluating." James racks his body in exaggerated horror. "What a nightmare."

"Nice pep talk." I cough out a laugh, grateful no more sandwich flies out. "But seriously, I feel pretty good about the song."

He tilts his head. "Did you decide on 'Today Was a Fairytale'?"

"Yep." I ball up my foil. "Can't go wrong with Taylor Swift. I just wish I could've brought Dolores."

Dolores is my mom's guitar. My mother always dreamed of being a singer, and I've always dreamed of making her proud.

Unfortunately contestants aren't allowed to use instruments in their audition, no matter how many times they beg.

Ask me how I know.

"She'll be with you," James says. I peek at him, and his jaw shifts. I don't know if he's talking about the guitar or my mom—neither of which could actually be here. Guitars aren't allowed, and my mom's been gone since I was a baby.

I don't even remember the accident.

"Look." James nods at the big brick building. A lanky producer in a hipster fedora emerges from a pair of sliding glass doors. He's got a bullhorn, and everyone who's been milling around stops their conversations to listen.

"Thanks for your patience," he calls out to the crowd. "Hopefully you all have your assigned numbers."

"Check," I say to myself, patting the square patch of paper safety-pinned to my sweater.

"If your number has an *A* at the top, you'll be first to head inside," he says.

I was randomly assigned to the *H* group, which means I've got a wait ahead of me. Still, the fact that *H* is the first letter of my name feels like a good sign.

My fingers slide up to the thin gold chain with the *H* charm. There's a small pearl in the center. My dad gave me the necklace for my twenty-first birthday. He said the world is my oyster. Then he made me birthday meatloaf.

It's a long story.

"Let's go, group A," fedora-man says. The contestants gather at the entrance, filing in behind him. I memorized the agenda for audition day, so I know they'll be led to an air-conditioned theater before waiting their turn in the room with the judges. That's why I wore this sweater in the first place.

Cold air outside. Cold air in.

Too bad I can't stop sweating.

A woman in a narrow pencil skirt with a platinum bob clicks toward the benches in cherry-red patent leather heels. Along the way, she examines everyone she passes. She's pretty. I'd guess in her late thirties. She's probably a secret talent scout for the show, sent out early to choose a few people to feature in the first episode.

I straighten, and reach up to smooth my braid. As the woman approaches our bench, her laser-sharp focus darts between James and me. Her eyes widen.

Can she see the boob sweat through my sweater?

Her white blouse is tucked into her skirt and accessorized with a thick black belt. She looks like she's never had boob sweat in her life. "Hello, there," she murmurs at James. Her lips are as red and shiny as her shoes. "Are you a *Hidden Talent* contestant?" she asks him.

He lifts a hand to his chest, laying his palm on pecs so well-defined I can see them through his long-sleeved Henley. "Me? No. I don't have any talent."

"Perfect." She reaches for her clutch, her long nails working the latch.

I put on an extra-bright smile because my dad raised me to be kind. Not to mention, I need to do well today, and this woman in the pencil skirt could give me a leg up. "I'm Hadley," I chirp. "Hadley Morgan. And I *am* a *Hidden Talent* contestant."

She lifts her gaze, and I stick out my hand. Unfortunately, I'm still holding a ball of foil full of sandwich crumbs. So I shove the foil at James, like that was my plan all along. As I shake hands with Pencil-skirt, I grin at her, trying again. "I like your shoes," I say. "You're with the show, right?"

She glances at the building, clearly trying to stay under the radar.

But I'm onto you, lady.

"I'm in group H, waiting to audition," I tell her, "but I'm totally prepared to sing right now in the square. I've seen them film stuff like that on earlier seasons. Is that what you're out here scouting for? People to showcase in the highlight reels? I'll bet you have a film crew waiting in the lobby, and you're going to contact them on a walkie-talkie you're hiding in your—"

"Hadley," she interrupts. "You did say your name was Hadley, didn't you?"

"Yes!" I beam at her. "Hadley Morgan. I'm twenty-one, and a North Carolina native from Harvest Hollow." Pencil-skirt offers me a small smile that's a little too close to pity.

"I'm sorry to disappoint you, Ms. Morgan, but I've got nothing to do with this show." She starts to hunt in her purse again.

"Do you need a tissue?" I ask. "I have a tissue in my bag."

She looks up. "I don't need a tissue." She flicks her eyes to the left. "I need him."

Him?

Gulp. Is she talking about James?

"He doesn't sing," I rush to say, but it's a ludicrous thing to tell her, considering she admitted she's not part of the show, and James already told her he's not a contestant.

He clears his throat. "I'm just here for Hadley."

The words thrum in my chest. *I'm here for Hadley*. My pulse races even though it shouldn't. And when he scoots an inch closer to me, my body vibrates with his closeness.

Pencil-skirt purses her lips.

"You might change your mind when you hear what I have to say." Wow. She's really not giving up. "You've got a great look," she continues. "Like Zac Efron." She peers down at him. "You could absolutely be Garrison Plum's son."

James scrunches his perfect nose. "The guy from the *Enforcer* movies?"

She nods. "The studio is planning a prequel when Magnetron's just coming into his power."

"But I think Zac Efron has a beard," I interject, and my cheeks get hot. "James doesn't," I add pointlessly.

The woman tips her chin. "James. Hmm." Hearing her repeat his name raises goose bumps on my neck. "We might have to come up with something snappier than James."

"James is already snappy," I say.

"Who's we?" he asks.

"I'm an agent with The Browne Agency," she says. "Ever heard of us?"

He hitches his shoulders. "Nope."

"I'm not surprised"—she glances around the square—"given our current location. We're based in Hollywood, but I've been traveling to *Hidden Talent* auditions across the country, in search of someone with the right ... *je ne sais quoi*. And you, young man, have *it*!" She bites down on the *T* so hard, I'm surprised spit doesn't fly out of her mouth. But I guess spitting stuff on James is my specialty, not hers.

"We don't speak French," I mumble, and my body slumps. This woman doesn't care about me at all. She pulls a wallet from her purse, and slips out a business card.

"My name is Pippa Sergeant, and I think we could do big things together."

Big things? I suck in air. *In Hollywood?*

She aims a crooked smile at James. "How would you like to be in the movies, young man?"

"He's a student," I blurt.

"He could be a star," she says.

"I have no talent," James adds.

"You look like this." She sweeps a hand up and down in front of him. "The rest we can work with."

"I'm not an actor," he insists.

"The Browne Agency works with the best acting coaches in the world. And the best agents." She lays a hand over her heart. "*I'm* their best. Besides, we're talking about superhero films. It's not like you'll be in the running for an Academy Award ..."

"Thanks," he says. "But I'm not interested."

I let out a breath, and my insides flood with relief. Not that I thought James would really consider leaving North Carolina. To be an actor? In Hollywood?

It's way too unrealistic and risky. He needs to get his degree first. Even if I *won America's Hidden Talent*, I'd still finish—

"Take the card," Pippa says, holding it out to James. "No obligation to call, of course. But I do hope you call."

He takes the card.

Three hours later, the *Hidden Talent* judges send me packing after the first round.

Three days later, James texts me from a plane to California.

Goober: We're about to take off. I'm so sorry. And Carson's still an idiot.

Chapter Two

LINK

Present Day

"Are you the *real* Magnetron?" A girl with curly pigtails props herself up in the too-big hospital bed. Her gown is covered in teddy bears, and she's got an IV line taped above her wrist.

"Shh." I glance around like I'm about to reveal a secret, then I sneak her a quick nod.

"Whoa." Her eyes are wide as frisbees. "You *promise* you're not one of those *pretend* Magnetrons my mom takes me and Griffin to see at the mall? They're always so fake."

"Nope. I'm the real deal." I plant my enormous red boots wide, and strike Magnetron's signature pose—fists at my side, elbows out at right angles. "See?" This is the stance Magnetron uses in all the *Enforcer* movies when he's about to melt one of his enemies by shooting laser beams from his pupils.

"You're my favorite superhero!"

I put a big glove over my chest. "I am?" I flash her a grin. "That's the best news I've heard since I found out I could cook bad guys from the inside out." I tilt my head at the door that leads to the nurses' station. "Don't tell the others, okay?" I use my deep Magnetron voice and try to stay in character, which is hard to do next to a hospital bed. We're at Highland Hospital in Los Angeles, but no amount of palm trees in the parking lot can change what this place means.

It's one thing to play Magnetron for the cameras, in full costume, reading from a script. It's another to be a superhero in front of a publicity team that's just trying to make me look good.

We're here staging photo ops to be splashed all over every social media platform known to man. But if you've read any of my interviews from the past five years, you'll know I never claimed to be an actor. Becoming a movie star kind of just happened to me. Now I feel worse than a fish out of water.

Scratch that. I'm more like a fish out of water that's been tossed into a frying pan before flopping over the edge into the fire.

But I get it. Poor me, right? It's hard to feel sorry for some random guy who got famous for looking like Garrison Plum's kid.

"And who are you?" I ask the little girl.

"I'm Violet. Violet Ludgate. And I'm going to be a singer like Taylor Swift."

"Yeah, you are." I smile and high-five Violet again as memories of Hadley clog my throat, and the old familiar ache of longing for her floods all major arteries. I hated seeing her with Carson, spent years wishing I was good enough for her. And even after I made a clean break for both our sakes, I'm still caught off guard by the reminders.

Not like you've been trying to forget.

"My brother's name is Griffin," Violet chirps, hauling me back to the here and now. "But he's home with my dad. My mom's in the cafeteria. She says the burritos here are going straight to her hips."

"Hmm." I nod, all seriousness. "Thanks for the tip."

"My dad says my mom's totally lovesick over you. Which isn't the real kind of sick. But she's going to be so sad she missed you.

So will Griffin. He's not in the hospital because he isn't *any* kind of sick."

"Well, I'm glad to hear that, for Griffin's sake, and I'm very happy to meet you, Violet." I reach my giant gray glove out for a high five, and she lifts her arm—the one that *doesn't* have an IV linked to it—and pats me with her tiny hand.

A part of me wants to ask Violet why she's here, but the other part is grateful not to know. That way I can pretend the reason she's in the hospital isn't serious.

Like a tonsillectomy. Something routine and non-life-threatening.

A nurse enters the room and gasps when she sees me. "Oh my." She's got Violet's chart pressed to her blue scrubs.

"Hey, there." I address the nurse, dropping my Magnetron voice for a moment.

"You're Lincoln—"

"I'm Magnetron," I say, cutting her off. "Do you need to get in here to check on Violet or something?"

The nurse's throat flushes—like she's got a neck full of hives—and she stutters, "Oh, no, no. No, no. I'm just ... no. Thank you. I'm fine."

It's been five years since I took this role in the *Enforcer* franchise, and I'm still not used to grown women finding this superhero stuff so attractive. I'm literally in a costume made of red rubber with oversized gray fists. Like a human magnet with fake abs.

To be clear, the abs underneath the suit are all mine. Youngblood Studios has had me working with a trainer since the day I signed my contract. But Magnetron's muscles are ... ridiculous. Real men don't have eighteen rows of abs.

A photographer comes from behind me and shoves his camera lens in poor Violet's face. He's got a body like a fire hydrant and the hair of a circus clown. He takes a series of close-ups of Violet without her permission. I'm sure Pippa will have her mom sign a waiver, but the fact that this guy doesn't even ask

Violet if she's okay with getting her picture taken rubs me the wrong way.

"Move closer to the kid again," he barks over his shoulder. When he turns back toward Violet, she recoils. "Now, you. Little girl. Stare up at Magnetron like he's your hero."

"He *is,*" she announces. "My *favorite* superhero."

"Don't tell me," the photographer grunts. "Show the camera."

Hackles rise along my neck. This publicity stuff is *not* part of the job I love. I glance at Pippa who's standing in the corner. She isn't paying attention, but that's my fault. I asked her to monitor the nanny cam on my phone while my dogs are home alone.

Our usual photographer, Sam, always tries to make our sessions as authentic as possible. He's a family guy with kids of his own. Twin girls who are five. He'd be way better at this than the fire hydrant clown.

"Hold still," he yelps at me and Violet. "Now do that high five thing you did with her before. Right. Again. Again. Good."

Violet and I recreate our high five, but it feels stiff and forced now, not like the real connection we had the first time.

"Hey, Pippa," I call out. "Why isn't Sam here today?"

She looks up from my phone. "First day of kindergarten for the twins."

"Great," I mutter. I don't begrudge Sam the chance to be with his family. His wife, Tanya, is an angel on earth, and their girls call me Uncle Wink. So I'm glad they're together today. I just wish Sam's temporary replacement wasn't so sleazy.

"Just a few more rooms to visit," Pippa says, as the guy snaps even more shots of me with Violet.

"Fine," I say under my breath.

"What's wrong, Link?"

"Nothing." I send up a silent prayer of gratitude that at least we're not in a wing with terminal patients.

"You're an actor." Pippa cocks an eyebrow. "This is all part of the job."

Violet frowns, her bottom lip in a pout. "You said you're the *real* Magnetron."

Thanks for blowing my cover, Pip.

"I am," I assure Violet in my best Magnetron voice. "And to prove it, I've got something for you." I stride over to the promotional bag on a chair next to Pippa.

"Is it a guitar?" Violet asks. When I turn, a grin spreads across her face. "Just like Taylor Swift?"

Again, my heart squeezes as I picture Hadley with Dolores, her mom's guitar. When she'd play in the quad, I let myself believe she was singing just for me. But deep down, I knew better. I wasn't right for someone so whole and happy.

"Sadly, what I've got isn't quite as good, but almost ..." I pull out a plastic rendering of Magnetron's secret weapon. "Surprise!" It's a red and gray magnet.

"Whoa." Violet claps her hands.

I cross the room and hand her the magnet with a broad flourish. "For my favorite Violet."

"Thanks, Magnetron," she gushes. "This is the best day ever. Griffin's going to be so jealous he's not in the hospital."

While she pretends to wield the magnet like a weapon, the photographer moves around her bed taking shots from different angles. Then he cuts his eyes to me. "Time to go, Link."

"Ahem." I tip my head, warning him with my eyes. "You mean *Magnetron.*"

He harrumphs. "Yeah. Right. Sorry, *Magnetron.*" He nods at the clock on the opposite wall. "I've already got enough shots of you and this kid. We need to move it along."

I square my shoulders and turn back to Violet. "It was a pleasure meeting you." I give her my best superhero bow. "You feel better soon, young lady."

She beams at me, her pale cheeks shining. "I will, now that I met you."

Man, her doctors better be good.

With a pit in my gut, I head out with the photographer hot

on my heels. In the hall, I pause in front of the nurses' station, looking both ways. Pippa probably knows which direction we're supposed to head next.

The photographer cranes his neck to talk directly into my ear. "Let's get you in with a kid who looks worse than that last one," he says. "A real sick one will tug on the ladies' heartstrings."

A low rumble begins in my throat, and heat flares across my chest. It's the kind of roiling swirl I'd expect from Magnetron if children were being reduced to a publicity stunt.

Before I can tell this joker exactly where to shove his camera, Pippa approaches carrying my phone and her bag of magnets.

"What's the problem, gentlemen?"

I grit my teeth. "The problem is this guy's a total—"

"Hey! Don't blame me," the photographer interrupts. "Andrew told me he wants every woman in America eating out of Link's hands when *Enforcer's Endgame* opens."

I groan. Andrew's my manager. He's stationed outside this wing making sure no paparazzi get through. I like Andrew well enough, but we don't always see eye to eye when it comes to career decisions.

He says that's *exactly* why he's essential—that I need a yin to my yang. Whatever. Andrew can be my palm-pressing yin.

My yang still wants to melt this photographer.

"Let's get this over with," I mutter.

"Too bad we're not allowed in the ICU," the photographer says. "Imagine the photo ops in there."

"These are kids," I growl. "Not photo ops."

He lowers his camera. "But I'd love to get shots of you hovering over the bed of some baldy with can—"

In a flash my fist connects with his jaw, but I'm wearing Magnetron's big rubber gloves, so I miss the satisfying crunch of bone on bone. The photographer stumbles backward, and his camera crashes to the floor. I take a step forward, and he backs up against the wall.

Pippa steps between us. "Link!"

"Don't worry." I meet her stern gaze. "I won't hit him again. This trash isn't worth it."

"You're going to regret this," the photographer spits out.

"You'll be fine," I say. "The glove saved you." That's when I spot a crew with cameras coming toward us down the hallway.

Paparazzi? How did they get past Andrew? They probably captured this entire exchange.

Uh-oh.

My gut clamps down.

This can't be good for Magnetron's yang.

Chapter Three

HADLEY

"Honey, I'm home!" Nina shouts this from the door of our two-bed, two-bath bungalow. I'm across the house in the kitchen, so I can barely hear her over the playlist blasting from my phone. We've been renting this place since we both got hired at Harvest Hollow High. That was last fall—one short year ago—but it sure feels longer.

When we met, Nina Bennett and I were just two newbies with fresh teaching credentials who wanted to live on our own. Now she's pretty much my best friend. A ride-or-die kind of girl. So I forgive her for loving math more than music.

Nobody's perfect.

"I'm in here!" I call out, turning the volume all the way down.

Nina's keys jingle as she tosses the ring into our key dish. We drove to school separately so she could stay late to finally finish decorating her classroom. I, of course, finished decorating mine the same day summer school ended. The cinder block walls of my room in the performing arts building are covered with posters of my favorite musicals and musicians, not to mention the best original songs written by last year's students. As an extra touch, I even lined the windows with strands of curling ribbon.

Just for fun.

Nina comes around the corner in her standard uniform of fitted trousers and a tailored blazer. I myself prefer bohemian skirts and oversized cardigans. Our math teacher versus choir director stereotypes are well-established.

"Oh, Hadley, no." She stops cold, her eyes narrowing under a fringe of bangs so dark and thick you can't even see her brows. "Did Carson call again?"

"Carson?" I slip a tray of my famous apple-crumble cupcakes from the oven and set it on the butcher block counter. "What makes you say that?"

She drops her bag onto a stool next to the island. "Because you turned into a one-woman bakery the last time he begged you for forgiveness."

Spoiler alert: Carson and I reconciled shortly after I bombed the *America's Hidden Talent* auditions. This was, coincidentally, also after James up and ghosted me.

I slip off my oven mitts. "I guess I did rely a bit on cupcakes for strength then."

"A bit?" Nina smirks. "I gained ten pounds, and you ruined your vocal cords singing 'We Are Never Getting Back Together.'"

"My vocal cords aren't ruined."

She rolls her eyes. "Not the point."

"Then what *is* the point?"

"The point is I don't mind living with Betty Crocker, I just hate when that little jerk makes you sad." Nina makes a noise in the back of her throat that's half scoff and half cough. The *scough* is her signature sound.

"First of all, Carson's over six feet tall." I grab a toothpick from a box in the spice cabinet. "And also, I'm not sad." I shrug. "I can't keep settling for someone who can take me or leave me so easily. I honestly never even think about Carson anymore."

I stick the toothpick into one of the cupcakes and steer my brain away from the man I *do* still think about.

James Lincoln. He left you easily too, Hadley.

So why can't I let *him* go?

The toothpick comes out clean, telling me the cupcakes are done, so I shove a fresh batch of batter-filled cups into the oven and set the timer for fifteen minutes.

"Well, if those cupcakes are just for us," Nina says, "two dozen seems like a lot."

"They're not for us. They're for Ms. Fudrucker."

Nina scrunches her nose. "And what did our illustrious principal do to deserve this bounty of baked goods?"

"It's not what *she* did. It's what I'm *not* going to do for her."

Nina takes off her blazer and lays it over her bag. "This sounds promising. Tell me."

I cringe. "I'm afraid Ms. Fudrucker's going to ask me to take over as newspaper advisor since Collette's going on maternity leave."

"Oh, she's definitely going to ask. You never say no."

"It's hard, Nina," I groan. "She was my principal when I was a student. Now I'm a teacher and she's my boss."

"Correction. The Fud is your colleague." Nina scoughs again. "And you can't even bring yourself to call her Felicia yet."

"Well, I'm determined to turn her down this time. And these cupcakes should soften the blow when I say *no*."

Nina's lips twitch. "Like how you said no when she asked you to cover two extra adjunct duties last year?"

"I was weak then."

Nina points at the cupcakes. "These aren't proof of strength. They're more like an admission of guilt. You're basically bribing The Fud to like you, and I don't want you to look desperate."

"I'm not desperate." I square my shoulders. "I'm strong. *So* strong. Like four-ply toilet paper strong."

"No such thing."

"Oh, yeah?" I come around the island and step up to Nina. She's five foot ten without her heels. In my ballet flats, I barely come up to her chin.

She snorts. "What are you doing?"

"*No* is such a short word," I say. "Two letters. One lonely syllable. Was it a syllable that used to hurt my soul? Sure. But that was the old me." I put my hands on my hips. "Anyone can turn over a new leaf, right?"

Nina puts her hands on my shoulders. "I think you might be losing it right now."

"Life is all about new seasons, Nina. Change is part of the deal. It's who I'm becoming this fall. I am Hadley Morgan: Professional leaf-turner-over-er!" I raise my hands triumphantly, while Nina shakes her head.

"Yep. You *have* lost it."

"Go ahead. Ask me anything, and I'll say no!"

"Did you make your famous cream cheese frosting for those cupcakes from scratch?" She puts famous cream cheese frosting in air quotes.

"That's not fair." I wince. "I'm a bad liar."

Nina's mouth quirks. "You can say that again."

"I'm a bad—"

"Oh, man." She cuts me off. "You're going to need more practice than I thought." She lifts a brow. "Do you want me to order a pepperoni pizza for dinner?"

No fair. I always want pizza.

"Noooo," I say, drawing the word out. Then I whisper, "But I definitely *do* want pizza."

"See?" Nina pokes my nose. "You already failed. Twice."

"Asking if I want pizza is below the belt," I protest. "You know I can't resist cured meats and cheese."

"The Fud hits below there, too. She plays off the fact that you're ridiculously sweet."

"I'm not *that* sweet."

"You're the sweetest people-pleaser I've ever met, Hadley. And The Fud takes advantage of that fact, hook, line, and sinker."

"I don't want to be a sinker." I suck in a breath, then slowly exhale.

Nina glances at the unfrosted cupcakes. "Can I have one?"

"Yes."

"Fail!" Nina grabs a cupcake and peels off the wrapper. It's polka dot and pink. As cheerful as I could get.

"You're right," I admit. "I have a problem. Help me, Obi Wan Kenobi."

Nina sets down the cupcake. "Repeat after me. 'Thank you for asking, Felicia, but as it turns out, I won't be able to accommodate your request.'" She pauses. "Now you say it."

I clear my throat. "NO!"

"Ha! You did it!" Nina bursts into applause while I curtsey across the kitchen. That's when my phone buzzes with a new text.

"It's probably my dad asking if I'm coming to meatloaf night."

Nina quirks an eyebrow. "Should I text him no for you, or are you prepared to do it yourself?"

I grab my phone. "If you did it for me, I'd hardly be leaf-turning, would I?"

Sure enough, the text is short but sweet, just like my father.

Dad: Dinner?

I type out a response, then show it to Nina before hitting send. She reads it out loud.

Me: Thank you for asking, but as it turns out, I won't be able to accommodate your request.

Nina chuckles. "You wouldn't dare."

"It's my dad. Of course not." I delete the text and start over.

Me: See you at seven. (Smiley face.)

Meatloaf night has been our weekly ritual for as long as I can remember. Over the years, my dad's experimented with every kind of recipe—from traditional ground beef to veggie. He's even tried salmon-loaf which makes me gag, even after I cover it with lemon juice.

Nina stifles a grin. "You said yes to meatloaf again, didn't you?"

I offer her a half smile. "You want to come with me?"

When I throw prayer hands back at Nina, a ripple of laughter bursts from her. Then she schools her face back into a flat mask of seriousness.

"No," she says. "See how easy that was?"

I pretend to pout, but I'm really stifling my own laugh. "You're so mean."

"This is what the kids call tough love, my friend."

As I move to the refrigerator to take out the homemade cream cheese frosting, my phone starts to buzz again, this time with an incoming call. "Is it my dad?" I ask over my shoulder.

Nina glances at the screen. "It's an LA area code."

I spin around, and our eyes sync.

James lives in Los Angeles. That's about all Nina knows about him, besides the fact that he broke my heart. I never could bring myself to tell her my old friend James is Lincoln James now.

"Want me to answer it?" she offers.

"No." My stomach lurches, and I set the bowl on the counter. "I don't know anyone in LA."

"You do."

"Don't."

"But it could be—"

"It's not." I open the cutlery drawer for a spreading knife. "Just more spam."

"How do you know for sure?"

"Because it's been five years, and I haven't heard a single word from him."

Tears prick the corners of my eyes, but getting all emotional is pointless. Nina meets my gaze, her dark eyes widening. The phone stops buzzing and we both wait for a chime of voicemail. When none comes, I slam the drawer.

"See? Spam."

"I need a palate cleanser now," Nina says.

"Me too."

"The usual?"

"Yes, please."

She takes my phone and scrolls my playlist to cue up the song. And as Taylor Swift tells her ex they're never, ever, ever getting back together, we grab hands and dance around the island, singing at the top of our lungs.

Chapter Four

LINK

"We've got a problem," Pippa says. She steeples her well-manicured fingers over her desk, and I drop into the chair across from her. I'd better get comfortable for this.

"Where's Andrew?" I ask. Normally, my manager would be here for a meeting where I'm in trouble.

"He had something else come up, but we both decided this can't wait." She sighs. "As usual, I'm pulling double duty for you, Link. *Triple* if you count the fact that the ever-enigmatic Lincoln James won't hire a personal assistant."

"Let me guess." I scratch at my chin, pretending to mull over the issue. The prickle of beard is satisfying since I'm only allowed to grow one in between movies. "Andrew's mad I haven't posted any pics of me and the dogs at the park yet. But you can tell him the paparazzi are on the case. Maybe I'll show up in that one magazine: *Stars. They're just like us.*"

Pippa peers at me over her tortoise-shell glasses. "Are you talking about *Us Weekly?*" There's a smudge of lipstick on her front tooth, which means she's been chewing her lip again. This is probably my fault. Pangs of sympathy for her have me squirming.

"I'm sorry, Pip, but I didn't rescue Scout and Jem for publicity. I loved those mutts the minute I saw their goofy faces at the shelter, and I'm not posting pictures of us bonding on social media."

"You don't even have any accounts, Link." She shoves her glasses up her nose and fixes me with a stare. "And you *do* realize that allows strangers to control your narrative with their fan pages."

"Let them. As long as my private life stays private."

Pippa screws up her face like she just bit into a raw onion. "Newsflash, Link: The more closely celebrities guard their secrets, the more audiences seek the dirt. And after what happened at Highland Hospital last week, you've got reporters digging."

"The thing with the photographer?" My throat heats up, and I'm right back in that moment. "Is it bad?"

Pippa's eyes are wide with disbelief. "You and your dogs must be living under a rock. The story is everywhere, Link."

"I called out a jerk taking advantage of sick kids."

Pippa throws up a hand. "All the public sees is Lincoln James —or worse, Magnetron—attacking a professional photographer we hired to be there."

"Andrew hired him. Not me." I straighten in my chair. "And he was supposed to make sure there weren't any paps around."

"Andrew was in the restroom, Link. He's a human. Humans pee."

My mouth slips sideways. "Magnetron doesn't."

"This situation isn't funny. If you'd let us hire a bodyguard—"

"Not interested." I lay my palms on my knees. "I already have you, Andrew, Sam, Dr. Kwon, and Ingrid. That's enough people in my inner circle."

"Ingrid's a trainer and Dr. Kwon's a therapist. They're hardly qualified to defend you. And even all five of us taking turns couldn't babysit you in every situation."

I run a hand through my hair. "I don't need a babysitter."

"Are you sure? Because ZTV is airing a highly unflattering video of you threatening a photographer as he cowers against the wall. The *National Tattler* has a whole spread of pictures. Every media outlet in town is speculating about why the man didn't press charges."

"Because he knew he was in the wrong."

She shakes her head, exasperated. "Because Andrew paid him off."

My hands ball into fists. "Did you hear what the guy said?" Anger presses against my ribs.

"It doesn't matter, Link. There's no audio to prove your claim that the photographer was being offensive."

"Fine. So one TV show and a tabloid are dragging me. People are smart. They can tell the difference between real life and a fake story drummed up for views."

"Don't be so sure." Her focus flickers to the wall covered with headshots of all the actors she represents. "This isn't just about you," she says. "You're putting me in a bad spot too."

"I'm sorry, Pip. I really am. But you said yourself I can't control the narrative."

"Nevertheless, this isn't the kind of publicity Youngblood Studios wants right before *Enforcer's Endgame* opens. Cal Youngblood is apoplectic."

Cal Youngblood is the grandson or maybe the great-grandson or some kind of privileged offspring from the guy who founded the studio. I should probably know this, but right now I'm too annoyed to remember the Youngblood family tree.

"He's overreacting," I say.

"He has the right." She narrows her eyes. "And I thought you wanted to be cast in their new series."

"The one with historical superheroes? Like if Bridgerton and Marvel had a baby?"

She cocks her head. "They're considering you for the role of The Vise-Count."

"And what kind of hero is that, exactly?"

"He's a member of Regency-era nobility who turns into an actual vise to crush his enemies."

A laugh jolts out of me. "Sounds realistic."

"It's going to be fantastic for whoever's involved. But that might not be us anymore." She purses her lips. "Andrew got word of another actor in contention."

"As long as his name doesn't start with a Chris ..."

She cocks an eyebrow.

Crap. "Is it Pine? Evans? Hemsworth?"

"It doesn't matter. Right now the entire internet thinks Magnetron is a bully," Pippa says, "which makes you a liability to Youngblood Studios. You're supposed to be a hero and a heart-throb, not the bad guy."

"That photographer wanted to exploit kids. He—" I cut myself off, unwilling to go there again.

Pippa leans over her desk. "Our only option is to divert the conversation about you to something else entirely."

I pick up the picture on the corner of Pippa's desk. It's of us on the red carpet at my first *Enforcer* movie. Pippa had already gotten me signed on to the next three films, and we're both grinning for the cameras. But I haven't forgotten the hollowness of that moment. My smile was forced. Attending something this important without any loved ones felt ... off. But that's how things had to be back then.

How I need to keep things still.

"So what's the plan?" I ask.

"Right now, fans are split between seeing you as a warrior or a villain. We're going to shift the focus to you not just being desirable, but also sympathetic. We want women worldwide to be swooning over you, then clamoring to mend your broken heart."

"Broken heart?" Doubt prickles the back of my neck. "I haven't even been on a date in ..." I take a beat. "A long time."

"That's why we're going to leak the news that you've been in a secret relationship." There's a fresh gleam in her eye. "And you're not just dating. You're *obsessed,* ready to put your whole soul on the line for your long-lost love. Once we've got the attention of every media outlet, she's going to end things brutally and publicly." Pippa sinks back into her chair. "When she crushes your world, the world's crush on you will be revived."

"No way." I set the picture back on her desk. "People aren't that gullible."

"People want to be in love, Link. They want to hope. To dream. To fantasize!"

I snort. "Not me."

"Regardless." She sniffs. "Andrew's completed test studies with random samples of past audiences, and the numbers show this will improve your status with everyone of all ages. Better than any Chris."

I shake my head. "There's not enough time to pull off the charade of me falling in love with some stranger before the premier. It's in a few weeks."

Pippa arches a brow so high it's almost lost in her updo. "That's why she has to be someone you already know. And I've identified the perfect candidate."

Huh. Someone I already know? Dasha Peet's the only actress with a recurring role in the *Enforcer* franchise. She's beloved by audiences, a good sport, and we get along all right. Still. I don't want to use her like that. I don't want to use anyone.

"Not Dasha," I say.

"Of course not." Pippa scoffs. "We can't have people disliking your costar for breaking your heart. And Dasha's manager wouldn't agree to the ruse even if Dasha did. More importantly, Youngblood Studios would forbid it."

I bristle. I don't like Pippa's plan, but I *really* don't like being told what I can and can't do. "The studio doesn't control me."

"Don't be naive, Link. You agreed to follow whatever publicity recommendations the studio makes as long as it's not illegal or immoral. It's in your contract."

I blow out a breath, absorbing the irony. "And lying to the fans isn't immoral?"

Pippa plays with the strand of pearls around her neck. "All is fair in love, war, and publicity."

My guts are swirling now. At least when I'm onscreen, audiences know I'm acting. They're paying to be entertained. But this is a whole other ballgame. "I'm not into manipulating the emotions of people who haven't bought tickets for the show."

"Well, Cal Youngblood already gave the green light for this plan," she says. "I'm afraid you're bound by your contract to at least *try* to rehab your reputation."

I grit my teeth. Hopefully Youngblood won't be able to find me a counterpart for this role. "If not Dasha, then who?"

"She isn't an actress." Pippa fiddles with a ring on her right hand.

"Uh-oh, Pip." I screw up my face. "What did you do? Make me a Tinder profile?"

"Perish the thought." She darts her eyes to my phone. "We're not doing this with someone from a site for"—she wrinkles her nose—"random hookups. We need your secret love to be wholesome and friendly. A real hometown girl." Pippa's ticking her list off on her fingers now. "She has to be willing to pretend to be your girlfriend, but also willing to break things off. The breakup is the key." Pippa drops her hands. "You have to be single at the end of this."

I smirk. "Any woman with half a brain would be more than happy to dump me."

"Very funny, Link."

"Seriously, Pip. No one in LA knows me well enough to play along with a scheme like this. Not even Dasha."

"But the woman I'm talking about isn't in LA. She's not even in this state." Pippa pauses, staring at me, poised to clock my reaction. "I've already initiated contact. She hasn't answered my calls yet, but we'll get in touch with her even if it means sending you to North Carolina."

A pit opens up in my stomach, and I almost slide out of my chair.

Hadley?

A highlight reel runs through my head of those warm eyes,

that smile, her goodness. How much I wish things could've been different between us. But Pippa couldn't possibly remember Hadley. They barely spoke that day. "No … what? How?"

"When you gave me your phone at the hospital, so I could monitor the dogs on your nanny cam"—she folds her hands primly—"I took the liberty of checking your apps while you were otherwise engaged. Imagine my surprise when I discovered you *do* have an Instagram account. With a handle and profile picture no one would recognize. @_Nuthing2C_here."

My heart slams my ribcage. *Yep. That's me.*

"And I couldn't help noticing you're only following one account," Pippa continues. "@THE_REEL_HADLEY_-MORGAN looked familiar, and after a bit of scrolling … it clicked. The girl from the auditions."

"She's off the table." I grunt.

"Nothing's off the table, Link. You should know that by now."

"I can't believe you went through my phone."

"I'm truly sorry." She grimaces. "But you keep your past so buttoned up."

Yeah. With good reason. I don't want my public life to bulldoze the private lives of people I love. They didn't sign on for that kind of scrutiny. So I flipped my name and dropped all my contacts.

Lincoln James has no history.

"And you figured you'd blow all that up for me?" My eyes flash.

"No. I …" Pippa pauses, her throat blotching. "What's done is done. And I apologize for the violation, but I can't un-know what I know, Link. The truth is, Hadley Morgan is perfect for this assignment."

"How do you figure?"

"She's more wholesome than apple pie." Pippa splays her hands. "She's got a job teaching at the same high school she attended, a close parental relationship, plus a roommate who's a good friend and a coworker. The girl is walking sunshine."

Yeah. I know. And I don't want to mess that up for her.

"Most importantly," Pippa adds, "she has no boyfriend."

Pippa must be assuming this because Hadley's posts with Carson disappeared months ago, and there hasn't been another guy in her feed since. It's all yoga and school and dancing around with her roommate these days. Not that I check in every day.

But you check in every day.

Pippa cocks her head. "I figured you follow Hadley—and only Hadley—because your connection was deep. And judging by your reaction right now, I'm right."

My gut twists. Yeah, I wanted our connection to be deep, but Hadley deserved better than I had to give. So I settled for being her friend. Then I walked away.

Erased my past.

"Absolutely not," I grit out.

"Be reasonable, Link. The girl ticks every box. She's the perfect partner in crime. Not that you'd be committing any crime beyond resuscitating the public's opinion of you."

I cross my arms over my chest. "She won't agree to do this."

"You haven't heard what Youngblood's willing to do in return for her cooperation. I think Hadley Morgan will jump at the chance."

"She won't. Trust me."

"I love you, Link, but I can't afford to trust you. My status as the Browne Agency's top agent is at stake thanks to your little outburst at the hospital."

"I apologized for that."

"And I accepted your apology." She lowers her eyes. "But for your own good and mine—for both our futures—I'm calling Hadley again. Now."

As I rise from the chair, Pippa taps at her phone. How did she even get Hadley's number? Did Andrew track her down? Heat floods my torso, and my chest goes so tight, I might as well be in a full-body tourniquet.

"Don't do it," I say. "Please."

"Too late." Pippa covers the mouthpiece. "Hadley just answered."

Chapter Five

HADLEY

I'm at my desk on a break between music history and advanced choir when my phone starts to ring again. I rarely answer unknown numbers. In fact, I rarely answer numbers I *do* know. But this same LA area code has called me six times this week without ever leaving a message.

What if Nina's right? What if it *is* him?

My stomach leaps like I've got a hoop in there to jump through.

After James left, I spent months waiting for any kind of update. A text. An email. Even a phone call.

Hey, Hads. Being a big movie star is amazing! I'm Lincoln James now instead of James Lincoln, but you probably knew that already. So thanks for asking me to tag along on those auditions even though I had no interest in being on the show. Sorry you got cut in the first round, and I became a movie star.

I always loved you.

Yeah. Fat chance, *Hads*.

After half a year of radio silence, reality finally sank in: I'd been ghosted by my old friend Goober. At least I *thought* I was his friend.

Hadn't we shared countless talks on the quad? Didn't he go

with me to all the movies Carson refused to see? He definitely listened when I admitted my doubts about being a good girlfriend or a loyal daughter. And yes, when I was single, I sometimes wished there could've been more between us. But it wasn't his fault he didn't see me that way. And he never took advantage.

James always treated me with respect.

Until he got famous.

Maybe he's calling to apologize, Hadley.

Would I even want to risk being hurt again? My pulse is in a sprint, and I can't help myself. I accept the call just before it goes to voicemail.

"Hello?" I manage to say, over a half-closed throat.

"Is this Hadley Morgan?"

Definitely not him. It's a woman with a husky voice. Probably spam, just like I thought.

"Hello?" the woman prompts. "Are you there?"

"Yes. I am. I mean, yes, this is Hadley."

"Wonderful. I'm Pippa Sergeant."

Oof. My heart pounds harder, and my esophagus constricts even more.

"I don't know if you remember me," she says, "but we met outside an old theater in Asheville. You were there with a friend." She pauses. "A friend who became my client."

I clear my throat. "That rings a bell."

See, Hadley? Your instincts weren't completely wrong. This isn't James, but it's about *him*.

"I happen to be with my client now," she says. There's another pause. "Excuse me. Can you hold for a moment?"

I frown and say, "Sure," but Pippa's already put me on mute. Glancing around the classroom to get my bearings, I focus on the poster from *Les Miserables.* This is who I am. A teacher.

Stay grounded, Hadley.

After what feels like an hour but is probably fifteen seconds, she returns. "Thank you for waiting," she says. "You're on speaker now. Is that all right?"

I suck in a breath, channeling every ounce of bravery I can muster. James must be listening. "What can I do for you, Ms. Sergeant?"

"My client and I have a proposition, and we're prepared to make our request worth your while."

A proposition? Our request? Worth my while?

My vision swims, and I'm afraid I might get sick in the trash can. Rubbing my eyes, I will my swirling stomach to settle. Things could be worse, I guess. I could be singing "On My Own" during the French Revolution.

"So, Hadley," Pippa says. "You may have heard about the unfortunate incident involving my client at Highland Hospital last week. We're hoping to reveal his softer side to the media, a loving man who's sweet and vulnerable. That's where you come in."

"Me?"

"Yes. We're asking you to help us stage a ... romantic relationship between you and my client. It wouldn't be real of course. And you'd have to sign a non-disclosure agreement promising not to reveal that the whole thing is fake."

"Fake?"

"Absolutely. Fake, fake, fake," she says, like a clucking hen. "My client would discreetly visit you in Harvest Hollow—just for a week or so—during which time our trusted cameraman would document your love story in photographs and video. You'd only have to keep my client's presence in town a secret while he's there."

"A secret?"

"Yes, that's the key. Nobody can discover you're a couple until our team decides to go public with the footage. This is for your privacy as well as his, and it's the only way we can control how your relationship is leaked."

"Leaked?"

"But you don't need to worry about that. Sam will handle all aspects of the filming."

"Sam?"

"Our cameraman. I've already provided him with a list of potential locations to capture your romance, although you're welcome to assist in selecting the best places to keep this project on the down low, of course."

"Of course," I say on the exhale. Not because I'm agreeing to any of this. I've simply become a parrot to Pippa Sergeant.

"You haven't asked any questions yet, Hadley. Do you have any?"

I have *so* many.

But it really doesn't matter. My answer is no. In fact, I'm full of so much NO, Nina would be proud. Not only do I have zero interest in this kind of subterfuge, I'm beginning to understand why James left in the first place. We have nothing in common now. Maybe we never did.

I open my mouth, take a deep breath ...

"No," I say.

"Fabulous," Pippa coos. It takes me a second to realize she must think I just don't have any questions.

"What I meant is—"

"In exchange for your time," Pippa interrupts, "we're offering you a guaranteed spot on the next season of *America's Hidden Talent*. Being known as Lincoln James's long-lost love should give you a boost in voting from the start. Like those people who use their fifteen minutes of fame to get on *Dancing with the Stars*."

All the air leaves my lungs.

"Pretending to be Link's girlfriend for a week is a small price to pay for that kind of big break, don't you think? If I were twenty years younger, I'd fake-date Link myself." Pippa gasps. "Wait! I just thought of something! Your couple name can be *HadLink!*" She hoots like this is a victory. "*HadLink* is perfect since you'll be breaking up with him in the end. Then *HadLink* will be no more. Get it? You two *had* a *link*!"

I gulp. "Breaking up?"

"Yes, that's the most important part of the plan. When the

time is right, I'll strategically plant the story that Link remained single all these years because he's been truly, madly, deeply in love with you forever. And once the world is rooting for him to propose to his old friend Hadley Morgan, you'll dump him on national television."

"I'm sorry," I say softly.

"What was that?"

"I can't pretend to be Lincoln James's girlfriend." I raise the volume of my words. "The truth is, the two of us were never even friends."

"I don't understand," Pippa says, and an uncomfortable silence stretches. "Aren't I speaking to the woman I met at the *America's Hidden Talent* auditions?"

"Yes," I say. "But the person *I* was with that day was named James Lincoln, and I haven't spoken to him since. My answer is no. I don't date ghosts."

Chapter Six

LINK

The next morning during my workout, my trainer must sense something's off. I've been punishing my body for two straight hours, and we're not even in the grueling days of pre-project or mid-film training.

"Link!" Ingrid barks. She's behind me, hands just under my elbows, spotting me as I work through reps with the dumbbells. "We want a shoulder press. Not shoulder murder. Take it easy."

Sorry, Ingrid. Not gonna happen.

Not with this constant swirl of emotions running through my head. Hadley's voice catapulted me straight back to the time we spent together. To the easy comfort I'd sink into by her side. During that call, I felt the tug of longing to protect her again, and the harsh reminder that I'm the one who made her hurt.

"Sorry," I grunt. "Got a lot on my mind." Like Pippa insisting I have to go to Harvest Hollow and convince Hadley in person. When I tried refusing, Pippa reminded me it's not just about repairing my reputation.

"Your privacy's at stake," she said. "And your mother's. Not to mention the trajectory of my career. Andrew's too. Even Sam. For all of us, you've got to do whatever it takes."

Whatever it takes. For all of us.

"Well, you're going to injure yourself," Ingrid warns me now. But blowing off steam at the gym is what I do. Free weights help me pump out anger. On the machines, I work through frustration. If I get sad—the emotion I avoid most—I zone out on the elliptical. Then there are my runs. On long stretches of shoreline, I dream about what life could be like if I jumped off the hamster wheel. But self-pity isn't a space I drop into and hang around in very long.

It just brings up the hurt. Not to mention survivor's guilt and shame.

Bottom line: Everything Hadley said to Pippa yesterday was true. James Lincoln is dead. I made sure of that the minute I traded North Carolina for Hollywood.

Back then, I didn't want anyone looking into my history—finding out who I was, who I loved, what we'd lost. The anonymity I gained was priceless. My mom's stability was all that mattered.

It still is.

The last thing we need now is reporters finding out we're related and pushing for interviews.

Talking about the past—publicly—would only dredge up her old pain. All those years spent in the hospital with Tommy. Then her deep spiral afterward. I'd sacrifice anything to save her from reliving that. But the way things were not that long ago still simmers just below the surface.

So this publicity stunt Pippa has planned now—this charade she's forcing me to do—has an alarm bell shooting out the top of my skull like a whale through its blowhole.

Okay, maybe that's not the right image, but you get me.

"That's enough," Ingrid insists. "Let's move to back squats."

We head to the rack, but I'm spinning out, worried about how Hadley's feeling after being ambushed by that call. Pippa begged her for help, and I did nothing to stop the madness. Hadley shouldn't feel like she owes me.

My choices are my own.

So we shouldn't use Hadley's kindness against her. She's such a giver, saying no has always been a challenge. And having to pretend would be the opposite of her nature. Not to mention staging a fake breakup on TV. I hate putting her in this position.

"Five reps," Ingrid says. "Concentrate." Her voice a command.

But what if my reputation stays on a downhill slide? What if Youngblood Studios doesn't want me for the role of The Vise-Count? Most of what I earned from the *Enforcer* movies went to paying off family debts, buying my mom a house, and setting up my own place.

If new contracts stop coming, I may not be able to continue to support either of us. Then there's Pippa. Andrew. Sam. They're all counting on my continued success. Sure, they have other clients, but I've been dominating their efforts for years. They took a chance when they championed a nobody like me.

Don't I owe them this too?

Pippa is convinced a fake relationship and breakup with Hadley can turn everything around for all our sakes. But what if Hadley can't forgive me for disappearing on her? I'm not sure I can even forgive my—

"Link!" Ingrid yelps. "Focus!"

Easier said than done.

As we switch from back squats to bench press, my brain starts building a list of reasons to avoid Harvest Hollow. Besides Hadley's rejection, another obstacle are my dogs. When I adopted Scout and Jem, I promised they'd never be abandoned again. Ever. Being gone for a couple hours is one thing. I've got that nanny cam to keep an eye out. But this trip would require a week or more of boarding.

Not an option.

Indiana Bones is the best and closest, but they book up weeks in advance. Plus, dropping off a couple of rescue dogs so soon after their adoption could raise red flags. I can't have red flags raised and travel to Harvest Hollow without reporters finding out.

I suppose there's one solution. It's not perfect, but it's the best I've got: My mother.

She loves Scout and Jem, and her place is already dog-friendly thanks to her border collie, Boo. Her place in Malibu has plenty of space, and they'd all be good company for each other. The stretch of beach there is safe and serene. A world away from the worst tragedy of her life.

And yet, I know my mom misses North Carolina. Those Blue Ridge Mountains. We both do. Until we moved here, we'd never lived anywhere else. Asheville's where our roots were planted. Where she became a mother.

Where Tommy is buried.

A loud growl bursts from me, and my stomach heaves remembering. I can't let my mom be dragged back to that time.

Whatever it takes, Pippa said.

That's it, Link. You have to go.

Chapter Seven

HADLEY

Friday morning before work, I do something I told myself I wouldn't do ever since I got that call from Pippa Sergeant.

I pull the shoe box from my bedroom closet.

The fact that I still have the box—and also that I moved it from my dad's house to this place—means nothing. Okay, maybe it means something. Just a tiny bit of a thing. But I keep it in the way back of my closet.

That's how minuscule the thing is.

"Did you get enough coffee?" Nina asks from the hallway. She doesn't come in, but I didn't bother shutting my door. *That's* how unimportant the box is.

"Yep." I glance at the mug cooling on my dresser. "You can have the rest. Thanks for asking."

Sitting cross-legged on the floor, I slip the lid off, preparing for an onslaught of nostalgia. On top is my college graduation announcement, the program for the ceremony, and the tassel from CU. My dad sure went overboard that day with a lei and balloons and a noisemaker. He took pictures and recorded every snooze-filled minute of pomp and circumstance. But holding these mementos after all these years, I feel ... nothing.

Yes, I was grateful for my degree and my dad's support. But

despite his pride—not to mention the relief I felt when I admitted I wanted to teach, not be a professional musician—that day held a tinge of melancholy for me.

This wasn't because most of my college friends had their mothers to help with their hair, iron their robes, and bobby pin their mortar boards. For better or worse, I was too young to remember losing my mom. I was just a baby when the car accident took her.

What made my heart ache at graduation was the friend who was missing. The one I wanted to see most. The one who should've been walking alongside me. But he was in LA busy filming a superhero movie.

"You want me to toast you a bagel?" Nina calls out.

"Yes, please. Thank you!"

I dig back into the box, and things start to get more interesting. There's the key to my senior year dorm room, which is the only item I've ever stolen in my life. It was an accident. I didn't even realize I'd taken the key until I'd fully unpacked a week after graduation. By then, no one had said anything, and I decided it could be a keepsake. I'd paid my dues as an RA for my hall.

Three years of listening to homesick freshmen.

Three years of navigating roommate wars.

Three years of trying to set an example of good behavior for everyone on my floor.

Along with the key is a stack of movie ticket stubs, and now my stomach flip-flops. I spread them on the floor. These were all the movies I saw with James.

The films that didn't interest Carson.

Next, I pull out an empty box of Goobers. If it seems weird that I kept memorabilia from a guy who wasn't even my boyfriend, then consider me guilty as charged. I probably wouldn't have saved this stuff if James hadn't left so abruptly. One day he was with me, my companion at the auditions, and the next he was gone. I think this was my way of reminding myself he was real. That at one time, he meant something to me.

I thought I meant something to him.

Now he just wants to use you.

"You want cream cheese?" Nina yells from the kitchen.

"Absolutely!" I yell back.

This trip down memory lane might be killing my appetite, but still. I'm not a monster.

In the corner of the box is a tight ball of foil, the same foil from that turkey sandwich on audition day. This was the last meal I ate with James, the last crumb I spit on his lap while talking with my mouth full. Gross, right?

Yeah. The whole situation is gross, and a sliver of regret slices through me. Things might've been different if I'd been brave enough to tell James how I felt about him, how thankful I was for his friendship. How he made me feel seen and safe just as I was.

Being with him was unlike being with anyone else, although I never put my finger on why.

I was drawn to him in a way I'd never been with anybody else. But I knew James didn't think of me *that* way. As anything more than a friend, I mean. When I first told him Carson had asked me out, a part of me hoped James would speak up and throw his hat in the dating ring.

But he just nodded, and said, "Have fun."

Speaking of hats.

I've got one that belonged to James at the bottom of the box. It's a CU ball cap he let me borrow one afternoon when he ran into me out on the quad. The day was blindingly bright, and I'd forgotten my sunglasses. He was late for a shift in the dining hall, and I'd been planning to study outside, so he gave me his hat. Then he told me to keep it.

Like a good people-pleaser, I did as he asked.

"Your bagel's ready!" Nina calls.

"Coming!"

I put the hat on now, tugging the brim down and wishing it still smelled like James—that warm, spicy scent that was his alone.

He never even needed cologne. The air was just always a little bit more delicious when he was around.

In all the years Carson and I dated—between our breakups and reconciliations—the guy never so much as loaned me a sweatshirt. Maybe it's because a part of him sensed he'd always been my default choice.

If so, that's totally on me. And maybe someday I'll have an occasion to apologize to him for that. Still, Carson has so much more to apologize to me for. And anyway, I didn't even know the depth of my feelings for James myself—not until I heard Pippa Sergeant's voice on that call.

All along, I'd been secretly longing for him to claim me.

Instead, he disappeared.

Chapter Eight

LINK

I spend a good part of Friday on the phone with Pippa and Andrew making travel arrangements. Then I FaceTime Sam.

Asking him to leave his daughters and pregnant wife to document my fake relationship fills me with guilt. The man lives and breathes for his girls, the kind of love I can only imagine. But he assures me with a sly smile he's fine missing a few tea parties and playing Pretty Pretty Princess.

Five-year-olds are the best.

So is Sam.

Next, I let my therapist know I'll be skipping at least one of our sessions. Maybe two. Dr. Kwon doesn't ask questions, and I don't offer details. I figure I'll talk everything through at our next appointment.

When I tell Ingrid I'm taking a break for the rest of the month, she doesn't put up a protest. I guess the prospect of not seeing me for the next week or so doesn't upset her.

Yeah. Me either, Ingrid.

As it turns out, packing my bags for fall in Harvest Hollow is a bigger hurdle than canceling on my trainer. Summer temperatures in that part of the state can linger well into September, but a quick check of the forecast shows the weather will be cool.

A sliver of excitement cuts through me.

So I stuff a suitcase with jeans and long-sleeved shirts, two wool scarves, and a coat. I also throw in a pair of joggers and a few sweatshirts, plus a couple of hats for anonymity. But let's face it: No one will be looking for Lincoln James strolling down Main Street.

On the drive to my mom's up Pacific Coast Highway, I keep the windows down, soaking up the sun. Scout and Jem are in the back seat, tongues lolling, eating the wind. They had rough lives before I rescued them, but that's over now. I made sure of that. Their trust and happiness are so pure. I'm going to miss these drooling goobers.

Goober.

I hear my old nickname in Hadley's voice, and my senses flood with memories. Instead of the cliffs on one side of us and the ocean on the other, I'm suddenly back in North Carolina. The roads there are flanked by green pastures with the mountains as a perfect backdrop. At this time of morning, a blanket of clouds still probably obscures the rolling hills.

If I close my eyes, I can see it. Smell the grasses. Taste the clean, crisp water straight from the source. There's no drought there. No smoke from brush fires. No earthquakes.

Yeah. Just hurricanes, Link.

Of course, the salty air and sandy beaches of the Malibu coastline aren't anything to sneeze at either. This place is beautiful. It's just never felt like home.

Nowhere in LA does.

Making a left off the highway, I turn onto a stretch of private properties that run along the water. There are sunset views here for days. And privacy. The sound of crashing waves twenty-four-seven. All in all, it's not a bad place to hide out from the world.

Most people living on this stretch of the beach are rich. A lot of them are famous. Everyone minds their own business. That's partly why my mom and I chose this place. To escape unwanted eyes and intrusive questions. No one here's going to subject my mom to a firing squad of questions about her life, her suffering.

No one.

Pulling up to the gate, I type in the code, and a long black gate grinds open. My mother's waiting in the open doorway in a pair of flowing pants and an off-the-shoulder tunic. Her long black hair is threaded with gray. She's barely nineteen years older than I am, but those years sure took their toll.

The dogs whimper with excitement, their tails going nuts. When I let them out, they scamper past my mom into the house on the lookout for their pal, Boo. The iceberg of guilt inside me melts a few degrees. Here, Scout and Jem will be well-cared for and safe.

That's the whole purpose of this place.

"James." My mother throws her arms wide, motioning me inside. She's the only one who calls me James now. That is until Hadley said it on that call. As if she's right behind me, Hadley's soft voice echoes in my chest. A shiver runs up my spine, and my skin breaks out in goose bumps. Good thing I packed long sleeves.

Too bad they can't protect me from the ghosts.

As we do whenever I visit, my mom and I head to the deck out back. A pair of red Adirondack chairs sit side by side, but I'm too restless to sit. Kicking off my shoes, I skip the three stairs and hop directly into the sand.

Scout, Jem, and Boo are already at the water's edge, jumping into the tide, getting wet and sandy.

I cast a sheepish grin at my mom. "They're gonna make a mess, huh?"

"Eh." Her smile is crooked. "I'm used to messes."

"Still, thanks for taking them on such short notice."

"Are you kidding? Boo and I are going to have so much fun." She shifts her gaze to the dogs frolicking in the ocean.

"Yeah." I snort. "Well. Don't let them ruin your couch."

"No promises." She comes over to wrap an arm around me,

and we both look out at the water. The sun is high and bright, no sign of the marine layer that can last well into the afternoon.

"I'll call you when I'm settled at the hotel, okay?"

"You'd better." She squeezes my shoulder.

"You sure you'll be all right while I'm gone?"

"I'm a big girl, James." She shrugs. "Protecting me isn't your job."

"I'm always going to try."

"I suppose I can't stop you, huh?"

"You cannot." My mouth slips into a sideways smile. "But you *can* watch my dogs."

"The least I can do." She pats my shoulder. "You're a real-life hero, Magnetron."

Chapter Nine

HADLEY

"Are my ears bleeding actual blood?" Nina shouts this at me halfway through the football game. For two straight quarters we've been sitting near some very enthusiastic trumpet and trombone players. As it turns out, choosing seats near the marching band wasn't the best idea I've ever had.

At least the kids are filing out to the field for the halftime show now.

Sweet, sweet relief.

Don't get me wrong. I love music as much as the next person. *More* than most people, probably. You know when someone asks you what you'd rescue first in a fire? My answer is Dolores.

For sure.

Instead of memories of my mom, I have her guitar. Still, at some point during all the lessons, recitals, and auditions, I realized what actually fills my soul is helping others love music too.

So I became a teacher.

Now I get to perform in front of my classes every day without the pressure of the spotlight. Luckily music appreciation and choir are kinder and gentler on my head than band.

Mr. Logan, our band director, is a saint.

"Your ears are fine," I tell Nina, although I won't lie. I did check for blood. We're in the middle of bleachers packed with football fans. Everyone's dressed for fall, but in our school's colors. It's a crowd of red and white hats, sweatshirts, and scarves.

"Next week I get to pick our seats," Nina says.

"For the homecoming game? Ugh." I wrinkle my nose. "I don't think I'll go."

"Why?" She sticks her lower lip out in an exaggerated pout. "Explain please."

"I got chicken pox my senior year." I shift my focus to the drum major on the sidelines waving his baton like he's guiding planes on a runway. "I couldn't go to the football game or to the dance."

"What?" Nina smacks my shoulder. "How come you didn't tell me last year?"

I shrug. "I didn't know you then like I do now." My answer's nonchalant, but my mind can't help sliding down the slippery slope to James Lincoln.

You didn't know him as well as you thought either, Hadley.

"I didn't care so much about missing the dance," I tell Nina, "but I was supposed to wear my mom's old dress. So. Yeah. Not a fan of homecoming." I push down a swell of regret, but ignoring thoughts of the past doesn't make them go away. For example, I became an expert at forgetting James, but that didn't stop him from reappearing.

"Your mom's dress? Wow." Nina nudges me. "That's so .... I don't know what it is. Weird? Cool? Retro?"

"Beautiful," I say. "Not me," I add. "*I* was covered in calamine lotion, but the dress was really special." I pause as my stomach churns. It was probably a dumb idea to borrow her dress in the first place. Wearing her clothes and playing her guitar won't make me any closer to her.

"What's it like?" Nina asks.

"Butter yellow with a belt made of fabric daisies," I explain. "Anyway, skipping the dance turned out to be for the best. My date was an idiot, which I discovered when he told everyone I couldn't go because I had mono from making out too much."

"Eww."

"Right? It's a good thing my dad never found out. He's always been so protective. Who knows what he would've done?"

"Yeah, your dad's a stud," Nina says. "Speaking of which." She nods toward the bottom of the bleachers. My dad's there climbing the stairs in his favorite jeans and an old Bobcats sweatshirt. His dark hair just started graying at the temples which gives him a distinguished, handsome edge. But the *Home of the Bobcats* seat cushion tucked under his arm takes his stud rating down a peg.

"Go, Bobcats!" Ms. Fudrucker squeals at him as he passes. She's in her usual Harvest High spirit wear with red and white bows in her ponytails. The woman's in her fifties, and she's never been married. Unless you count her job.

"Nice cushion," she hoots, shaking her foam finger. My dad offers her a head bob, and I duck in case she turns around and spots me.

"I'm coming, girls," he calls out. He's carrying a to-go carrier with three drinks from Cataloochee Mountain Coffee.

"Probably pumpkin spice lattes," I whisper to Nina. "His addiction to fall-themed beverages kicks in hard every September."

He reaches our row and inches his way down the bleacher, holding out the carrier so Nina and I can both grab drinks. "The line at Catty's was extra-long," he says, "but you know I had to."

"Thanks, Dad." My cup is warm even through the sleeve, and I take a tentative sip. "Yum."

Nina grins at him. "Yes, thanks, Mr. Morgan."

"It's pumpkin spice latte," he says.

The Morgans are nothing if not predictable.

"*Nice cushion*," Nina says. It's a perfect imitation of The Fud. He drops down onto the bench next to me and sets the carrier on the ground. I'm between him and Nina now.

"I've had this same seat cushion since Hadley was the mascot here at Harvest High," he says. "I used to watch her jumping all over the sidelines in a Bobcat costume every Friday night."

I wince, remembering. "More like sweating all over the sidelines."

"Well, I never missed a game," he says, "and I even rejoined the booster club now that you're a teacher here."

"See?" Nina says under her breath. "Stud."

"What's that?" my dad asks.

"I said, 'Sweet,' Mr. Morgan."

"Listen. If you don't start calling me Ray, I'll show up next time with a cane." He rubs his hands together. "So. What did I miss, ladies?"

"Well, the Bobcats are up twenty-one to ten," Nina tells him.

"Thanks, but I can see the scoreboard. I don't need bifocals yet. I'm talking about gossip." His blue eyes twinkle. "Come on. Spill the tea."

"Well, *Ray*," Nina leans in, "your daughter started saying no to people this week, and I must say, it's a pretty good look for her." She bumps me. "Did you tell your dad about your recent act of bravery?"

My act of bravery? No, I did *not* tell my dad about saying no to Pippa Sergeant. But hold on. I didn't tell Nina about that either.

"Hadley actually stood up to The Fud," Nina says, patting my back.

Ahhh. *That* act of bravery.

"It was no big deal," I hurry to say. "I just turned her down when she asked me to fill in as the advisor for the newspaper."

My dad's gaze shifts down to Ms. Fudrucker, who's still frantically waving her foam finger. There's an empty space on both sides of her, and my heart squeezes a little.

Note to self: *Next time, maybe sit with Ms. Fudrucker.*

"Must've been hard to say no," my dad says. "That woman sure has a lot of team spirit."

"Yeah." Nina chuckles. "At the pep rally this morning she came out in a Bobcat cheerleader uniform. Believe me, you do *not* want to see our boss dressed like one of the Kittens."

Even as she says this, the band finishes its remix of "Uptown Funk" and begins to march back to the stands. That's when the football players emerge from under us with a loud Bobcat roar.

They charge out along the 50-yard line to start the second half. The cheerleaders drop down from their pyramid and burst into backflips and cartwheels across the field.

When they start leading the crowd in a cheer, Nina and I yell at the top of our lungs.

"Pump, pump, pump it up! Pump that Bobcat spirit up! Keep, keep, keep it up! Keep that Bobcat spirit up!"

"Careful not to lose your voice," my dad warns me as soon as the cheer is over. "A choir teacher's got to protect her instrument."

"I'm off until Wednesday," I tell him. "For staff development."

Every fall, our district gives teachers a break right before progress reports go out. Luckily Ms. Fudrucker's always been pretty cool about how we use our time. We can plan parent conferences, work on grades, or hold any necessary department meetings.

Glenn Logan—the band director and orchestra teacher—is the only other member of my department. We already decided we're plenty developed.

No need to meet.

"Four whole days." Nina snickers. "I can't *wait* to start developing."

"I'm going to work on a new arrangement for my a cappella choir's fall festival song," I say.

Nina nudges my arm. "Just promise me you won't let The Fud talk you into taking on the newspaper."

"Right." My dad arches an eyebrow. "I need to hear more about my daughter's total rejection of Ms. Fudrucker."

"Well, it wasn't a total rejection," Nina says. "Hadley did bake her famous apple-crumble cupcakes to soften the blow. But our girl is making progress." A dimple creases Nina's cheek. "Now she just needs to start saying yes to adventure and spontaneity."

"Hey." I square my shoulders. "I'm not afraid of spontaneity and adventure."

Nina snorts. "Meatloaf night doesn't count."

"What's that about meatloaf night?" my dad asks.

I turn to him and paste on a grin. "Nina's been telling me she wants to come to our next meatloaf night."

She squawks, but before she can officially protest, my dad beats her to the punch. "Wonderful!" He's beaming now. His Ray Morgan special. There's no way Nina can refuse. "I think the salmon loaf's up in our rotation," he says.

I nod, biting back a laugh. "I do believe you're right, Dad."

"I don't eat fish," Nina says, arranging her face into a mask of disappointment. "Too bad."

"I'm happy to switch things up for you," my dad says.

Yep. This people-pleaser didn't fall far from her father's people-pleasing tree.

Nina's face shifts into a cringe. "Switch things up to what?"

"I'll surprise you," he says. "Mystery meat!"

Our quarterback throws a long pass for the first down, and the crowd goes wild. My dad looks out at the field, missing Nina's expression of horror.

"Mystery meat?" she says under her breath.

I can't help giggling. "You're gonna love it."

"I might fake an illness," Nina says.

Pippa's voice is a gong in my head.

Fake. Fake. Fake.

Chapter Ten

LINK

"This is a terrible idea." I say these words under my breath, but Sam chuckles from the driver's seat. We're in a gray four-door sedan that Pippa had waiting for us at the Asheville Regional airport. She rented the most nondescript car available trying to keep my presence under the radar.

I slip on my green beanie and a pair of dark sunglasses.

I hope I don't look like a spy.

"Maybe it won't be as bad as you think," Sam says. "But yeah. It probably will be."

"Thanks, man." I wince. "That's great. Super helpful."

Sam's aware this trip is kind of a homecoming—for better or worse—so he offered to take the wheel. This leaves me free to soak up the winding roads and rolling hills between the airport and town. On either side, we're surrounded by stretches of tree-dotted greenery. The Blue Ridge Mountains serve as a backdrop. The desert landscapes and chaparral of California are nice, but who needs palm trees and a cactus or two when you can have this?

You *do, Link. You need LA and the career that goes along with it.*

LA is where your mom is.

She's why you're doing all this.

The reminder loops in my brain for a solid forty-five minutes. As we get closer to Harvest Hollow, though, another motivation claws its way to the surface: Hadley Morgan.

My guts are in a swirl, wondering how she'll react when she sees me on her porch. Will she shut me down? Slam the door? Slip on that same sunny smile I've thought about every day for the past five years?

Hope flickers in my chest, and I flash back to the first time Hadley and I met. She thought I was just another CU undergrad looking for a snack at the vending machines. When she teased me for snagging the last two boxes of Goobers, I gave her one. Then she smiled.

The world lit up.

This became our habit, showing up at the same machine at the same time every day. We'd take turns buying doubles of our favorite stuff to share with each other. Since I was always in custodial coveralls, she assumed I was part of the CU work-study program. I liked that she believed I was trying to subsidize tuition. So I never did tell her the truth—that I wasn't on work study. I wasn't even a student at CU.

I was part of their full-time custodial staff.

To be clear, I wasn't ashamed of my job. Not even a little bit. I was proud of supporting myself. Being on campus made me feel like anything was possible. I dreamed of taking classes at Blue Ridge Community and moving on to CU. I wanted to make something of myself. Wanted to be more.

Do more.

But my mom was already working three jobs to chip away at bills accrued at multiple hospitals. The debt felt like a mountain and a pit at the same time. I wanted to take her burdens away, not waste money on a four-year college. So I swallowed the dream. Lived vicariously through Hadley.

Let her think what she thought.

"Hey." Sam digs into the bag of mini-pretzels he got on the plane. "You all right, man?"

"Yeah." I keep my focus out the window. "Just thinking."

"Nervous?"

"That's one of the many, many emotions I've got brewing."

Sam grunts but leaves me to my thoughts.

So. Many. Thoughts.

The farther we get from the city, the more the properties spread out, with homes tucked into all the lush nooks and crannies along the mountains. There are big farmhouses with wraparound porches, and cozy homes that look more like cottages. Most are custom built with lots of acreage between them. There are no fences here. No sidewalks. Just ample space to breathe.

Too bad your breath keeps catching, thinking about Hadley.

Sam points out The Summit, an impressive hockey arena where Harvest Hollow's minor-league hockey team plays. "Huh. I wonder if Logan Barnes is in there practicing with the Appies right now."

"Probably."

He's one of the best players out there, but after an injury (plus one unfortunate incident of fighting with a fan) he got kicked down from the NHL and signed to the Appies.

"Man, he's amazing." Sam shakes his head, then eyes me sideways. "Too bad he couldn't control his temper."

Heh. Sorry, Barnes. I know the feeling.

Surrounding the enormous arena are a few strip malls with restaurants, bars, and hotels. Then our route gives way to planned communities, neighborhoods with more structure that somehow manage to maintain their charm.

I've never been to Hadley's hometown, but the entire region feels familiar. The warmth of recognition seeps through my bones. Along with this truth: I miss North Carolina.

"Yeah, I can see why." Sam nods.

Guess I said that out loud.

The leaves still on the trees here have turned a brilliant yellow, or they're on the roadside collecting in drifts. The quaintness of this place seems at odds with my goal: To pull one over on the residents of Harvest Hollow.

My stomach twists.

We pass a fire station, then a cluster of buildings that form the high school. The adjacent baseball field is straight out of a storybook. The marching band's practicing in the football stadium. Out front, a marquee reads Home of the Bobcats.

Sam tips his chin at the sign. "Is that Hadley's school?"

"Yup." My palms grip my knees, and my heart hammers harder.

Continuing into the heart of town, Sam and I eventually find ourselves in a large square with the courthouse, City Hall, and post office. The architecture is a stately combination of weathered red brick and stone. Above one of the buildings is a clocktower. In the center of the square is an enormous fountain in a pond surrounded by parklike grass and stone benches.

The black streetlamps are all wrapped with fall-colored ribbons and strung with strands of white lights. Signs about a harvest festival hang in every window.

I make a mental note of the date.

Hadley should be publicly ending things with me by then. *If* she agrees to go along with the plan in the first place.

"In half a mile, turn right on Maple Street," the GPS announces.

"Maple." Sam raps the steering wheel. "Like the tree? Or the syrup?"

"I'm guessing tree."

"Either way. This place couldn't get any sweeter."

We cruise past cafes and shops, each one more inviting than the next. On one corner is The General Store, followed by Cataloochee Mountain Coffee. There's also a gift shop called An Apple A Day.

I'll let you guess what their theme is.

In Bloom clearly sells flowers. Book Smart's got a display of paperbacks in the window. There's a novelty shop called Hollow-

Ween with grinning jack-o'-lanterns and skeletons made of … dried apple cores.

I'm sensing a pattern.

"Hollow-Ween?" Sam chuckles. "I think I like this town already."

"Speaking of places with puns for names." I point out a new-ish looking bar advertising trivia night. "Tequila Mockingbird. Pretty clever."

Sam puffs out a breath. "Says the man who named his dogs Scout and Jem."

"Like I said. Clever."

Some of the businesses have their doors propped open with sandwich boards to tempt people in. Others sport small bistro tables out front. A few have roll-up garage windows. On one corner a couple of straw-stuffed scarecrows wave from Adirondack chairs. Above all, the sentiment in Harvest Hollow seems to be this: WELCOME FALL.

Before I moved to a place without seasons, fall used to be my favorite. Crisp air. Smoke curling out of chimneys. A crunch of leaves underfoot. Pumpkin spice just tastes better when it's not eighty degrees out. The truth is, Los Angeles doesn't feel like home.

It's just some place I live now.

By the time we reach Hadley's neighborhood, my palms are clammy, and my head's on fire. When I slip off my beanie and check the mirror, Sam snorts. "You look gorgeous, Magnetron."

"Don't make me melt you, Sam."

On or off set, I rarely think about my appearance. When *People* magazine named me one of the thirty sexiest men under thirty, I was … mortified. But Hadley and I are about to see each other for the first time in five years. I don't want to be covered in flop sweat.

Why am I so nervous?

Sam pulls up to a low curb and parks under a tree with half-bare branches. "Welp. That's her place." He cuts the engine and nods at a cream-colored bungalow across the street. “It’s cute,” he says.

The roof is sloped and an apple-red door marks the center of the property. The curtains in the window are mostly drawn, but there’s a small space someone could peek through. In her yard two large maples are surrounded by loose leaves. A yellow rake propped against one of the tree trunks doesn’t look like it gets much use.

“I’ll stay out of sight, while you do your thing,” Sam says. “Holler if you need me.”

My blood pressure skyrockets. Hadley’s in there right now, probably.

“She does yoga on Saturday mornings,” I say, still staring at the house. “Then she practices piano. Plays guitar. Works on her lesson plans.”

“Ummm.” Sam clears his throat. “You know this how?”

“Social media,” I say. “Reels. Stories. Pictures.”

“Whoa.”

I turn to face him. “What? Nina tags her a lot.”

“Nina?”

“She’s Hadley’s roommate, but she spends a lot of weekends with her boyfriend. Hopefully Hadley will be home alone.”

Sam shakes his head. “You’re sounding a little like a stalker, my friend.”

“Yeah.” I wince. “I heard it too.” I toss my beanie in the back seat. “But I swear I only check in on Hadley to make sure she’s good, you know?”

“Uh-huh. Sure.” Sam smirks. “And exactly how often are you checking in?”

I run a hand through my hair. “You may have a point.”

“It’s all right.” He socks me gently on the shoulder. “You’ve got this. Hadley Morgan’s gonna be putty in your hands.”

I frown. “I don’t want her to be putty.”

“Then that would make a great opening line.” Sam’s mouth goes crooked, but his eyes are soft. Sympathetic. Maybe this is what being a dad does to some men, but in my history, there was a shortage of men around, period, let alone ones with any degree of compassion. "Don't worry. You've got this, Link. *Or* you'll do it all wrong."

"Thanks for the vote of confidence."

"Either way." He salutes me. "Good luck, man."

Unfolding myself from the car, I jog across the street and up the walkway. The closer I get, the more my chest constricts, but I force myself onto the porch. After ringing the bell, I stuff both hands in my pockets, staring at the door like it's a ticking bomb.

Will Hadley look through a window, or call out to ask who's on her welcome mat or—before I can formulate a third option, the door flies open. And there she is.

Here she is.

"Hey." I duck my head, and Hadley's eyes go wide, lashes fluttering like butterfly wings.

She is stunned.

She's stunning.

She slams the door in my face.

Chapter Eleven

HADLEY

Oh no, oh no, *oh no, oh no!*

OH NO!

This can't be happening. I must've fallen asleep during yoga, and now I'm having one of those nightmares where you're supposed to take your finals in college, but you can't remember where any of the rooms are, or if you've even attended a single class.

AM I FAILING OUT OF COLLEGE?

I put a hand to my chest, and take a long deep breath, resting my forehead against the door. No. I'm awake in my home. Safe and sound. *Nothing to see here, Hadley.* I've just started to convince myself I imagined this whole situation when—

Knock, knock, knock.

NO.

I am *so* not prepared for Lincoln James to be standing on my porch. I'd be less shocked to discover a unicorn out front. Or a barbershop quartet. Or some guy with a camera crew saying I just won the lottery.

"Please, Hadley." The gravelly voice on the other side of the door shoots a shiver up my spine. That is *no* unicorn, and I've never bought a lottery ticket. Seriously. What do I do? I haven't even showered yet. I'm still in my sweaty yoga clothes.

What is HE doing here?

Knock, knock, knock.

"I came here to talk to you," he says, like he read my mind. Like he's a MINDREADER. "But I don't want to do it through a door. I need to apologize."

Huh. What's that about?

Maybe he actually feels terrible about letting Pippa put me on the spot with zero warning. Or he might regret totally disappearing from my life. Or he could just be sorry I still haven't showered after yoga.

Either way, if my once-upon-a-time friend wants to get something off his chest, I guess I can let him say his piece. For a minute. Then I'll kick him to the curb and send him back to LA for breaking my once-upon-a-time friend heart.

Swallowing hard, I smooth my ponytail, and slowly open the door. I'm awake and in total control. Then I see him.

Oh, no. He has a beard now. This could be trouble.

"Hey, Hadley." His voice is deep and resonant. I break into full-body goose bumps.

"What do you want?" I manage to say, although my breath hitches on the *you*, and comes out more like you-hoo. *Not* the strong beginning I was hoping for.

"I know I shouldn't have dropped in unannounced," he says.

"That's not an answer." I tip my chin to meet his gaze.

"I came here to plead my case." He pulls his hands from his pockets and lifts both palms, like he's surrendering.

"Well." I put my hands on my hips. I want him to see me standing my ground. "I already heard everything I need to hear from that woman."

"Pippa."

"I know who she is. I remember that day."

"Right." His eyes flicker with something that looks like regret, if regret had an actual look. "I really wish those auditions weren't just a bad memory now."

I shrug. "I barely think about that time."

"Really?"

No. Not *really*. He knows better than anyone how much I wanted to prove I could try something new. To show Carson I was as wild and fun as the next person. As it turns out, wanting to prove myself to my ex was pretty shallow motivation.

No wonder the judges sent me packing.

"Okay." I incline my head. "You want to plead your case? Go ahead."

"Here? Now?" His neck tenses. "In the doorway?" His eyes sweep down the length of me to my feet before popping back up again. That's right, once-upon-a-time friend. I'm in sweaty yoga tights and a tank top.

Deal with it.

"I'll give you one minute," I say, arching a brow to feign confidence. But what I really want to do is grab the afghan from the love seat to cover up.

"All right." He clears his throat. "I ...uh ... I'm sorry Pippa ambushed you the other day with her whole fake-dating idea, but she's absolutely serious about that spot on *America's Hidden Talent*." When he gulps, his Adam's apple dips. "And even if you say no to helping me—which I would totally understand—I'll still convince her to get you on the show. You deserve that."

I puff out a breath. "*That's* how you want to use your sixty seconds?"

"No. I—"

"Stop."

He shakes his head. "Sam was right."

"Who?"

"I'm doing this all wrong." His words are slow now and halting. "It's just that ... you ... I ... I'm nervous." He blinks, and the corners of his eyes soften. He almost looks like Goober again.

"Well." I plant a hand on my chest. My heart's really

pounding now. "I didn't become a professional singer," I say. "I'm a music teacher."

He ducks his head. "I know."

"And I don't perform in public anymore," I say.

"Then this could be your chance to get back on that stage."

"The performing arts building is my stage. I help kids feel good about themselves. No matter how skilled they are. No matter how talented or ... not." I pause to swallow, remembering the one positive thing that happened at those auditions. I realized I loved music—so, so much—but I'd gone there for all the wrong reasons. Now I sing for a hundred right ones.

My students.

"They're all individuals," I continue, "just doing their best, you know? And I get to bring the joy out in them. *That's* the magic."

"That's amazing," he says.

"It is."

"*You're* amazing."

Whoa. Did he really just say that? "*You* disappeared on me."

He flinches. "Yeah. And I had my reasons at the time, but I won't bore you with them now."

"Ha!" I cough out a small laugh. "I would've *loved* a reason five years ago. Even a boring one." I sniff, then realize he smells good. *Not* the best discovery when I'm in sweaty workout clothes. "You know, it took me a while to realize I must not have meant as much to you as I thought I did back then. Like, we weren't best friends, obviously." My voice catches. "But I thought we were ... something."

I still have your hat, I think. *In a box. With old tin foil.*

"We *were* something." He drops both arms down to his sides. To be honest, he looks kind of sad and vulnerable. And it almost works. Until I remind myself he's been trained to convince audiences everywhere he's a superhero. Why wouldn't he try that act on me—someone who has a history of trusting him?

"Time's up," I say.

"Huh?"

"Your minute. It's over."

His shoulders sink along with his arms. "The last thing I wanted to do was hurt you, Hadley. But I hurt you anyway. And I'm sorry."

"Oh. So sorry you thought you'd just show up and apologize, and I'd agree to Pippa's publicity stunt?" I feel my throat begin to blotch. "I'm not a stunty person, you know." I scrunch up my nose, realizing that didn't come out quite right. "I'm not public either. I'm not .... publicly stunted." I pause for a gurgling breath. Why do I sound so spluttery?

Because you're authentic, Hadley. Stammering is normal when you're flustered.

"Those two words," I try again, "publicity and stunt—they're so manipulative."

He bobs his head. "I don't disagree."

"So you admit we'd be manipulating people," I say. "Not just any people. Your fans. How can you feel good about that?"

"I never said I felt good about it."

"Then why play along?"

"I owe Pippa," he says a little too quickly. "And Andrew, my manager." The tips of his ears turn red. "They've had my back over and over, but the video from the hospital—those pictures, what the tabloids are saying about me—"

"It's not true," I say, wishing I weren't so motivated to defend him.

"*I* know that." A grimace takes over his face. "But once reporters smell blood, they go digging for more."

I consider this comment for a beat. "Journalists aren't sharks. They're just doing their jobs."

"Maybe," he says. "But I still made Pippa and Andrew's jobs impossible at the worst possible time. So I need to turn things around for their sake."

"Fair enough," I say. But he averts his eyes, which tells me there's more to the story. I need to investigate. "What's in it for you?"

He blows out a breath and rubs a hand along the back of his neck. "Youngblood Studios is considering me for a new role," he says. "It's a multi-film contract that could mean a lot of money. Which, if it happens, would be good for Pippa and Andrew."

"And also for you."

"Yeah." He slowly meets my gaze again. "Living in California's expensive."

"I'll bet."

"But another actor's in consideration now," he adds.

I chew my lip, nodding. Processing. I still feel like there's something else he's not telling me, but I can't put my finger on it. "So what's the role?" I ask.

"That's not important." His brow furrows. "Trust me."

"You're the one asking for help." I shrug. "*I* get to decide what's important."

"Fine." He drops his chin. "It's this new franchise featuring superheroes set in Regency times," he mumbles to his toes.

This gets my attention. "As in the 1800s? Like in England?"

"That's the one," he says, lifting his chin.

"Huh. *That's* unexpected."

"Experimental is more like it," he says. "The screenwriters claim, and I quote, 'They're going for a unique blend of romance and action. Like nothing that's ever been on film before.'" His mouth slips sideways. "I'd be playing a character called"—he takes a beat—"The Vise-Count."

"The what?"

"The Vise-Count." His lip twitches, but he quickly schools his face back into serious mode. "He's a nobleman who turns into a giant vise to fight his enemies. Like *Pride and Prejudice* meets an auto body shop."

"Oh wow." I'm tempted to tell him Mr. Darcy isn't technically a nobleman. Still, a half smile tugs at my lips, as I picture

Link dressed like Colin Firth while simultaneously morphing into some kind of garage equipment. "And you *want* this part?" I ask.

He rakes a hand over his scalp. "I *need* this part."

Nina's voice whispers in my head. *You* need *to start saying yes to new things. You* need *spontaneity and adventure.*

Need. Need. Need.

"And me pretending to be your girlfriend," I say, considering the opportunity. "That will help your reputation?"

"Pippa thinks so," he says. "She wants Sam, my photographer, to follow us around capturing stolen moments like we're a real couple. The only difference is we'll be keeping our relationship a total secret."

"Our *fake* relationship," I emphasize.

"Right." He glances around, like he's already worried about being caught. "Pippa says the secretive part will up the ante when our relationship is revealed. Apparently, people really love to think they've scooped a story. Or that they've solved a mystery."

I arch a brow. "Or discovered HadLink."

"Exactly." His mouth quirks again, and I flash back to how easy it used to be to make him smile.

"So Sam will take pictures and videos of us?" I ask.

He nods. "And when the timing is right, Pippa and Andrew will unleash the photo evidence of our romance on every social media platform known to man."

I splay my hands. "And the crowd goes wild."

"That's the plan." He shrugs. "Then we'll arrange a time for a very public proposal, at which point you'll say no and break things off with me."

"And why would she want me to do that? Can't we just be a cute couple?"

"You want to be a cute couple?"

"No!" *No. No. No*. See, Nina? I'm getting better at saying that word too.

"I know you don't." He nods. "It's just that Pippa thinks it will be better if I look like a crushed puppy in front of the whole world rather than some guy in a happy relationship."

"I'd never crush a puppy," I say, huffing out a nervous laugh. I came a little too close to letting him think I actually want HadLink to be a thing. "Crushing puppies seems more like something Dasha Peet would do. Or maybe not Dasha. But her character. Ice-Sis."

"So you've seen the movies."

"Maybe."

He chuckles, shaking his head. "Well, that's one of the reasons Dasha didn't get this part."

"Oh." I take a small step backward, not loving the reminder that this is just a role, and I'm a means to an end. Then again, maybe this is a chance to advance my own goal in the process.

Spontaneity. Adventure. Just say YES, Hadley.

"Okay. So let's say we do this, and I dump you." I reach down to adjust the neckline of my yoga tank top. "Then what happens?"

"Pippa's hoping everyone will feel sorry for me. Like, *really* sorry." He grimaces. "The idea is that women everywhere will think they might be the one to heal my broken heart."

"Because if someone like *me* can get you, anyone can, right?" My lungs start leaking air again. "I'm just a nobody. Totally average."

"Trust me." He meets my gaze. "You are anything but average."

Gah! Did he really just say that? My throat twists up like a Twizzler. I used to buy packages of Twizzlers and use them as straws for my Coke and Dr. Pepper. But right now, I couldn't get a drop of soda through my throat-straw if I tried.

"What if I can't pull off this charade?" I choke out.

"You don't have to do anything except let Sam take pictures. He's great at his job. And so is Pippa. She and Andrew will work their magic with whatever footage Sam manages to get."

"Oh." I fight a flinch imagining my very *real* self being

reduced to fake captions and hashtags. They'll be using smoke and mirrors to manipulate moments that actually happen, turning them into something else entirely.

"It's only for a week or so," he says. "Which means even if you hate the plan—even if you hate *me*—this is all temporary."

"I don't hate you," I blurt, emotions bubbling up inside me. After all these years, I'd convinced myself my feelings for him were locked up tight. But Pippa's call sent me into a nostalgia spiral that's only getting worse. I have to regain my control. "Before I agree to help," I say, "we have to set up some ground rules."

"Anything." He exhales long and loudly. "Whatever you want, I'll do it. Or not do it. Either way."

"Wow." I fold my arms across my chest. "I've never seen this desperate side of you."

"I wouldn't say I'm *desperate*."

"What would you call yourself then?"

"Fine," he says. "I am desperate."

I drop my arms and offer him a slow clap. "Glad you could finally admit it."

"All right." The corner of his lip twitches. "Hit me with your terms." He nudges my arm, just below my bicep. "But not literally," he adds. "You look like you've been working out."

"Heh." A blush crawls across my cheeks, but I remind myself this is just a game for PR purposes. So I straighten my spine and present my demands. "Rule number one: No unnecessary touching."

"Whoa." He chuckles. "Starting out strong."

"That's not an answer."

"Yes. I mean ... no. Yes to no touching that isn't for the sake of pictures." He ducks his head. "I'm a gentleman, and you're doing me a favor. I wouldn't take advantage of the situation."

"Good," I say. "Next rule: We can never be alone together." Not that I don't trust myself, but ... I don't trust myself.

"Agreed," he says. "The whole point of this plan is for Sam to be with us filming so Pippa can leak evidence of us as a couple. Being alone would defeat the purpose."

I nod, slowly. "You know pretending we're a couple won't be easy for me."

"Me either."

"Ha!" A small laugh puffs across my lips. "You're an actor, Link. You make a living being fake." He jerks his head like my words stung him. And regardless of how much his disappearance hurt my heart, I don't relish the thought of hurting him now. "I'm sorry," I say softly. "I didn't mean to suggest—"

"Here's the thing." He steadies himself against the doorframe. "My roles don't require much acting. I spend my days being told what to say and how to say it. Where to stand and how to move. I jump off bridges and buildings. I get into car chases that end in explosions. I do more trading places with my stuntman than mustering up real emotions."

"Ah." My lip tugs up. "You're telling me a made-up superhero like Magnetron doesn't have deep feelings?"

"I'm not actually Magnetron, Hads."

Hads.

The old nickname sends a flutter through my insides. "Duh," I say, ignoring the wings beating in my stomach. "So if you're not a great actor, you think you can successfully pull off being in love with me?" I'd been aiming for a lighthearted tone, but he takes my hand and sparks fly up my whole arm.

"Truly, madly, deeply," he says.

"Whoa." All my brain cells start swishing like a bowl full of goldfish. So many fins chopping at the water.

"See?" He quirks a brow. "I can be pretty romantic for a superhero."

Oof. I *knew* he was acting. This week-or-so is going to be dangerous. "No *old* nicknames," I blurt. "You can't call me Hads. That's the third rule." Hads makes me weak for him, and I can't risk being weak.

"That might be hard for me," he says. "Hads is a habit."

"We haven't spoken in five years, Link. Surely you can resist calling me Hads for one week."

He lurches like I socked him in the stomach. "You called me Link."

I wrinkle my nose. "That's not a new nickname," I say. "That's your real name now. You changed it." *And then you erased all evidence of the person I used to know.*

"Yeah, I guess I did do that."

"And your real girlfriend would call you Link, so me calling you James would be weird and confusing. You have to be Link to me. Only Link. That's who you are now. And anyway, we're both just acting."

"Okay." His jaw shifts. "You're Hadley. I'm Link. What else?"

What else? What else? There's still so much I want to know about what happened back then and about who he is now. And I don't have much time before I'll have to end things. Before he'll leave me again.

"If I agree to be your fake girlfriend ... I get to ask you a question at the end of each day, and you have to swear to answer honestly. You can't back down or hem or haw or tap out."

"Like truth or dare?"

"Yes. But *without* the dare."

"All right." He makes a small noise in the back of his throat, like a grunt of concession. "So one Q & A session per day until our breakup?"

"Yep."

"Agreed." He scrapes a hand along his beard. It's a bashful move that would be adorable if I knew he was being genuine. But how can I tell the difference between what's true and what's a part he's playing? I can't tell. That's the answer.

"What else?" he asks.

"That's it." My mouth goes dry. "Four rules. I don't want to overly complicate the situation any more than it already is."

His nod is quick and tight. "Do we have a deal then?"

I exhale. This might be the stupidest move of my life. What would Nina tell me?

Adventure. Spontaneity. Say yes, Hadley.

"Yes," I say, and he startles, like he can't quite believe I agreed either. Then before I can change my mind, I say, "Now what?"

He shakes his head, pulling his phone from his pocket. "Pippa looked up some places for photo ops in Harvest Hollow." He taps at his screen. "She thinks these spots could be perfect for getting romantic shots without being discovered. Here." He holds up his open Notes app so I can scan Pippa's note titled Operation HadLink.

The woman clearly did her research on what Harvest Hollow has to offer, but most of what she's listed would be impossible to pull off without an audience right now. This season attracts tourists like no other time of year, and the fall festival is right around the corner.

I stifle a laugh. "If Pippa thinks we can fly under the radar feeding goats at Harvest Farms on a Saturday afternoon, she's barking up the wrong sugar maple."

"Yeah." Link shoves his phone back in his pocket. "I warned Pippa this might not work." A shadow passes over his face, convincing me I was right before. There's definitely more to this situation. Something he's not admitting.

"Hey." I reach out and touch his elbow. Thankfully he's wearing a Henley. After all these years spent trying to forget he existed, I'd probably turn to dust like a vampire in the sunlight if I touched his actual skin. "Are you okay?" My question is soft, all traces of teasing gone.

"I'll be fine," he says, but the words are full of stones. "I'll always be just ... fine. And there's absolutely nothing fair about that."

I swallow hard, and something shifts inside my chest. I've got no idea what's happening for Link right now, but his vulnerability turns my insides to mush. I said yes to this ruse because I wanted to bring spontaneity and adventure into my life. But if I can help Link now, I want to try.

I know I shouldn't care. I don't *want* to care. But every time Carson tore me down, Link was there for me with no other motive than to be my friend.

So no matter what came after that, and even though I'll probably get hurt at the end of this, I can do this for Link.

Maybe then I'll be able to leave the past where it belongs for good.

"I've lived in this town my whole life," I say. "Well, except for those few years at school. But I've got some ideas up my sleeve, if you'll let me play around with Operation Hadlink." I peer up at him, until our eyes are in sync.

"You'd do that for me?"

"I would." I nod, then tilt my head. "First things first, though. Tell your photographer he can come out now."

"Huh?"

"The guy with the camera." I point over Link's shoulder. "Red hair. Blue sweatshirt. Behind the trash can. He's with you, right?"

A smile breaks across Link's face, bright like a sunrise and even warmer. "You hear that, Sam?" he calls out. "You're gonna have to get a whole lot better at hiding."

Chapter Twelve

LINK

"Well, it's not the Ritz," Sam says, kicking his feet up on the low coffee table. "But this place is a whole lot quieter than my house." He drops back against the sofa and stretches his legs out with a sigh. "I might even take a nap."

The Maple Tree Inn may be short on bells and whistles, but it's clean and comfortable, which is all we need. This isn't a honeymoon. Our time here has an expiration date. For our stay, though, Pippa got Sam and me a suite.

There are two medium-sized bedrooms with attached bathrooms off a shared living space, and a small kitchenette with a microwave and toaster oven. A functional desk sits across the room from the couch. A flat screen TV takes up half the wall. Both our closets are stocked with extra pillows, and the carpets are freshly vacuumed. The fact that the decor is all apple-themed is comforting.

Apples remind me of Hadley.

"I'm just glad no one recognized me coming in the back entrance," I tell Sam. He checked in on our behalf, then I used the parking lot entrance, bypassing the lobby and going straight to the elevator. Opening the slider now, I step out onto the balcony.

Considering the modest nature of the suite's interior, the

view is more impressive than I'd expected. On our side of the inn, miles and miles of greenery stretch into the distance. There are groves of trees and flat pastures, then mountains rising to the clouds. A bird swoops overhead before soaring across the sky. I breathe in for the count of six, hold it for seven, then blow it out for eight.

Just like Dr. Kwon taught me.

When I turn back toward the suite, Sam's already out like a light, snoring softly on the couch. So I shut the slider and take a seat at the table on the balcony to FaceTime my mom. Her smile fills the screen so quickly, she must've been waiting for my call.

"Hey, baby," she says. She's on her deck sitting in one of the Adirondack chairs.

"How are the dogs?" Might as well get that out of the way first.

"Full of sand and seaweed." She chuckles. "My furniture may never be the same. But I'm used to that by now."

"I can't thank you enough, Mom."

"You already have," she says. "And it's the least I could do. So how's it going there?"

"So far so good." I offer her a sheepish look. "Hadley's being more cooperative than I deserve."

"She agreed to help?"

"She did. Which is good, otherwise this trip would've been for nothing."

"Except to see her."

"Yeah."

"And to be in North Carolina again."

"On that note." I flip the phone to show her the mountains. The sun's still making its slow descent, but we've got a couple hours of daylight before it sinks below the horizon. The air is chilled, and the breeze is perfect.

This space smells like home.

"I really miss that view," my mom says. Her tone is soft and wistful. "I miss everything about North Carolina."

I flip the screen so it's facing me again, and prop it against a potted plant on the table. It's a sweet touch that makes the place feel more homey.

"You could always move back," I say. "We can sell your house in Malibu and get you one in Asheville. Someplace quiet. Somewhere that's still under the radar." Even as I say this, my stomach twists like an old knotted rope.

"No." She shakes her head, and the wind off the ocean blows her dark hair. "The beach is beautiful here, just different. And anyway, I just want to be where you are." She offers me a small smile. "You're all I have left, James."

"Yeah." I nod, my heart splitting a little at the seams. "Me too."

As if they feel left out of the conversation, Boo, Scout, and Jem bound up behind my mom and take turns lapping at her face while she shrieks and laughs, pretending to shoo them away. "You dogs are a total mess!" she warbles.

"You know you love it," I say.

"I think they wanted to remind me I still have them. Muddy paws for the win!" She shrugs, as she always does when she's ready to change the subject. "So, anyway, what's the plan now that you're there?"

I glance over my shoulder through the glass. "Well, Sam's crashed at the moment."

"Ah." She grins. "Good for him."

"He grabbed us a couple frozen burritos at The General Store to tide us over until we can figure out where to eat without being recognized."

"Chicken or beef?"

"Both, I think. Try not to be jealous." I huff out a laugh. "We'll probably just unwind here until it's time to meet Hadley for our first photo shoot."

"And where's that going to be?"

"Harvest Farms," I say. "Hadley's idea. According to her, it's like autumn threw up over there. But in a good way. They've got a cider press and a pumpkin patch. Hay rides. A petting zoo. Apparently all the commercial stuff shuts down at six on weekends. Hadley says the corn maze will be deserted by seven, which gives us just enough time to take pictures before it gets dark."

My mom arches an eyebrow. "Sounds kind of fun, actually."

"I guess." Sam also pointed out the light at sunset will make shots of Hadley and me that much more romantic. Just the thought of it raises goose bumps on my neck.

Or maybe that's from this breeze on the balcony.

"We're going to park down the road out of sight and slip in through the exit," I continue. "Apparently there's a big farmhouse on the property, but it's set so far back, Hadley says no one will see us."

"Hmm." My mom cocks her head. "Hopefully you won't get lost in the corn maze."

The prospect of being stuck with Hadley among rows and rows of corn stalks makes my pulse speed up, until I remember Sam's going to be there taking pictures. "At this point, I'm just hoping the plan works."

My mom sighs. "Would it be the end of the world if it didn't?"

My teeth clench up and I force them open again. "The paps are on high alert now, looking to dig up anything on me they can. But that's not good for ... Magnetron." I don't want to admit I'm more worried about her than my image. Questions from reporters would only make her relive the pain. I can't let her spiral again. Not when she's finally good. "Until Youngblood casts their new film, I need to give the media something else to sink their teeth into."

"Something that's not real," she says.

"Better than the alternative."

"Which is stuff about me. About us. About—"

"Yes." I cut her off.

"I said it before, and I'll say it again. Please don't do this on my account." Her voice goes soft and she drops her gaze. When she won't make eye contact, I know she's struggling, and I hate that my fame makes her a target.

"Mom."

She lifts her chin. "You and Hadley shouldn't have to lie because of me."

"We aren't lying. We're just letting the public draw their own conclusions and failing to correct them if they're wrong."

Jem runs over, pressing his snout into her hand. "So Sam taking pictures of you and Hadley alone in a corn maze is—"

"Something people do in the fall," I say. "This town is practically a shrine to the season. That's all real. And Hadley is an old friend of mine. And I really do care about her." My throat tightens. "That's the truth, Mom." *More than you know. More than Hadley knows.*

More than I've been willing to admit to myself.

Behind me there's a tapping on the glass, and I jerk around just as Sam slides open the door. "Sorry to interrupt," he says, waving at my mom. "Looking good, Mrs. L."

I smirk. "Stop flirting with my mom. You're a married man."

He cuts his eyes to me. "I'm the most married man in the USA." He splays his hands. "Speaking of which. Is *People's* sexiest single under thirty ready for the best frozen burrito of his life?"

* * *

Two hours later, Sam eases our rental car off the main road and parks behind a copse of maple trees. The expansive property of Harvest Farms is just ahead of us, but from here we're well out of sight. The sun's sinking toward the horizon, and the air's much cooler now, so I grab my beanie from the back seat and pull it on. Climbing out of the passenger seat, I assess the area for possible discovery, but we're off the main road, and no one else is driving by. Sam joins me at the back of the car, his camera bag in tow.

"Nice shades." He smirks, nodding at my sunglasses.

"Nice face." I smirk back. But he's got a point. The sun isn't exactly high in the sky now. So I slip off my Ray-Bans and toss them into the car. The evening is quiet except for a pair of birds cawing in the branches overhead. Soon Hadley's orange Volkswagen beetle appears in the distance, chugging toward us like a giant jack-o'-lantern.

She drives slowly, crunching over fallen leaves to park under the other side of the trees. Meanwhile, Sam and I wait for her, kicking at pebbles, making tiny clouds of dust. When she hops out of the car—wearing cuffed jeans, lace-up boots, and a cable-knit sweater the same blue as her eyes—my mind skips back to when she'd meet me at the vending machines in pajamas or mismatched sweats.

Her hair would be piled on top of her head in a messy blonde bun, her face fresh-scrubbed, eyes sparkling. Whenever I saw her, she was nothing short of luminous. Even when she'd get made up —in lip gloss, mascara, earrings, heels, the whole nine yards—Hadley still seemed comfortable in her own skin. All easy beauty. Kindness. Humor. But her good nature was never enough for Carson. No. He wanted some hot daredevil by his side.

Man, I hated that guy.

He didn't see her. Not the real her. Which seems impossible since there's nothing to see in her but realness. I don't think Hadley Morgan's ever pretended to be anything she isn't. Not a single day of her life.

Until now.

My chest constricts with equal parts guilt and regret. I'm the one who talked Hadley into faking this relationship. I should've just told Pippa and Andrew no way. Let the chips fall where they may.

It's not too late, Link. You can still back out.

So what if I don't turn things around and get the public feeling sympathy for me? What's the worst that could happen?

Enforcer's Endgame could be a flop.

The role of The Vise-Count could go to someone else.

But the truth is, my mom's debt is already paid off, and I've got her set up in a house she can stay in for the rest of her life.

Still, Cal Youngblood's invoking the part of my contract that requires me to do any publicity the studio demands. If I'm in breach of our agreement, they could go after the money I've already been paid. That would be bad for my mom. For me. For Pippa. For Andrew.

Then there's Hadley's guaranteed spot on *America's Hidden Talent*. I get that she's moved on to teaching now, and that's what makes her happy. But singing always meant so much to her. A way to connect to her mother. And I don't want to be the one who takes away her chance to make it big as a performer.

"Hey," Hadley approaches with a small wave. When she tucks a strand of hair behind her ear, she's so adorable, my heart skips a beat.

"Thanks for coming," I say, meeting her gaze. "I still can't believe you're willing to do this for me."

"Well, don't be *too* grateful." A smile tugs at her lips. "I'm just using you for the chance to be a little wild for once."

"Whoa." Sam chuckles. "I think I like you already."

Hadley cuts her eyes across the adjacent field over to the corn maze. "I told you this place would be empty after hours. We got lucky that tonight's not scheduled for a haunted corn maze."

Sam and I exchange a glance. "Haunted corn maze?"

"Like a haunted house on Halloween." She shrugs. "It's kind of fun, but it does get pretty spooky."

Sam grins at her. "We'll keep you safe."

We, Sam? Thanks, but I can do that just fine on my own.

Hadley nods at the deserted parking area in front of the farm. "We can head around the back, and stay out of sight."

"Lead the way," I say. Together we trudge away from the road toward the edge of the corn maze that's farthest from the farm. Hadley's up front and I'm right behind her, close enough to catch the scent of apples. It could be from the cider press, but Hadley always smells like apples. Maybe she's always carrying a little piece of this town in her.

Sam follows at a distance. As we're about to enter the maze, he says, "Hold up."

Hadley and I both freeze and turn. He's standing with his camera up, but he drops it. "No, don't look at me." He waves at the maze. "Just go slow, and I'll get a couple of shots of you two slipping into the corn. It'll make for a great caption. Something like 'Lincoln James and his longtime love Hadley Morgan sneaking in for a little after-hours fun.'"

"HadLink," I say under my breath.

She tips her chin. "Huh?"

"Our couple name, remember?"

"I do," she says. "I just didn't hear you."

My shoulders hitch. "Do you hate it?"

"I don't know what I think. Being one half of a celebrity couple is new territory for me." Her cheeks pink up, or maybe it's the lighting. Either way, I swear she's never looked more beautiful.

"Go," Sam prompts. "But take your time. Even slow motion wouldn't be bad. I'll just hang back and do my thing. Forget I'm here."

Without thinking, I put my hand out stretching toward Hadley's, and she dips her gaze, letting me grab on to just the tips of her fingers.

The charge is electric and shoots straight up my arm. I almost pull away, but she nods, and spins around, gently tugging me toward the corn. As we enter the maze and turn the first corner, I watch the back of her, moving through the stalks. This is the first time we've touched since ...

I can't remember the last time we touched.

The truth is, Hadley always seemed a little out of reach no matter how close we got. At first, we were just two people bonding over our mutual love of chocolate-covered peanuts. But I knew from the beginning she was way out of my league. Here was this funny, smart, bright light of a woman who was wanted by both parents and cherished by her father. She deserved so much more than I could give her. I felt like the best I could offer was friendship.

But even after we started planning off-campus meetups—coffee, dessert, movies—I still didn't open up to her. Vulnerability and trust just weren't my thing. But Hadley?

She shared a lot.

Maybe she needed an ear because she was an RA who spent so much time listening to others. Either way, I heard all about her dad. Her mom. Her music. Her goal of finishing what her mother couldn't. All the while, I kept at least a sliver of distance between us. For my own safety. Selfishly protecting myself.

How could I tell her I wasn't a student? That my only parent was in a mental hospital, and we were drowning in debt?

In the end, it didn't matter, because by her third year, Hadley was either dating Carson, or they'd just broken up. She'd be doing the "will they or won't they get back together again" dance.

I'm a lot of things, but I'm not *that* guy. The one who jumps in on another man's girlfriend. Even if the man is more like an idiot. Instead, I stood by, hoping she'd figure out she could do so much better. But I never thought I was the so much better she deserved.

She glances over her shoulder now, lets go of my hand, and skips away. "Hadley? Where are you going?"

She disappears around a corner, and Sam comes up behind me. "What's she doing?" he asks.

"I have no idea."

We follow the path she took up around the same bend, and there she is, standing on a pile of hay bales.

"Sam." She nods at him. "Get your camera ready."

"Will do, boss."

"Hey, Link." Hadley grins. "Catch."

Chapter Thirteen

HADLEY

So jumping off a hay bale into Link's arms *seemed* like a good idea at the time. I pictured Sam capturing the moment on film, something kind of fun and a little romantic, and wholly authentic, since Link wouldn't see it coming. Otherwise the pictures would look fake and planned, right?

I was aiming for adventure and spontaneity.

Until I crashed into an unsuspecting Link, knocking him to the ground.

"OOF!" I land on top of him, and all the air is forced from my lungs. Now we're both sprawled in the dirt, and I'm flailing like an upended turtle. Except for the part where I'm not upended. I'm lying directly on top of Link.

"Are you all right?" I manage to blurt, my body pressed against his. But Link doesn't respond.

Oh no. DID I KILL HIM with my spontaneity and adventure?

"Say something," I gasp.

His chest starts to heave beneath me, and he raises his arms straight up on either side of my body, like he's a zombie. Or in the act of surrender. What's going on?

"Arrrgh," he chokes out, then suddenly laughter's bursting from him in great big gulps.

"I'm so sorry!" I struggle to scramble off him, but he drops his arms, wrapping them around me. My body heats up at his touch, despite the awkwardness of the moment. Why is he hugging me? This doesn't seem like a hugging situation.

"Help," he manages to wheeze, and I realize Link isn't trying to hug me. He's trying to get his bearings while all my weight is still on his torso. I probably knocked the wind right out of him. Not to mention he's laughing so hard, he probably can't breathe anyway. Still, the sound is so infectious, I start to giggle too. I'm partly embarrassed, and a little surprised, but mostly relieved I didn't crush Magnetron to death.

"Are ... you ... all ... right?" I ask the question again, this time stammering through my own giggles. His eyes finally meet mine, and we've both got tears in the corners. My face is just inches from his.

Link's brows fly up as he takes in just how close we are. And before my next heartbeat, he flips us both over, with me still cradled in his arms.

Whoa. Magnetron's been working out.

Instinctively, I start to wriggle free, and he releases me, gently lowering my body to the ground. I scramble to a crouch with a whole lot less grace than I imagined when I first came up with this idea.

Behind us, Sam says, "Don't stop now, kids. This is fantastic!"

Link and I both jerk our heads in his direction. "How about a little help?" Link grunts at Sam.

"No way, man." Sam shakes his head from behind the lens. "I'm still recording. We'll edit the sound out, but I can't be in the shot. Keep going."

Without another word, Link leaps to his feet, then he grabs my hand to haul me up. I stumble into his arms, then take a big step backward. Link's gaze sweeps downward, taking me in, and his mouth slips sideways.

"You got a little something ..." He begins, but then his voice trails off. He's pointing at my sweater. When I look down, I see I'm covered in straw and dust and dirt.

"I got a *lot* of something." I pat myself down, scraping off strands of dry hay. When I realize Link's not doing the same, I freeze and look up at him. "What?"

He reaches out and brushes my lip with his thumb. "You missed a piece," he says. His voice is rough, like a dried corn husk. A trail of heat follows his touch, and my insides quiver. I'm basically one big Jell-O mold now, except with two arms, two legs, and one heart banging my rib cage.

Oh, Hadley. How did you think—even for one second—you'd be okay pretending to be Link's girlfriend? You're already a total mess and you're only a few hours into this week.

"And cut!" Sam calls out, off to the side.

Link's thumb is still hovering at the edge of my mouth. "We're not on set," he says to Sam, eyes still pinned to mine.

"I'm aware of that, Einstein." Sam chuckles. "I just wanted you to know you could stop pretending now."

Link drops his arm.

Too bad I wasn't pretending.

"Seriously, though," Sam says. "That was totally brilliant, Hadley."

My throat flushes. "You think so?"

"Yeah. Link didn't see that coming, so all the shots I got were off-the-cuff and adorable."

Link sweeps his gaze over to Sam and arches a brow. "I'm *adorable*?"

"Hadley's adorable." Sam smirks. "*You're* a guy who got taken to the ground by a person half your size. But that'll play great to the audience. Exactly the kind of stuff we want them to see."

"Audience. Right." Link adjusts his beanie. I ignore the heat blooming across my cheeks and beat the rest of the dust and straw off my clothes. All the while, I give myself a silent pep talk:

Remember that's what this is about, Hadley.

Getting perfect images for your fake love story is what you're here for.

Not genuine feelings.

"The best part of this week," Sam continues, "is I don't have to fight for the exclusive. I'm usually stuck trying to scoop every other freelancer with a camera. But no one knows we're here."

Link nods, brushing excess dirt and straw off his jeans. "I liked the part where I didn't have to trade places with a stuntman in the middle of a scene I could do myself."

"I liked the part where I didn't break any of your bones," I chirp. Link and Sam both stop to stare at me. "What? I thought we were sharing our favorite parts."

"You weren't in any danger of breaking me," Link says, and the edge of his mouth curves up. "I'm not that fragile." He stamps his feet, stirring little clouds of dust. Then his face breaks into a genuine smile.

And there go my insides, spinning faster than a windmill in a hurricane.

"It's time to move on, my friends," Sam says, interrupting my Don Quixote metaphor. "We're wasting the last bit of light." He hikes up his camera bag. "So. What's next, Hadley?"

I lead them through the corn maze, which—I might add—they both would've gotten lost in if it weren't for me. Then we head to the pumpkin patch where Sam takes pictures of Link and me tossing mini-gourds at each other. After getting footage of us climbing to the top of the giant pumpkin pyramid, I point out a big green tractor in the middle of the field.

"We should pretend to drive that," I suggest.

As it turns out, the seat's so small, I have to sit on Link's lap to fit.

"Link. Put your hands around her waist," Sam says. "Lean back against his chest, Hadley. Get closer. You're not going to electrocute each other."

Says you, Sam. Says you.

When the sky finally gets too dusky for shots with natural

light, Sam waves at us to climb down. "Careful," Link says, helping me off the tractor. His grip is strong and I feel safe, even in the midst of my awkward clambering. He pulls out his wallet and retrieves two hundred-dollar bills, stuffing them in the tractor seat.

"Wow. What's that for?"

"We would've paid to do all this stuff if we weren't sneaking around."

"He does this kinda thing a lot," Sam says. "Some worker will find the money and it'll make his day."

"Or her day," Link says. His eyes meet mine in the gathering dark. I blink and open my mouth to thank him, but Sam speaks again first.

"Well, this has been a great shoot," he says. "And you both seemed totally real and believable the whole time," he adds. "There was just the right amount of surprise, clumsiness, and laughter to make the romance feel real."

"That was all part of my plan," I blurt, then my face flames hot. "I mean, the clumsy part. I was going for less pretend-y stuff and more couple-y."

"Well, it was genius." Sam grins. "I loved the look on Link's face when you jumped off the hay bale on top of him ... and then when you couldn't stop blushing...You're *still* blushing."

I press a palm to my cheek.

"Anyway, the shots I got were perfect," Sam says. "And the video footage is even better. I'll send everything to Pippa and Andrew tonight to be sure we're on the right track. But I think they're gonna flip." He secures the camera back in the bag. "So what's on tap for tomorrow, kids?"

I'm still recovering from my runaway blush when Link says, "Pippa suggested going to the top of the clocktower. That sounds interesting."

"We can't," I rush to say. "The clocktower's in the town square. It's attached to the courthouse, City Hall, and the post office."

"Ah." Link nods. "So those buildings probably won't be open on a Sunday."

Sam tilts his head, considering. "I think we should save the clocktower for a night shoot anyway. Pictures of you two at the top with the town all lit up in the background will be amazing."

My stomach lurches, not so much a windmill anymore as a plummeting elevator. The truth is, I can't be up that high. The pumpkin pyramid was already testing my limits. Okay, that's an exaggeration, but still. I feel silly admitting I'm afraid of heights after claiming I'm all about adventure and spontaneity.

"The public's not allowed up in the clocktower," I say.

Link's mouth slides into a lopsided grin. "You could've just said that in the first place."

"Too bad." Sam rubs his chin. "I figured that would be a great place to do some canoodling without being spotted."

Link's brow hitches. "Canoodling?"

"It's a word," Sam says. "Trust me."

"I have a different idea," I pipe up, and they both turn to face me. "Let's go to the movies. Considering your job, it'll be ironic, or meta, or whatever. I used to work at the theater back in high school."

Sam's eyes brighten. "I saw that place on our way through town. The Cineplex?"

"That's the one," I say. "Meet me at the far end of the parking lot tomorrow. Eleven o'clock." I aim an arched eyebrow at Link. "There won't be any red carpet, though. So no tuxedos, okay?"

He coughs out a laugh. "I'll do my best."

"And don't be late," I warn, wagging a finger. "The first matinee starts at 11:15."

Sam scratches his head. "Won't the employees notice Lincoln James showing up at the movies?"

I grin at them. "Trust me."

* * *

Nina's text comes in later while I'm in my bathrobe, brushing my teeth. I've been a ball of nerves all day wondering what to tell her about Link. A part of me hopes she'll approve of a plan this wild. The other part worries she'll think I'm insane. The thing is, Nina's always got a lot of opinions. And they're almost always strong. And she's usually not wrong.

Nina: What's up, Chuck? You have a good Saturday?
Me: Yep. Just gonna crawl into bed now with my new book and get a good night's sleep. Try not to wake me when you get home. Also: My name's not Chuck.
Nina: That's why I'm texting. I won't be home for a few days.
Me: ???

A wave of relief washes over me. At least for now, I won't have to defend my decision to fake-date Lincoln James. And I'm all about putting off discomfort as long as I can. It's kind of been my life's motto.

Nina: Since we've got staff development coming up, I decided to develop elsewhere.
Me: Elsewhere meaning ...
Nina: Meaning Gavin's family's cabin. They invited me to go with them.
Me: !!!! They've never invited you before.
Nina: Which is why I'm jumping at the chance. I need to make a good impression while I have the opportunity. Wish me luck!
Me: Luck!
Nina: NOOOO. You're supposed to say I don't need any luck, and that I'm awesome and they're going to love me.
Me: You don't need any luck, and you're awesome and they're going to love you. But.
Nina: But what?
Me: Not as much as I do.

Nina sends me back a string of heart-eye emojis, then a GIF of two little kids tackling each other in a hug. I smile and wipe a smudge of toothpaste from my mouth, then crawl into bed like a carcass full of mixed emotions.

It feels weird, not explaining what's going on to Nina yet. She has no idea I know Lincoln James. She's only aware my friend from college moved to LA and ghosted me. Telling anyone I was once close to Lincoln James felt a little desperate, like I was trying to be fame-adjacent. Even worse, I was afraid people might think I wasn't telling the truth.

Even my dad doesn't know my old friend is now the actor who plays Magnetron. And if I'm being totally honest, not talking about James allowed me to keep the temporary joy of our friendship frozen in time. We're like a fossil preserved in amber.

Until a few days ago, that is.

Bottom line: I'm not ready to tell all this to Nina yet. I've barely processed anything myself.

So this trip with her boyfriend just bought me a few more days to explain things to my heart.

LINK

I spend most of the night lying awake, counting Sam's snores through the walls of our suite. It's no worse than counting sheep, I guess. And if the poor guy's getting some rest, I'm not about to disturb him.

Sam Rollins is the closest thing I've had to a good friend since I moved to LA. Sure I trust Pippa and Andrew, but I can't ignore the fact that their financial success directly correlates to mine. No shade to them, though. I needed to make money just as much as the next person. And they've stuck by me even when I haven't made things easy. But they're as often frustrated by me as delighted.

Sam, on the other hand, seems to genuinely *enjoy* being my sidekick with a camera, and he's so good at what he does, I know he could get another gig in a heartbeat. There's no shortage of people in Hollywood looking to add a loyal photographer to their team. But I've only let a few see me without my mask. I'm talking about the figurative one, not my Magnetron mask, if that wasn't abundantly clear. Anyway, I like keeping Sam happy, so I let him snore the night away while I relive every second of the time I've spent with Hadley.

The shock on her face when she saw me on her doorstep.

The way she made me work to get her to agree.

Her spontaneity at the farm, not to mention her softness, strength, scent.

All the best *S* words.

Suddenly I remember her rule about getting to ask me a question at the end of every day. So before I can stop myself, I grab my phone. Answering Hadley will be easier via text than a face-to-face conversation anyway. This way, I can think through my response and she won't be able to read my expressions.

Cop out?

Sure.

Cowardly?

Indeed.

But also, smart, and self-preservation has been my MO for as long as I can remember. I'm awake anyway. Maybe she is too.

I kind of hope she is too.

Me: You forgot to ask me your daily question.

A minute passes. Then two. I figure Hadley must be asleep. After all, it's past midnight. I haven't adjusted to the time change yet, but this is Hadley's zone. So when her text finally does come in, I have to chuckle.

Hads: Who is this?
Me: Are you really wasting your first question on that? Or did you get *multiple* people to agree to brutal honesty today?
Hads: I just need to know if I'm dealing with James or Link.
Me: Why don't you decide who you're asking? Maybe you've got different questions for each of them.
Hads: I'm honestly surprised you reminded me about this after making sure I couldn't ask you a single question for years.
Me: I'm a man of my word.
Hads: I'll have to take your word for that. Okay. Let me think for a minute.

Me: Take all the time you need. Sam snores like a pack of wildebeests. I'll be awake all night.
Hads: A pack of wildebeests is called a blender.
Me: A blender of wildebeests? Did you just make that up?
Hads: Yes. But I'm supposed to be the one asking the questions.
Me: GIF of Clint Eastwood as Dirty Harry aiming a gun with the word SHOOT.
Hads: ...
Hads: ...
Hads: ...

As she composes multiple texts—then most likely deletes them—I can't help smiling at the ease with which the two of us slipped back into texting. Like no time has passed. Like I didn't move away and leave her hanging without a real goodbye.

Hads: Okay. I've got my first question. Where did you end up getting your degree after you dropped out of college to become a famous Hollywood celebrity?

Oh wow. I don't know what kind of question I expected from her, but I'm unprepared for this one. In fact, I'd hoped for something along the lines of *did you miss me* because it would've been so much easier for me to admit I missed her every single day in a text rather than face-to-face. Instead she's going with something that could be stickier.

Me: I didn't.
Hads: Become a famous Hollywood celebrity?
Me: Get my degree.
Hads: Why not?
Me: That's more than one question.
Hads: GIF of Dirty Harry saying "Go ahead. Make my day."
Me: ...
Me: ...

Me: ...
Hads: Ghosting me again? (skull emoji)

My gut clamps down.

Me: I'll explain another time. It's a longer story than I can get into on a text thread at midnight.
Hads: Is Sam's blender of wildebeests too distracting?

I'm composing a response when my phone buzzes again, but it's not Hadley.

Pippa: Sam sent me the footage from Harvest Farm. Your fans are going to eat this up. All ages and genders. Everyone's going to love HadLink. And when she breaks your heart, theirs will break for you. Great acting, Link.

Acting. Right.

Me: Yeah. The farm was Hadley's idea. I'm letting her run with the plans if that's OK with you. She knows the best places and times to go around here.
Pippa: Of course she does. Hometown girl. That's why she's perfect for this role. By the way, Andrew's hoping for something a bit more passionate tomorrow to ramp things up. He suggested shots of you and Hadley kissing. Make-out sessions encouraged.

I grip my phone as stones fill my gut. I'm surprised I don't crack the screen.

Me: I'm not going to pressure her.
Pippa: Of course not. We know you're a gentleman. But maybe she'll WANT to kiss you. What woman doesn't want to kiss Lincoln James?
Me: You.

Pippa: Touche. Anyway, take the compliment and do the best you can tomorrow. Be charming. Woo the girl. And remember, this is good for everyone. Not just you.
Me: You never let me forget.

As soon as Pippa and I sign off, I send Hadley one last text.

Me: Sorry for disappearing like that. Pippa interrupted. But I want you to know I had fun at the farm today.
Hads: It wasn't tooooo terrible.
Me: Thanks for playing along.
Hads: Whatever. I'm using YOU to prove I'm full of spontaneity and adventure.
Me: Mercenary. (skull emoji.)
Hads: On that note, we should get some sleep. I'll see you at the Cineplex tomorrow. Then I get to ask you another question. That's the deal, right?
Me: Right. And you're not tooooo terrible either.
Hads: Wow. Not too terrible? Thank you so muchness.
Me: Muchness?
Hads: Autocorrect. I was going for sarcasm. My gratitude isn't THAT big.

Hadley's gratitude may not be *that* big, but I still lie awake for hours with a smile on my face. The next day, just before eleven, Sam parks under the trees at the far end of the Cineplex lot. As we climb from the car, I quickly scout for anyone who might be curious about our identities, but there are only two other cars on the opposite side of the lot.

"Coast is clear," Sam says.

"Yeah. Everyone else must be at Harvest Farms taking pics on the tractor or getting tackled in the corn maze."

Sam chuckles and checks his phone. "Welp. Eleven on the dot."

"She'll be here. Hadley's always on ti—" Before I can finish my sentence, she appears around the corner coming from the alley behind the building. Her blonde hair falls loose over her shoulders and she's wearing a forest green sweater, navy leggings, and knee-high boots. When she spots us, her eyes brighten like blue lightbulbs, and my insides do a somersault.

I don't think I'll ever get used to what this woman's face does to me.

I'm not sure I want to get used to it.

"Hey there, men." Her expression is full of mischief. "Ready for another round of super-secret celebrity pictures?"

"Ready," I tell her. "No tuxedos, per your instructions."

Her gaze travels slowly from the ground up, starting with my cross trainers, then gray jogger pants, and ending with the black hoodie I threw on over a T-shirt. Suddenly I'm bashful, wanting to please her more than I probably should, especially since this project ends with a mandatory breakup.

"Is this all right?" I ask, my voice almost catching on the question. That's how much I want her to say *yes*.

She does one better by saying, "You're perfect." Then she makes a noise like a squirrel gagging on a mouthful of acorns. "I mean what you're *wearing* is perfect." As her cheeks flush, she quickly backtracks. "No one would ever suspect you're anyone special."

"Believe me, he's not special," Sam confirms, nudging my elbow. "You should've heard this guy snoring last night."

"A real blender of wildebeests, huh?" she asks.

Sam snorts, then tilts his head. "Wait. What?"

Hadley glances over her shoulder, her face is still flushed. "I parked behind the building. The alley's deserted right now." She turns to address me. "But put your hood up just in case we're spotted."

As I tug the hood over my hair, Hadley reaches for the strings and yanks them taut until my face is a small circle poking out of the cotton. The scent of laundry detergent fills the air, and Hadley takes a good long sniff.

"It's Tide," I say.

"What is?"

"That smell."

"I wasn't smelling you."

"My mistake." My mouth quirks. "I just thought you should know I do my own laundry."

A smile tugs at her lips. "Everyone does their own laundry, Link. That isn't something to brag about."

"Not in Hollywood," I tell her. "We've got services that come door to door, pick up your stuff and deliver it, washed, dried, fluffed and folded."

"This conversation is totally scintillating," Sam says, "but will there be a big tub of buttered popcorn to stick our faces in anytime soon? Asking for a friend."

"No, but I brought snacks," Hadley says, patting the purse slung across her. "We can't go in the front entrance or to the concession stand. It's too risky. The ticket taker or someone in the theater might recognize you."

"So what do we do?" I ask.

"Follow me." Hadley grabs my hand and heads down the alley behind the buildings. The hand-grab almost seemed like an afterthought for Hadley, but it's definitely a before-thought for me.

In fact her touch dominates *all* my thoughts right now. Heat spreads from my fingers, up my palm, past my wrist, to my elbow, over my biceps, and across my chest. It's a whole-body onslaught one section at a time.

Like I'm being trampled by a blender of wildebeests.

Around the back of the building, all the doors are painted the same color as the stucco, so they're basically camouflaged except for the metal handles. As we approach the first door, Hadley peeks back at us, her blue eyes twinkling.

"When I worked here in high school, the latch on the back entrance never closed correctly. The employees would leave it unlocked during business hours so their friends could sneak in. If we're lucky ..." Her voice trails off, and she whips around to try the door, hauling it open. "EEK!" She giggles. "Still works."

"Wait." I hold back. "We're breaking in?"

"I'll leave enough money in a cupholder for the three tickets we would've bought," she says. "They'll find it when they clean up after the show."

I still hesitate.

"This is the only way we can sneak you in without anybody recognizing you. Which is the whole point, right? Then Sam can take pics of us in a darkened movie theater. Very couple-y."

This rule-breaker side of Hadley is one I never would've expected. While I'm not about to cheat a small movie theater out of their ticket prices, I'm good with the idea of leaving a bunch of money behind as a surprise.

There's not a chance I'm letting Hadley do it, though.

"Come on," she says. Sam hoists the strap of his camera bag higher on his shoulder, and we both follow her into the dark. As the door shuts behind us, I start blinking fast, trying to adjust to the pitch black. The smell of popcorn hits my nose like a fist. Underneath that is a hint of sugar.

"Is that cotton candy?" Sam asks.

"Shhh," Hadley says. "The previews have already started, so hopefully the usher's finished his sweep. This way." The three of us slink along a hall with tiny lights set at intervals where the walls meet the floors. It's like a miniature runway, and Hadley floats toward another door. She peers inside, and, after a moment, motions us forward. We're in the back of the theater now, slinking along the second to last row.

Sam sinks into an aisle seat just behind us, keeping a discreet distance while still having an angle to take pictures. In the meantime, Hadley scoots farther down our aisle, finally pulling me into the collapsible seat next to hers.

The Dolby surround sound is pretty good for a theater this size, and as a preview for a movie with all three Hemsworth brothers slides into a high-speed chase, booming music pulses in my chest. Or maybe that's just my heart throbbing for Hadley.

Overhead, a thick ray of light beams across the room onto the screen.

We made it.

I can't believe nobody spotted us, until I survey the rest of the theater and realize there are only three other people in here and they're down in front. This would never happen back in LA. Then again, I don't make a habit of going to the movies on Sundays before noon.

For the first fifteen minutes of the film, all I can think about is Sam taking pictures of Hadley and me in the dark. Again it dawns on me that I've asked her to compromise her ideals. Then again, she seems into the idea of throwing caution to the wind for once. Then Pippa's voice bombards my brain—reminding me what could go wrong if this doesn't work.

I glance sideways, just an inch, so Hadley doesn't catch me examining her profile. For at least a minute, I just watch her watching the movie.

The light flickers, playing over the curve of her throat, the jut of her chin, the swoop of her nose. When her lips part, ever so slightly, I fight the urge to rub my thumb along her mouth. We're sitting so close, I soak up her scent. Like rain and apples and sunshine. I just want to inhale her so that combination can live in my lungs forever.

Is that weird?

Yeah, man. Super weird.

After another full minute, she turns, and I quickly swing my gaze back to the screen, acting like I've been paying attention the whole time. I'm not sure she's fooled, but she leans over the armrest, her lips pressed close to my ear. "So far so good," she whispers.

"Yeah," I say, staring straight ahead.

"I can't even tell if Sam's getting any shots of us."

"He is. Trust me. He's really good at what he does."

She offers a small nod. "Shouldn't you put an arm around me or something?"

My throat goes dry, but somehow I manage to croak, "Good idea."

At least I've got her permission.

When I do throw an arm over her shoulder, the total awkwardness of the move floods me with embarrassment. I've got no smooth moves when it comes to Hadley. We might as well be a couple of kids on a first date with their parents chaperoning.

Then again, my mom was always at the hospital with Tommy or too busy working to monitor me back then. And I never even met my dad, so I sure didn't get any lessons about how to be a man from him. I never sat through any talks about how to respect women. I'm flying blind here, without any guideposts. No role models.

Just my pulse picking up.

Man. I really am a teenager around Hadley.

She snuggles into the crook of my arm, like she was always meant to fill this space, and the emptiness that's been threatening to swallow me whole suddenly disappears. Just when I'm feeling out of my depth, completely overwhelmed, surrendering to self-pity, Hadley brings the exact comfort I need.

As if my body has a mind of its own, I reach for her hand with my free one. At first she just sits there, frozen, her eyes glued to what's happening onscreen. Then slowly, as if we're part of a slow-motion montage, she twines our fingers together.

As we hold hands, I hold my breath. Holding. Holding. Holding.

Hadley literally takes my breath away.

A wave of something crests in me—a fierce desire to protect this woman. To bring her some of the comfort she brings me. But if this is how I feel on only our second day together, how will things go when I'm on a stage ready to propose, with cameras aimed at us as she dumps me?

Probably no worse than she felt when you disappeared.

Sharp pains stab at my ribs. I hate that I'm the one who hurt her. And now Andrew wants me to ramp things up romantically? To be a bit more passionate? Hadley may have her own agenda of spontaneity and adventure, but I refuse to be the guy who takes advantage. So me moving in for a kiss?

Not gonna happen.

A deep rumble comes from inside me, and Hadley slowly turns and tips her chin. In the darkness, I can barely make out the outline of her, until the light from the movie screen glows across her face.

"Hey," she whispers softly.

"What?" I whisper back.

"You think we should kiss now?"

And that's when my brain explodes.

Chapter Fifteen

HADLEY

In the darkened theater, Link's black eyes glimmer down at me. Maybe it's a reflection from the screen, but either way, the light around his pupils is getting closer. Closer. Closer. He moves as subtly as a glacier, gathering me in with the arm that's already around my shoulder. Then he untangles his hand from mine. What's he going to do?

You suggested kissing, dummy.

My mouth goes cotton-dry as he reaches up to the spot where the neck of my sweater dips. Then he traces one fingertip along my bare collarbone. The hitch in my breath won't be caught in any pictures or video, but I'm beyond caring now. Link's touch is deliciously slow and achingly tender. Warmth builds in my stomach, radiating out like rays of sunshine.

He dips his chin, and my lips part, almost as if they're attached to him by strings.

Speaking of which, his face is only inches away from me. I suck in air, anticipating the feel of his lips pressed against mine. All these years, I never let myself imagine what his mouth would taste like. The scruff of his dimples along my skin. Well, almost never.

I can't help what happened in my dreams.

Still, now that the moment's almost here, I surrender to the inevitability. I'm letting go and perfectly powerless in the presence of my attraction. This man is drawing me to him like metal to a magnet. Like Magnetron.

I'm about to kiss Magnetron!

Our lips brush—just the briefest, barely there touch—but I pull away, alarm bells clanging in my head.

Link is acting, Hadley! Remember?

His brow furrows, but his eyes are soft and tender. He doesn't look upset. He's just concerned. Or maybe this is all part of his training.

In the articles I (may or may not have) read about Lincoln James, I know he's been studying with some of the best acting coaches in the world in anticipation of his next role. Not the *Enforcer* franchise. Something bigger. Better. That Regency superhero role, probably.

The Vise-Count.

Securing the part is the reason he needs his reputation rehabbed in the first place. Link's only pretending to date me as a means to justify the ends. It's just another role to him.

Until last week, he wasn't interested in kissing you at all.

My stomach heaves, and I feel sick. Regret unfurls inside me.

"Are you all right?" he asks.

No.

"You said Sam's good at his job, right?" I choke out.

"He's the best." Link's voice is scratchy now, like sandpaper. Wow. He really commits when he's performing.

"Then he must've gotten footage of us already," I say.

"I'm sure he has." Link's Adam's apple dips, and he pulls his arm from around my shoulder. I miss the weight of him already.

"Okay." I turn my face back toward the screen, willing my pulse to stop its screaming.

"I'm sorry," he says, his breath warm in my ear. "I thought you said we should kiss. But I must've misheard you."

"I meant *pretend* to kiss," I say, my eyes still glued to the screen. I can't risk seeing Link's face if he looks disappointed. Even knowing it's an act, I might lose my resolve. "This is all pretend, isn't it?"

"Yeah." I feel shoulders slump beside me. He's not used to being turned down. I wonder how many starlets he's made moves on since he moved to Hollywood. I know of a few he's been linked to. Dasha Peet. Celie Houston. Arden Lords. My internal organs start churning even worse when Sam pokes his head between us.

"You two look like you're ready to go."

Gee, Sam. Is that because of how far I'm leaning away from your actor friend?

By way of response, Link grunts. Then he digs in his pocket, slipping a wallet out.

"I've got this," I say.

"No way." His eyes flash. "This is my gig. You don't pay."

His gig. Of course. How could I forget?

He peels another two hundred-dollar bills free—just like he did at Harvest Farms—and stuffs it into the cupholder.

Then without another word, the three of us slip out of the theater the same way we came in.

Chapter Sixteen

LINK

Out in the parking lot, the three of us decide to drive back to Hadley's place to regroup. From there we can figure out where to take pictures without being spotted today. Apparently, Hadley's roommate is out of town with her boyfriend until Tuesday, which is good news for us.

As curious as I am to meet Nina after seeing her on social media for the past year, the next few days will be much easier with her gone. At least in terms of staying under the radar.

Instead of heading through town this time, we follow Hadley down a back road the GPS didn't suggest when we came to Harvest Hollow.

"Man, I miss knowing a place so well, you've got the shortcuts down pat," I say.

Sam shrugs. "Yeah. But new adventures have their own appeal. Take it from a guy who's lived in Southern California his entire life. It's not a bad place to be stuck, if you have to be stuck. But still."

"You're stuck?"

"Exactly."

We pull up to Hadley's house and hop out to meet her at the

front door. I've got to admit, I'm excited to see inside her place. She made me stay on the porch last time. This feels more intimate. Like a step in the direction of us becoming friends again. Not that Hadley will want to keep the relationship going after this week is over.

Not like we'll be allowed to keep things going.

Pippa and Andrew both emphasized the success of this plan rests on Hadley crushing my heart and not looking back. There can't be any evidence of us staying in touch after our breakup. The whole point is to make me sympathetic in the eyes of the public. I'm supposed to be a broken man in need of healing. Not to mention single.

And attainable.

"Hey," Hadley says, throwing the door open like she did yesterday, except this time she sweeps an arm out to invite us in. At least she's welcoming Sam. And I follow.

The front room's about the size of my living room in LA, but mine's all exposed brick and ductwork. Her bungalow feels like a home, while my place feels like an industrial loft.

Two overstuffed couches face each other with a distressed wood coffee table between them. There's a vase of daisies in the center.

Nice touch.

Hadley didn't know we'd be coming over after the movie, so she must keep fresh flowers around just because they're lovely. I'm not surprised. Her dorm room was always cozy and inviting. She had extra pillows and blankets for people to sit and colorful tapestries on the wall. The warmth of her space helped the kids on her floor who were homesick. She always made them feel like they belonged.

I felt like I belonged.

"This is it," Hadley says, her gaze skittering around the room, like she's trying to see it through our eyes. "Home sweet home." In one corner is a roll-top desk. In the other is an L-shaped computer table with a laptop and printer. She nods across the house toward a farm table with four spindle-legged chairs. "The kitchen's that way," she says.

Sam clears his throat. "Can I use your bathroom? We couldn't go back at the theater."

"Down the hall, first door on the right," Hadley tells him. "But the bras hanging over the shower rod aren't mine." As soon as she says this, her face blooms red. "I don't know why I said that."

"I get it." I shrug. "You gotta wash those delicates by hand."

Hadley raises her brow, an unasked question in her eyes.

"Not that I have any actual experience with washing lingerie," I quickly add. "The head of wardrobe just likes to talk a lot."

Great, Link. Way to make Hadley think you're a creeper who discusses underwear with women. See also: You are, in fact, discussing underwear with a woman.

Nice touch.

"So." I scrape a hand along my beard. "Can we start over?"

"Sure." She turns toward the kitchen. "You want some lemonade? It's pink. I like it better than the other kind."

I look past her to the french door just beyond the dining room. The door is mostly glass with a wood frame around it. But there's a man out there on her back property peering at us through the window. My pulse starts racing and years of gut instincts kick in. Trespasser.

Paparazzi.

My first priority is to protect Hadley. Not just her in general, but her identity and her privacy. After plenty of practice with this kind of intrusion, I grab her by the shoulder and pull her to me, shielding the back of her head with my other hand.

"Don't turn around," I grunt through gritted teeth. My heart's throbbing now and my chest has become an angry vise. I'm used to this kind of invasion in my own life, but I hate knowing someone else is the target now because of me.

My insides are screaming. *Stay away from Hadley!*

"What's wrong?" she asks, her blue eyes round and innocent.

"You'll be okay. I've got this." I keep one arm around the back of her while I lift the other one, spreading my palm out to face the pap. I'm hoping to block him from taking pictures, but Hadley blinks up at me.

"Link."

Oh, man. She's scared now. I never want her to be scared.

"I'm so sorry, Hads." The nickname slips out before I can stop myself, and she takes a quick step backward, sliding free from my embrace. "I should've known this would happen," I growl to myself. I just didn't think they'd find me here. Or so soon. "Pippa had a plan," I say. Hadley and I lock eyes. "Your home wasn't on the table. I swear if Andrew sent these guys, I'll fire him so—"

"Sent who?" Hadley looks over her shoulder, following my gaze to the trespasser.

"I'll handle this." I stride past her toward the french door, a man on a mission. "You stay here."

"Link!"

"This isn't your problem, Hadley."

"It's not your problem, either," she says, pointing at the glass. "That's my dad."

Huh?

Now I want to crawl under the rug in Hadley's dining room and stay there until I stop feeling like an idiot.

An overreacting idiot.

An overreacting idiot who jumped on a figurative white horse to rescue a damsel in distress.

From her father.

Hadley opens the back door to let in a man who's carrying a large reusable shopping bag. He's in a sweatshirt and a ball cap with his brim pulled low. That was what got me thinking he was spying on us in the first place. Once he's inside, he pulls off his hat, and his face crinkles into a grin. It's the kind of genuine smile that reaches his eyes.

Nice touch.

"I thought you'd never get home," he says to Hadley.

Her gaze careens between the two of us. "What were you doing out there, Dad?"

"Your front door was locked, so I came around back to see if I could get in." He sets the bag on the dining room table. "I got a dozen apple cider donuts from Catty's. I thought I'd just drop them off for you and Nina." He cuts his eyes to me and must notice my furrowed brow. "That's Cataloochee's, in case you didn't know."

"Right." I nod. That place was on Pippa's list of potential spots to take pictures. "Cataloochee Mountain Coffee?"

His eyes twinkle. "Exactly." He turns to Hadley. "I also brought a Tupperware of leftovers from our meatloaf night."

Meatloaf night?

Hadley shifts her weight, clearly not sure how to play this situation. "That's very sweet, but you didn't have to do that."

Sam emerges from the hallway, and Hadley's dad takes in another surprise visitor. "So who are your friends?" he asks Hadley.

Friends. Right.

"Dad, this is Sam," Hadley says, starting the introductions.

"Nice to meet you, sir." Sam extends his hand, and Mr. Morgan pumps it enthusiastically.

"Call me Ray."

"All right, sir. Ray."

"Not *Sir* Ray. Just Ray."

"If you say so." Sam's face splits into a grin, but he avoids making eye contact with me. He's probably unsure about how to handle Hadley's dad showing up. But Ray Morgan turns my way, sticking out his hand.

I must outweigh the man by a good fifty pounds, and I'm at least half a foot taller, but his grip is firm and strong. I get the feeling Hadley's father would fight paparazzi for her too.

"I don't think I've had the pleasure," he says, squinting at me. "But you sure do look familiar."

My throat tightens, and I glance at Sam, who's looking at me now, amused.

"Dad, this is James," Hadley interjects, saving me from having to decide how to introduce myself. "We know each other from college."

"Ah!" Mr. Morgan beams, his focus ping-ponging between me and Sam. "You're Hadley's school friends. Wonderful!"

Hadley arranges her face into a half smile without actually confirming that Sam's a part of our CU past. Technically, she's telling the truth, and I admire her even more for how hard she's working not to lie.

"That explains why we haven't met," her father continues. "All the years Hadley was at Carolina U, she'd always make the drive home for meatloaf night. Hardly skipped a week, so I didn't have to visit her on campus much. Except for move-in and move-out days, of course." His chest puffs up with fatherly pride. "It's pretty great having a daughter who makes time for her old man on the regular."

"I'll bet it is," Sam says, probably thinking about his own twin girls. "I hope mine do the same." Then he quickly adds, "When the time comes."

He's also trying not to lie.

"Still, I did miss out on visiting her at school," Hadley's dad says. "And meeting her friends. Sam and James, huh?" He scratches the salt-and-pepper scruff at his chin. "Yeah, I think I remember Hadley talking about you two."

Sam's mouth slips sideways. "Well, I *am* pretty memorable."

Great, Sam. Thanks.

My stomach is a jumble of relief that actual paparazzi haven't converged on Harvest Hollow, and that Ray Morgan must not be a fan of the *Enforcer* franchise. He said I only look familiar to him, so he's clearly got no idea I'm Magnetron.

This is all good news. Still, a sliver of disappointment slices through my gut. Hadley clearly didn't talk enough about me over the years for her dad to recognize the name James. I can tell Ray Morgan's only pretending he knows who we are.

"Well, I've got plenty of food for everyone," he says, surveying the rest of the room. "Where's Nina? Probably with Gavin, I'll bet."

See? Nina is a friend Ray Morgan knows all about.

"She's at his family's lake house," Hadley tells him. She cranes her neck to peer out the window at the front of the house. "Where's your car, Dad?"

"No car. My bike's out back," he says. "I wanted to get a good ride in before the first real cold snap hits. And I sure do love the crunch of leaves under my wheels." He turns to Sam and me. "You boys in town early for the fall festival?"

"Sam's a photographer," Hadley quickly answers for us. "He's here working on a shoot of fall foliage." Her voice hitches only slightly. For someone who's not good at telling tall tales, she busted that one out like a champ.

"You should really get out to Harvest Farms then," her father says. "Beautiful place, especially this time of year. Fun too. They've got a petting zoo with baby goats, and a pumpkin patch. I think there's a homemade cider contest next weekend. And their haunted corn maze is really something."

"We went there yesterday," Sam pipes up.

"Ah. Well then, you know all about it already." He splays his hands. "So. What's on tap next?"

"That's what we're trying to figure out." Sam shrugs. "I wanted to get some shots from the clocktower, but Hadley says it's off-limits to the public."

"She's right." Her dad's eyebrow soars, like the arch of a clothes hanger. "Not just any ordinary Joe is allowed to climb to the top. So it's a good thing we ran into each other."

"Dad." Hadley's lids drop, and she shifts her weight.

"And why is that, sir?" asks Sam.

"It's Ray," he says. "And I've got keys to the place."

Chapter Seventeen

HADLEY

Thanks a lot, Dad.

My stomach plummets like I just fell off the roof of the clocktower. Meanwhile, Link and Sam exchange quick glances, before Sam turns to my dad again.

"Do you really think we could get up there, Sir Ray?"

"Absolutely," he says. "The tower stairs are accessed from the atrium next to the post office. And yours truly is the postmaster. I've got keys to let in the guy who services the clock." He beams at us. "I'd be happy to give you two a tour of the whole place."

"Oh, no, no." Sam throws his hands up. "We wouldn't want to inconvenience you."

"But that's a very generous offer," Link adds. Of course he and Sam don't want my dad going with them to the clocktower. They're not really interested in taking pictures from the highest point in town. They're only interested in getting social media shots of Link and me.

"It's no trouble," my dad says. "As long as you can wait until tomorrow. I've got plans tonight."

"Poker?" I ask.

"Something like that," he says.

"The trouble is ... uhh—" Sam scrambles for an excuse, "You

see ... we really need to get all our photo shoots done as soon as possible."

"Because we ... won't be in town for long," Link chimes in.

"Ah." My dad nods. "I understand."

No, Dad. You really don't.

"Maybe we could go with Hadley tonight," Sam suggests. Then he nudges Link like the idea's just occurring to him. "That is if it's really no trouble, and if you don't mind lending her the key."

My mouth goes as dry as old beef jerky, and my dad responds before I can.

"Ahh." My dad makes a face that's half regret, half grimace. "I'm afraid Hadley can't take you."

Link swings his focus over to me. "But we *need* you," he says under his breath. Beneath his statement is a silent plea. I have to be in all the shots Sam takes. Without me, there *is* no fake relationship.

"You need her for the pictures?" my dad asks. "I guess I can understand why. There's no one prettier in this whole town, or—if you ask me—in the world. In my opinion, Hadley could be a model. She's that gorge—"

"Dad," I interrupt. "They don't need a model, and you're obviously biased."

"I'm not biased." My dad shrugs like a man who believes wholeheartedly in what he's saying. "Your good looks are a fact not worth debating. And anyway, you didn't get them from me." He turns to Sam and Link. "My wife was the real beauty. I'd say we were high school sweethearts, but we *actually* met in elementary school." He slips his phone from his pocket and hands it to Sam. The screensaver is a picture from their wedding day. "That was the happiest day of my life, next to when Hadley was born."

Sam, the only photographer in the room, studies the picture, head on an angle. "She really is beautiful," he says, handing my dad's phone back.

"We lost Maureen when Hadley was a baby," my dad says.

"But you being her friends and all, Hadley probably told you about that already."

Cue more stomach plummeting from me. I told Link about my mom back when he was James, but this is new information for Sam, and I'm not sure how he'll handle it. Luckily, he just shifts his weight, lowering his lids. "I'm so sorry for your loss."

"Thank you." My dad throws his arm around me. "But my wife wouldn't want us to be sad. That's not the kind of woman she was. If she could, she'd tell both Hadley and me to make the most of every day here, until we're reunited again."

He nods, and I look up to see a soft smile on his face. My dad's so relentlessly positive, I've heard him say something along these lines more times than I can count. "I was blessed every minute I had her," he tells Sam and Link. "She was a real angel on earth." He pats my back. "Now she's watching over us."

I hazard a glance at Link, but his expression is unreadable. He knows about my mother, and that I'd hoped to make her proud. He's aware I wanted to keep her memory alive with my music. But I also told him I was too young to remember her. And that's the truest source of sadness for me. I felt an aching guilt admitting I can't miss a woman I never really knew.

I still feel like that.

It's a strange kind of place to land, losing something you never had in the first place.

My dad clears his throat, pocketing his phone again. "Anyway, as I was saying, you won't get Hadley to go on that photo shoot with you."

"If she's got lesson plans to work on this afternoon," Link says, "we can be flexible with our timing."

My dad looks at me, a twinkle in his eyes. "Oh, no. That's not the problem," he says. "I guess my daughter never got around to telling you."

Link tilts his head. "Telling us what?"

"That she's deathly afraid of heights."

Deathly afraid. Interesting way of putting it, Dad.

But when you're told from your earliest days that your mom died in a car accident, you do what you can to *not* have any accidents of your own. Especially avoidable ones. "He's not wrong." I gulp. "I'm so sorry, *James*. And Sam," I add quickly.

"Nothing to be sorry about," Link rushes to say. "We'll figure something else out."

"Awww, don't feel bad." My dad pulls me in for a hug, before turning to address Sam and Link again. "I'd tell you to try harder to convince her, but I know from experience my girl will still say no. You must know her ex from college. He was a real son of a—"

"Dad!" I slide out from under his arm.

"Pardon me," my dad says, both palms up as an apology. "I suppose I shouldn't speak about anyone in those terms. Even a weasel like Carson."

Link grunts. Then his dark eyes go even darker. "And you aren't wrong, sir."

"Probably not. Still. I shouldn't resort to the same kind of low blows he'd toss out."

Link huffs. "At Hadley?"

"No. I wouldn't have let him near her if he did that." My dad exhales a long breath, full of frustration. "But I just can't respect a man who'd pressure a woman to do something she doesn't want to do. Not when he claims to love her."

"Yeah." Link's jaw shifts, and he balls his hands into fists. "That doesn't sound like love to me."

"That's what *I* told Hadley," my dad says. "But Carson made her feel awful about herself. And he put her in a position where she had to keep on refusing him, which made her feel even worse."

Link's just standing there, hands fisted. "Nobody should make anyone say no more than once. Ever. Man or woman."

I make a small noise in the back of my throat, and my dad turns toward me again. My insides are roiling, but I'm so full of embarrassment and nerves, I can't force myself to speak up and stop him. "Let's see," he says, lifting a hand. "There was the hot air balloon, and the bungee jumping." He raises his fingers to help him count the times I let Carson down. "But the skydiving was the worst, wasn't it, Hadley?"

Wow. My dad might as well be writing a book for *The New York Times* Bestseller List: *Hadley Morgan: A Study in Disappointment.*

"I guess so," I manage to say.

He swings his gaze over to Link and Sam. "Every time I thought she'd finally gotten free of him, he'd worm his way back in."

I square my shoulders. "Not the last time, Dad. Carson knows it's definitely over now."

"About time you severed that cord." My dad nods. "And I, for one, say good riddance to bad rubbish."

Link clears his throat. "Don't worry." His voice still sounds full of sand. "I would never ask Hadley to do something she's not onboard with one hundred percent." He turns to me. "Forget we brought it up."

The edge of protectiveness in his tone cracks something loose inside me, and I suck in a great gust of air. "I'll do it!" I blurt.

Laughter trips out of my dad's mouth. "Do what?"

I plant my legs wider. "Climb to the top of the clocktower."

"*Yeah,* you will," Sam says, reaching a hand out to slap my palm, then he hesitates. "Unless you want to say no ..."

Link chimes in even as Sam and I are high-fiving. "Please don't do this on my account." His tone is gruff, and I feel the weight of it all the way to my toes. "I never would've asked if I'd known you were scared of heights."

"*Deathly* afraid," my dad adds, putting extra emphasis on the word deathly.

So. Not. Helpful.

"I know you wouldn't ask," I tell Link. "Which is exactly why I'm saying yes. I can be spontaneous and full of adventure, remember?" I gulp down a lump in my throat. "That's my goal, anyway. And you can help me get there."

"Hmm." Link shifts his weight, like he's considering pulling the plug on the whole endeavor. Sam tilts his head, waiting for Link. After all, this is Link's publicity stunt.

"Okay," Link says, his eyes locking with mine. "But we can call things off whenever you want. No warning. No problem. Just say the word if you're getting too high."

Sam snickers, and I think he'd be wagging his tail now if he were a puppy. Link tosses a frown his way. "Right, Sam? We'll stop whenever Hadley says we're too high?"

"Of course." Sam winks at me. "But I'm willing to bet she's braver than she thinks."

Sam might be wrong.

But I hope he's not.

Chapter Eighteen

LINK

For the rest of the afternoon, over apple cider donuts and leftover meatloaf, Ray Morgan regales Sam and me with story after story about Hadley. As a little girl, then as a teenager, and finally as the young woman I used to know. She sits across the table from him, laughing the whole time, her cheeks pinker than the lemonade.

She's even more adorable than I remember.

Not because she's embarrassed. I'd be kind of a jerk if I enjoyed her discomfort. It's more like she's flushed with memories of growing up safe and secure. Carefree, even. I wouldn't know what that's like.

Scarfing down a second helping, I can't help wondering what my life would've been like if I'd had a father who was a part of it. Even a little bit. Even a stepfather.

Later, when Ray hands Hadley keys to the clocktower building, the trust he puts in us stirs something in my chest. This is what it's like to believe in the goodness of others.

I want to believe in that too.

By the time we arrive downtown, the night is almost fully dark. Sam and I wait in the paid parking lot at the edge of town square. The giant fountain is all lit up now, shooting water into the sky. When the cascade drops down, a spray of sparkles ripple in the surrounding pond.

The effect is almost magical.

Thanks to the streetlamps decked with twinkle lights, the whole square is bathed in a soft, welcoming glow. From our position we can watch people strolling in pairs or small groups, but we're mostly out of sight ourselves.

Across the lot is City Hall, the courthouse, and the post office. Rows of overhead lights finally flicker on as Hadley enters the adjacent building. She said she wanted to scope out our route, even though her father assured us the place would be deserted. Sam kicks a pebble across the asphalt and stuffs his hands in the pocket of his hoodie.

"I know Hadley's dad gave us a key," he says, "and that we've got actual permission to be here from the literal postmaster, but I still can't help looking over my shoulder." Even as he says this, he bounces a quick peek behind him. "I feel like climbing the clocktower when the building's supposed to be closed is ... ummm..." His voice trails off, and he taps at his chin like he's looking for just the right word.

"Illegal?" I finish for him.

Sam barks out a laugh, then rubs his hands together like a gleeful villain in one of those old black-and-white movies. "I was going to say sexy, but if breaking the law gives these pictures the extra juice we need, I say let's go with that." He's full-on grinning now, his teeth bright under the streetlights.

"You're getting a kick out of this project, huh, rebel?"

"Maybe." A smirk splits his face in two. "My life's pretty boring these days. The pictures I take for you are all commissioned. I don't have to hustle anymore. Which is good in its own way. But yeah, I'm not mad about this gig. Feeling like we could get caught at any moment is kind of fun."

"I'm glad my predicament is bringing you joy, man."

"You'll get it someday."

"Will I?"

"When you become a dad. Suddenly your whole life revolves around sippy cups and minivans. Nap times and snacks."

"Not every dad. Just the good ones. And I won't qualify."

"Ah, come on." Sam huffs out a breath. "You'd be a totally good dad."

My gut churns, and I run a hand through my hair. I'm not going to share with Sam the fact that I can't picture myself as any kind of dad. Good or bad. I certainly don't see myself as the kind of family man he is. Not that I wouldn't want to be if I could. I've just never had that role modeled for me. I've got no blueprints for being a husband or father. It's like those LEGO kits that come with specific instructions on how to assemble the whole thing brick by brick. And the outside of the box comes with an age recommendation.

AGES 8+.

I'd need the box for a grown man who never had any kind of paternal figure. Sure, my mom tried her best, but I couldn't be her priority. She was overwhelmed—and rightly so. We rarely had time for playfulness. For fun.

Which is why my LEGO kit's just a bunch of random pieces in all shapes and sizes. Yes, there are building blocks inside, but I've got no guidelines for how to put them together. I've also got no interest in talking about this with Sam. So it's a good thing Hadley appears in the doorway of the building.

"There she is," Sam says, nodding at the clocktower. Hadley lifts a fist in the air. This was the all-clear signal we'd agreed upon.

"Showtime," Sam announces. He bounds across the street wielding his camera with the enthusiasm of his five-year-old twins. At the curb, he turns and grins at me.

Man, I want this guy's LEGO instructions.

As we reach the steps to the side entrance, Hadley waves us in. There's a shine to her cheeks, but I can't tell if it's excitement or nerves. Maybe a little bit of both. What I do know is I'm on alert, waiting for clues she might not be up for this. At the first sign of apprehension, I'm calling things off. I refuse to let my publicity stunt cause her a moment of fear.

We follow Hadley into the atrium between the post office and the clocktower. Before we left, Ray Morgan let us know we're not allowed in the post office. It's government property and off-limits. Still, the wall dividing the two spaces is made of glass. On the postal side, there's a service desk with windows separating customers from employees. Those sections are empty now. So is the security station. I guess in a town like Harvest Hollow, guards don't work twenty-four hours a day, especially on the weekends.

"The stairs to the clocktower are down here," Hadley says, leading us to a long hallway on the right. Overhead there's a hum of lights. Past a set of public restrooms and a water station there's a utility closet. I slip a couple of bills from my pocket and slide them under the door. Hopefully the custodian who finds them could use the money.

Hadley turns, and a smile tugs at her lips. "Nice."

As we continue down the hall, I hazard a glance at Sam. He's in old-timey villain mode again, tiptoeing behind her, having the time of his life. Hadley pauses in front of a large wooden door, and her shoulders creep up slowly. Then her chest expands like she's drawing in a deep breath. I'm about to ask her if she's all right, when Sam calls out to her first.

"Hold up, Hadley." He turns to me. "You're hanging back too far, Link. Get right up next to her."

I do as he says, and the scent of apples and cinnamon fills the shrinking space between us. Hadley's nearness is thrilling. But more than that, I'm worried about how she's feeling. Her eyes are wide and bright and vulnerable. I just want my heart to grow tentacles that can wrap around her and tell her everything's going to be all right. Then again, heart tentacles would probably be freakier than the clocktower.

"You okay?" I ask her quietly.

"Mmhmm." She offers me a quick nod. "I just keep telling myself this is an opportunity for adventure and spontaneity."

"Now go on ahead," Sam says, encouraging us. "I want to catch you two sneaking into the stairwell together. I'll do a burst of shots of you unlocking the door, opening the door, and heading through the door, sneaking looks back over your shoulders like you're trying to escape the public eye."

I clear my throat, and wait for Hadley to make the first move. She pins me with a gaze, then her focus dips to my mouth. When she licks her lower lip, I just about spontaneously combust.

"Perfect, Hadley," Sam says. "Keep doing stuff just like that. Brava, girl. Brava."

Oh, man. Sam might as well have dumped a bucket of ice water down my back. His praise is a cold reminder that Hadley's just pretending. This whole week is about her using our situation to find adventure and spontaneity. And tonight she's trying to prove to herself she can do something she's always been afraid of.

"Hey, Link." Sam lowers his camera. "You're gonna have to get your head in the game if you want to keep up with our girl."

Not our *girl, Sam. Mine. Mine. All mine.*

And I don't want to just keep up with this woman.

I want all of her.

"I already got some great still shots of Hadley making googly-eyes at you," Sam says. "She's really pouring it on thick, man. These pictures are so great."

Just pictures. Not reality.

"Link?" He snaps his fingers behind us. "You awake?"

"Yeah," I grunt. "Sorry." I shake my head to escape the stupid silent meltdown mode I've slipped into.

"Get closer to Hadley," Sam says. Without a word, I shuffle right up to her like I'm a robot on autopilot. Make that a robot with human senses.

The small space around her body feels warm and smells like apples and sunsets and every good earthly thing. She inserts the key in the lock and meets my gaze again. My eyes search hers like they can read what she's thinking. When she takes a beat to inhale deeply, the sound of her breath makes my pulse quicken.

"Good, Link," Sam says. "Not as good as Hadley, but you definitely look like a man in love."

Love.

A strangled noise fills the back of my throat. I feel like I'm swallowing my own tongue.

"Keep this up," Sam says, "and the public will absolutely lose their minds over HadLink."

Hadley gulps, and I bob my head, hoping she understands I'm offering encouragement, not trying to force any of this on her. She swings her focus to the key in the lock, and I follow her lead, putting my own hand over hers.

Together we turn the handle.

The feel of her skin weaves a web of warmth that spreads from my wrist, up my forearm, past my elbow, before radiating throughout my body.

"Kids, this is amazing stuff," Sam says. "I'm going to switch to taking video of you both now all the way to the top of the stairs. Take your time. Really connect. Just keep acting like you're obsessed with each other."

"All right," Hadley breathes out softly, like she might be struggling for air.

Is she scared?

Just playing a role?

If she's pretending, she's a better actor than I've ever been.

We enter the stairwell holding hands, and I lead the way up the first flight, waiting for her between each step. Midway up, I glance over my shoulder to check on her. "I'm okay," she says. "You?"

"Yeah. Great." I shift my gaze beyond her. Sam's still at the base of the stairs, his camera aimed at us.

"I'm going to hang back now," he tells us in a low, slow voice. "I'll probably stay a whole flight below you. I should probably stop giving directions too. I want to capture anything you might say to each other organically. So I'm going silent. Forget I'm even here. Don't get tripped up by that or be self-conscious. Try to stay natural and authentic. We might even be able to use your dialogue in a clip. Or we can always edit out your words if we have to."

Dialogue. Just like a movie. I can do this.

Hadley and I reach the first landing, our fingers still entwined. There's something so comforting about holding her hand. It's a tangible connection to the past, and I'm bringing her with me straight toward the future. So even though I know this isn't real, I give her hand a squeeze, and she grips mine back like I'm the life preserver and she's the castaway being rescued.

At the second landing, I pause to check on Hadley. Her cheeks look sucked in and hollow, but she says, "Don't worry. I can do this."

"Have you always been afraid of heights?" I figure this line of questioning works for a couple who's getting closer. Curiosity would be part of that. And concern. And I *am* genuinely curious and concerned about Hadley. Not just for the camera.

Not for the camera at all.

"Maybe." She presses her lips together, like she's considering her answer. "I'm not sure you can tell you're truly scared of something until after you've tried it. The only time I was ever at the top of a tall building, I was totally terrified. And I can confirm the term shaking like a leaf is a literal thing." She huffs out a small laugh. "So I suppose the answer is yes, I've always been afraid, I just didn't know how much until we were up there."

We.

Who is we?

I'm tempted to ask, even though the answer might be Carson. I don't want her thinking about her ex right now. But I also don't want to stop her from processing the memory. This could be important for her. So instead of asking who she was with, I focus on the location. "Where were you?"

She swallows hard, like the fear still lives in her throat. "The top deck observatory of the Empire State Building."

"Whoa." I offer her a small whistle, legitimately impressed. "That's over a hundred floors, isn't it?"

"Yep." She wrinkles her nose. "And I hated every one of them." She shakes her head, then nods to indicate the stairs.

"You ready to move on?" I ask, the double meaning not lost on me.

"More than ready." She leads the way.

While we're climbing the next flight, she pauses to glance back at me. "My dad's the one who took me to the Empire State Building, by the way. On our one and only trip to New York City." It's like she'd read my mind wanting to know who she was with.

"Cool," I say, with a shrug, hoping not to audibly sigh with relief.

"He told me sightseeing in Manhattan was on my mom's bucket list, so it ended up on mine."

"By default?"

"Something like that."

"How was the flight?"

"We drove. Road trip. I've still never been on a plane."

"I don't think I knew that about you."

Her lids flutter. "There's a lot we don't know about each other yet."

Yet.

"I guess you're right," I say.

"But I want to learn everything," she tells me. She glances down the stairwell, probably checking to see if Sam's catching this. Then she turns and starts to climb again.

By the time we reach the second-to-last landing, my heart's banging like a jackhammer. On this level, there's a window, framed by weathered wood, and set high in the stone. It's just above Hadley's line of vision, and I decide not to ask if she wants a boost in case she's nervous and feels pressured. But my fake girlfriend has her own plans.

Hadley slides up next to me, her eyes squeezed shut. "Adventure and spontaneity," she murmurs. Then she rests a hand on my shoulder, whispering, "Just for balance."

As I put an arm around her waist to steady her, a small tremor shoots through her body.

"Scared?" I ask. Her answer is a tight nod. And yet she slowly opens her eyes, sweeping her gaze out the window. Beyond the glow of the fountain and the square, miles of her hometown stretch below us, glittering and golden under the night sky.

But all I see is her.

"Ohhh." She sucks in a long breath, her blue eyes widening with wonder. "It's so beautiful," she sighs.

"Yes," I say. "It is."

Chapter Nineteen

HADLEY

Link's arm is still at my waist, and he strengthens his hold on me. He's been doing his best to keep me safe, taking each flight at my pace. I've never felt so protected by any other man. So valued. So seen.

Exactly, Hadley. Remember, being seen is the whole point of this.

That's right. I've almost forgotten Sam's below us in the shadows of the stairwell taking pictures and video.

"And we're not even at the top yet," I say, slipping back into the role of Link's secret girlfriend stealing a private moment with him. "There's a platform for the bells above the clock faces. We'll be able to see even more from there." This is all part of the adventure, part of my attempt at spontaneity. Plus, we're supposed to be overheard. "I can't imagine anything better than this," I add. "But I know it will be better, since I'm with you."

My pulse accelerates at the thought of being even higher than we are now. But the nerves rattling around my insides are sharing space with butterflies now. The same butterflies that took wing the moment Link wrapped his arm around me.

I find myself sinking into him, my back pressed against his chest. But I must be imagining his heart pounding through his sternum. It's just those butterflies trying to beat their way out of me and into him.

When a low noise rumbles in his throat, I break away from the stunning view of Harvest Hollow, ready to replace it with a better view.

I slowly turn in his arms, and Link gathers me to him. His embrace is like a safety net, a strong tether to the earth, no matter how high up we get.

"Hadley." My name is a vow on his lips. As I gaze up at him, his eyes drill into mine. Then they flick to my mouth and stay there.

A low moan escapes me.

I'd be embarrassed, but this is perfect for the photo shoot. Or the video. Or whatever Link's team is going to post. The world will see I'm not some predictable woman with no surprises. That's what this is about. It can't be about my heart or the way it's singing right now.

Link lifts his free arm—the one that's not holding me—and tenderly brushes the hair off my forehead. Running his fingers down the length of a single strand, he gently tucks it behind my ear.

I slide my hands over the swell of his chest, tipping my chin up as I fist the collar of his shirt. We stumble back against the stone wall, and he tugs me toward him, lowering his face to mine. Holding my breath, I imagine the taste of his lips. But when he's only inches from me ... he freezes.

"Don't stop," I whimper.

"Hadley," he groans.

"Hey, guys!" Sam calls up to us. "This is probably a good time to take a break. I've gotta pee again. Sorry. Tanya says I have a bladder the size of a walnut."

Link growls and takes a full step backward. My hands feel empty as I let him go, and I already miss his body heat. Suddenly I'm aware of every stair we've climbed to get here. How high we are. With a shiver, I wrap my arms around my middle. I liked it so much better when the arms around me were Link's.

"Now that we've stopped, I'm not sure I can make it to the top," I tell him softly.

"That's okay." His eyes are black, nothing but pupils boring into mine. "I told you we don't have to do anything you're not comfortable with."

"I remember," I say. "And I trust you." Still, I can't help feeling jarred by the sudden distance between us. I glance down into the stairwell and Sam's already gone. We're not on film now. So I tip my chin up. "Can I ask you something?"

He rakes a hand over his beard. "Like the daily question thing?" When I slowly nod, he says, "Sure. We might as well do that while we wait for Sam."

Sam. Again. Right.

It's all about the camera.

I sink back against the wall like I'm seeking support. "You told me you never finished your degree, and you said it was a long story. But I guess I just want to know why." I pause to swallow hard. "You were so close to the finish line." My voice drops to almost a whisper. "Do you have any regrets?"

Do you regret leaving me?

That's the question I really want to ask. But if he said yes, I'd have to assume he felt coerced into the answer. And if he said no ... Ouch.

Link blows out a breath, then he works his jaw, like it's suddenly gone tight. "I didn't get my degree when I left CU because ... I was never enrolled in the first place."

"What?" His statement punches all the air out of my lungs. I feel flipped around, like I'm flying on a trapeze, dropping down with nothing to catch me. "That's not possible."

"It is."

"But ... we used to talk about school all the time." I blink at him, bewildered. "You walked me to my classes. We always knew each other's schedules. You were there when I committed to being a music major."

"Yeah." He grimaces, almost like this hurts. "You talked about your plans. I knew where your classes were. We'd meet up on the quad and at the dining halls. But if you think back and really remember, I was mostly just listening. Encouraging. Supporting."

"You were everywhere on campus, though," I say. "All the time. Doing different work-study jobs all three years."

"Work, yes." He grits his teeth. "Study, no."

"You lied to me?"

"No." He takes a beat. "You assumed I was enrolled, but I never told you that directly." His voice is full of regret now. Deep, guttural regret. And my brain's on a loop, replaying all the moments we spent together, every time Carson and I broke up, and I'd secretly hope James might throw his hat into the ring.

His metaphorical hat. Not the real one I still keep in my box of college mementos. The one I tried smelling just a few days ago.

And you had no idea who he was this whole time.

"Why didn't you tell me you weren't a student?"

"Because I wanted to be a student, more than almost anything. I wanted you to think I was."

"But ... but ... I wouldn't have cared." This comes out as a strangled stammer, but even as I hear myself say it, I know I'm misplacing the blame. I shouldn't be mad at Link for not making sure I understood. I'm mad at myself for being so blind. I only saw what I expected to see.

"*I* cared," he says.

My knees buckle, and I stick a hand out to brace myself against the wall. The stone is cold and rough under my palm, and if we weren't almost to the top of the clocktower, I'd probably run down.

"I'm so sorry," he says. "I—"

"Stop," I interrupt, my throat heating up with mortification. "This is totally my fault for thinking we were closer friends than we were."

"But—"

"Please don't make me feel even more stupid than I already do. You don't have to explain to me why I couldn't see what was right under my nose. You must've thought I was the most self-absorbed person on the planet, going on and on about my plans for school and not realizing you weren't even participating in the conversation."

"But I did participate," he says, his gaze skating back and forth, assessing me. "And I was taking classes at the community college. Just a couple at a time. So I didn't have very many credits by the time I met Pippa. Not enough to make it worth pursuing a degree."

I'm glad it's too dark for him to see my face flushed with embarrassment. If I'd ever imagined there was a chance this man might have feelings for me, those thoughts are gone now.

I was just a spoiled coed while he was busy working like a grown man.

"Hey, lovebirds," Sam calls out to us from the bottom of the stairwell. "You two ready to head to the top now?"

"No," I blurt before Link can answer. "We're done for tonight."

LINK

After a silent car ride back to The Maple Tree Inn, I storm into our suite, kicking off my shoes so violently, one of them smashes into the wall. That's when Sam must've figured something's up with me. If not sooner.

"Who puked in your pumpkin spice latte?" he asks.

"Hadley," I mumble.

His eyebrows fly up. "Do tell."

"I don't mean she actually puked."

He smirks. "Yeah. I didn't think so." He flops on the couch in our shared common space while I pace between the balcony and the kitchenette. "But I could tell something was off when we left the clocktower," he says. "I would've brought it up sooner, but I was afraid you'd yell at me in the car."

"I don't yell."

Sam cocks an eyebrow.

"Okay. I yell a little. At the paparazzi when they deserve it. But I'm not mad at Hadley. At all. I'm honestly mad at myself. She just threw me for a loop tonight. And now I'm feeling all ... I don't know."

"Loopy?"

I freeze in my tracks. "Off-balance," I admit. "Like I'm questioning everything. Totally unsure of all my life decisions. Wondering if I've ever done a single thing right."

Sam nods, putting his socked feet up on the coffee table. "That can happen around attractive women. Also smart women. Kind-hearted women. And Hadley's all of those things, so I'm not surprised you blew it with her."

I drop into the chair by the desk. "I never said I blew it."

"But you did, though, right?"

I run my hands through my hair and groan. "I told her something I should've admitted years ago, and now I look like a liar, which is bad. Even worse? I made her feel stupid for not seeing the truth in the first place."

Sam picks up a throw pillow and tosses it at me. "When I mess up with Tanya—who also happens to be beautiful, smart, and kind—I just tell her I'm sorry. And I always am. Well." He shrugs. "Almost always. There was the one time she backed the car into—"

I throw up a hand. "I'm not sure I need the history of the few arguments you've had in your completely perfect marriage."

At this Sam guffaws. "Tanya's perfect for *me*, but there's no such thing as a perfect marriage. There are just marriages. And you either decide to stick around forever, or you don't. That's it."

I harrumph. "A decision, huh?"

"Yeah, man. You didn't think what happens with you and Dasha onscreen was real life, did you?"

"No, I just never saw a man stick around, that's all. My mom never did get married. Not that her getting married was some kind of obligation." I wince. "Man. This is all coming out wrong."

Sam's quiet for a stretch, his goofy side-grin slipping away. "Your mother's a good woman. If she wants a partner, she'll find one."

"She says it's too late for that now."

Sam cocks his head. "Tanya says it's never too late for love. And I'm inclined to agree with her. Anyway, back to your screw-up with Hadley. Did you apologize to her?"

"I tried," I moan. "But I didn't get very far."

"Why not?"

"You and your peanut bladder showed up asking if we wanted to go to the top of the tower."

"Walnut," he says. "I have a walnut bladder."

"Not the point," I mutter. "After you interrupted, Hadley ran down those steps so fast, it was like she'd never been afraid of heights." I lean back and spin around in the chair, staring up at the ceiling. "Leave it to me to be such a jerk she had to push past her biggest phobia."

"Hold on," Sam protests. "One? Don't give yourself that much credit. Two? Heights is probably not her biggest phobia. Three? You have a rental car. So, go see her now. Try harder, man."

I straighten. "Try harder to what?"

"To say you're sorry. Remember that old 80s movie Tanya made us watch with that guy holding up the boom box for his girlfriend playing a forgive me song on her lawn?"

"*Say Anything*?"

"Right. That one." Sam splays his hands. "So grab your metaphorical boom box and go to Hadley's house right now. Beg her to listen to you. Explain yourself. Help her understand. And don't come back here until you've made things right with her."

I rub my chin like it's a lamp and a genie might pop out to solve all my problems. "You don't think I should give her space?"

"You gave her five years of space, man. How'd that work out for you?"

I flinch just as my phone starts ringing. Not a text. A call. My manager's contact is on the screen. I haven't spoken to him in days. So I hold it up so Sam can see. "I gotta take this," I say.

Sam nods. "I was gonna FaceTime Tanya, anyway."

"Great. Say hi to your perfect wife for me."

"Done." Sam nods at the phone. "After you talk to Mr. Manager, go find Hadley."

"Yeah, yeah."

He points at me. "Promise."

"I will," I say. Then I answer the call. "Hold on a second," I tell Andrew. "I'm heading out to the balcony." Once outside, I take in the view again, and gulp down a big gust of evening air. "Hey, man." I collapse into a chair. "I'm glad you called. I owe you an update."

"Let me go first," he begins, and his tone of voice does not bode well for me. "You're not gonna want to hear this ..." His sentence trails off.

"I think I know what this is about." Andrew wants to tell me directly to ramp up the romance with Hadley. This is vintage Andrew, not trusting Pippa to be the messenger. And even though I know Pippa can take care of herself, I feel the need to defend her.

"It's all right." I switch the call to speaker and lay the phone on the table. "Pippa already told me you want Hadley and me to turn up the volume—like more on-camera affection—and we're working on it."

"Sam sent me the footage." Andrew clears his throat. "It's a good start. More would be better."

I lean toward the phone. "Just so we're clear, I refuse to push Hadley or make her feel even a little bit uncomfortable. Respecting her is my biggest concern."

Andrew harrumphs. "Maybe it shouldn't be."

"What are you talking about?" I frown. I don't like where this is going.

"I'm not talking, Link, I'm warning you. The paparazzi are on the prowl."

"They always are."

"Well, they're sharks in the water now. And thanks to you, they've tasted blood. Just enough to be whipped into a frenzy."

"What taste?" I sink back into the chair. "Pippa hasn't even shared any pics from Harvest Hollow yet."

"I'm referring to what happened at Highland Hospital."

"Ah." This again. The photographer with the big mouth. I

flash back to Violet with her pigtails and her IV telling me she loves Taylor Swift and Magnetron. "The guy deserved it, Andrew." A vein on my forehead begins to throb. "You know it as well as I do."

"We could argue that all day and get nowhere, Link. What matters now is these reporters are looking for intel on you and your family. They're going for the jugular, and I hate to say it, but we might be too late to turn this ship around."

"So what do you recommend, then?" There's a stretch of silence on the other end, and a ridge of goose bumps rises along my neck.

"Look. This isn't easy for me, Link. But I want to be upfront with you, okay?"

My teeth clench. "Okay."

"I've been in talks with somebody else. Another actor Youngblood's considering for The Vise-Count."

Now my throat goes tight like my teeth. "He isn't a Chris, is he?"

"I'm not at liberty to say."

"Flint Hawthorne?"

"All I can tell you is he's a whole lot more palatable than you are right now."

"Got it." I nod even though he can't see me. "So you're taking on a new, more palatable client. Which means there's a conflict of interest, huh?"

"I'm not saying you and I have to end our professional relationship. I just thought I owed you the tru—"

"Message received," I interrupt. "And you know what? As long as we're telling the truth, you and I don't really see eye to eye anyway. I'm the one who got you into this mess, and I can get you out. So this is me letting you off the hook."

"Link."

"It's a good thing, Andrew. Take the win. You deserve a fresh start managing someone who's more ... palatable."

"Come on, Link. Don't be like that."

"I'm just being honest. Pippa and I can take it from here. Or maybe we can't. Maybe everything's going to blow up in our faces. But either way, you and I should end this now while we're still on good terms."

"Are you serious?"

"I'll honor our contract and pay you, but you're not obligated to me anymore. And don't hold back on signing Chris or Flint or whoever. Thanks for everything, man. Seriously. Good luck."

I cut off the call before he can say another word. My chest is full of invisible ball bearings running a track around my torso. Metaphorical bees are buzzing in my head, stinging at my eyes. I'm not sure how to handle any of this.

Getting the role I'm not positive I want.

Fulfilling my contract with Youngblood.

Believing in Pippa.

Protecting my mom.

It's all too much.

The one thing I *do* know is I need Hadley.

Now.

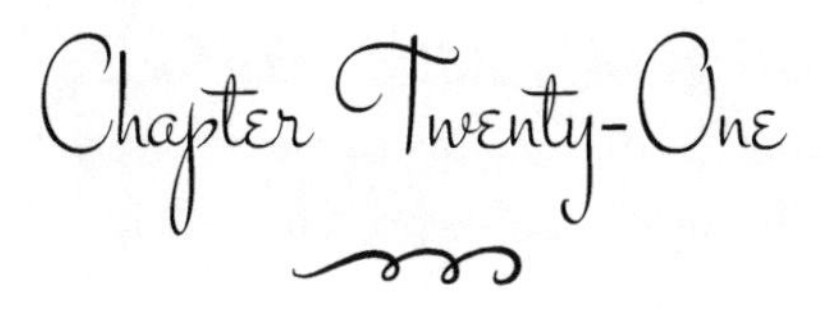

Chapter Twenty-One

HADLEY

After the debacle at the clocktower, I race back to my place to take a cold shower. Then I take a hot one. Then a bath. Lather, rinse, repeat.

Now I'm in my flannel pajamas and a terry cloth robe—feet stuffed into fuzzy slippers—brushing my teeth so hard I probably won't have any gums left. But even after all that, I've still failed to wash the traces of Link off me. His incredible scent has seeped into my nose, my head, my brain, my—

Nope.

Not my heart.

I have to erase him from there for sure.

Before James left North Carolina with Pippa, I thought he was a completely different person than the one he turned out to be. Did I imagine all our talks about him starting his own business someday? No. He had dreams. I'm sure of it.

I assumed he was a business major, and he never corrected me. To be fair, he also didn't share much about his specific classes. Music majors and business majors don't have many in common. But he seemed to be driven by big dreams. Bigger than most of the other students in my hall. I thought this was evidence of future motivation. But it's just more evidence that I never really knew him. And that's really the bottom line, right?

I didn't know James Lincoln at all.

I try to read, but I'm too restless, and it's too early for bed. Even if I tried, I don't think I'd be able to sleep. So I call Nina, but she doesn't answer. Not a surprise. There's no sense leaving her a voicemail because she never checks those anyway. Neither of us do. We aren't the phone call type. We're definitely text first, ask later people.

So I send her a message.

Me: Hey, Nina Bean—hope you're having fun with Gavin and his family. Is their cabin nice? I'll bet it's nice. Gavin is so nice. You deserve nice. Have I said nice enough times? See also: I miss you. Why does it seem like you've been gone forever when it's only been two days?

I know the answer to my own question. The past two days have been wild. Like off-the-charts abnormal. The kind of circumstances no one would believe. And the fact that Nina knows nothing about what's going on makes the whole situation even stranger.

I really want to tell her, and I'm sure she wouldn't say anything. Who'd believe her anyway?

Hey, my roommate is pretending to be Magnetron's girlfriend so Lincoln James can rehab his reputation and score a new movie role.

Yeah right. I can't tell her about this madness over text, though, can I?

Well. Maybe just a hint in a follow-up message.

Me: Things have been weird here, by the way, but I can't share the details yet. I CAN tell you it has something to do with that LA area code, and with me finally saying yes to adventure and spontaneity. I think you'd be proud. But please don't say anything to anyone until we have a chance to talk.

As soon as I hit send, a cold wave of guilt floods through my body. Whether or not James/Link/Goober was totally honest with me, I'm dancing along the edge of betraying his trust. I should just unsend the text, eat the rest of those apple cider donuts, and lie awake all night counting sheep.

Strong plan, Hadley.

I go back into my messages to fix my mistake, but before I can unsend my last text to Nina, another one comes in.

Link: Can you come outside?
Me: Huh?
Link: Please.
Me: Why?
Link: Look out your window.

Tightening my robe, I pad to the front of the house, turn on the porch light, and peek through the curtains. The moon and the street lamp offer just enough light for me to see Link on the front lawn. He's holding Nina's rake—the one we pretty much never use. Beside him is the neatest pile of leaves I've ever seen. The kind of leaf pile you'd expect on a fall ride at Disneyland. Perfectly rounded.

What on earth?

He rests the rake against the tree trunk and offers me a small wave. I throw open the door, stepping out onto the porch. "What are you doing here?"

He glances at the rake, and a flush creeps up my throat. I mean, I guess it's obvious. I really am so dumb.

"An act of service," he says, his shoulders hitching. "It's kind of what I do."

My heart swishes, because yes, this behavior definitely tracks. When we were in college—correction, when *I* was in college and

James worked there—he was always a doer. Not just because his job required it, but because it was his instinct to help. I personally witnessed him throwing away random trash left out on the quad, helping the vending machine guys unload their trucks, and bussing tables in the dining hall.

Generosity was intrinsic to him. I always admired that.

Now my emotions are a jumble, twisting my lungs, making it hard to breathe. He takes a step toward me. "I know we're not supposed to be alone. That was one of your rules, which is why I asked you to come outside."

"We're alone out here."

"Yes." He glances around. "But there are a couple of big trees. Better than nothing."

I clear my throat. "Thank you for raking."

"You're welcome. But that's not why I'm here. That was just my lead-in." He bobs his head. "Can we talk, please? Like adults? Not like the kids we used to be?"

I glance at the porch swing. "I think that can be arranged. Want to sit? Or should we stand out here by the leaf pile?"

"Sitting sounds good." He comes toward me, pushing his hands into his pockets. He's wearing his beanie again, hair poking out beneath it. There's an air of vulnerability and sweetness around him—the man who raked my leaves, the one who's trying to abide by my rules.

How can I stay mad at this person?

Together we sink onto opposite sides of the swing that runs the length of the porch. The cushion is thin, and the swing gently rocks as we settle in. I turn to face Link, adjusting the edges of my robe. I'm wearing multiple layers, but I still feel exposed. Flannel and terry cloth.

I couldn't be more frumpy.

"You drove off so quickly," he says, "I didn't get a chance to truly apologize to you. And I am so, so sorry."

"No." I draw in a breath, soak it up, then exhale slowly. "You were just trying to be honest with me back there at the tower, and I totally freaked out. I'm sorry I overreacted."

"You have nothing to be sorry for. I'm the one in the wrong, and I don't think it was an overreaction." His gaze skitters over my face. "For the record, there's a reason I never told you the whole story. But I don't want to rationalize or make excuses now."

"If you want to share, I won't think you're trying to rationalize or make excuses. I know you better than that." At least I *thought* I knew him better. And I'd still like to think so.

"Okay." Link nods and rubs at the back of his neck, taking his time before speaking again. The night air is cool, and half a moon peeks through the trees. The branches are mostly bare, like wooden fingers reaching out to grab the stars. Under different circumstances, this moment might feel a little romantic.

Minus the flannel, and the terry cloth.

"I'm listening," I tell him.

He exhales, shoulders sinking. "I liked being seen as a student," he says. "More specifically, I liked *you* seeing me that way. I knew you had the wrong idea, and I didn't correct you. That's my fault. But it was a dream of mine to go to CU. And when I was with you, I kind of felt like I got to live my dream. In ways big and small, your friendship made me feel like I deserved to be a student."

A seam of feelings splits straight through my heart. On the one hand, I love that my friendship helped him to dream. On the other hand, that's all he saw me as then.

A friend.

"You did deserve to be a student," I say. "You still do deserve that if you want." My nose starts to sting. "You could go to school now, you know."

He shakes his head and adjusts his leg an inch closer to mine. His jeans next to my pajamas are a study in contrast. He's cool denim.

I'm plaid flannel.

"Nah," he says. "I don't think the professors would appreciate Magnetron showing up in an economics lecture."

"You won't know unless you try."

"That time is over. I did what I had to do. It was just a means to an end." He takes a beat and the porch swing sways.

What did he *have* to do and why? I don't want to disturb the flow of this moment by asking, but I need to keep this in my back pocket for a daily question later in the week.

"I don't have many regrets," he adds. "Except not being honest with you sooner." He exhales, and my heart flounders. When he did try to be honest with me, I lost it and took off without letting him explain. He probably thinks he can't rely on me now.

Maybe he can't.

"And that's the other reason I came here tonight," he continues. "Say the word, and I'll call this whole charade off. You don't have to do this anymore. I'll just figure out another way to protect whoever might be caught in the crossfire."

I assume he's talking about Pippa and Sam. He's already told me how much they count on him. But there's a depth to his gaze that makes me think there's something else he's worried about. So I won't let him give up our original plan because of me.

"We can still make this work, Link. I want to do this for you. *With* you." Before I can stop myself, I lean forward and touch his knee. He looks down at my hand, and gulps.

"We may be fighting a losing battle," he says. "Andrew—that's my manager—he's going to work with the other actor the studio is considering for their new franchise."

"And you think he'll get the role instead of you?"

Link shrugs. "Probably for the better. Who wants to be a Regency-era superhero anyway? The idea's kind of ridiculous."

"I think it's kind of sweet." I swallow hard. "I think millions of fans would want to see you as The Vise-Count."

He grimaces. "It might be too late."

"I don't believe that," I say. "I always tell my students it's never too late to go after something they want."

He huffs out a laugh. "That does sound like you."

"And you didn't give up when I first told Pippa no." I offer him a small smile. "You came here to plead your case in person."

"Don't remind me." He ducks his head, sheepish. "I put you on the spot and took advantage of a friend. A friend I know has trouble saying no."

Friend. He said it again. Twice.

The good news is this eliminates all confusion. He really doesn't see me as more than a friend. As long as I remember that, I can keep my heart safe. I'll embrace our ruse without ambiguity. My goal wasn't romance, anyway. I just wanted to be spontaneous and adventuresome with no strings attached.

"The truth is, I'm the one who's been using you now," I say.

A crease presses into his forehead. "How do you figure?"

"Thanks to you, I finally said yes to something without being sure about the outcome. That's huge for me, you know? Like stepping out onto a high wire with no net." I tilt my head. "My whole life, I stuck with what was known and safe. I avoided taking risks or trying anything remotely new. I turned down a lot of opportunities for fun." I scrunch up my nose. "Think about it. The biggest thing I ever did to put myself out there was audition for a TV show along with thousands of other people." A sigh leaks out of me. "It's probably why I kept going back to Carson."

"That guy." Link grumbles. "Idiot."

"But his patterns sure were predictable, which was easier than taking a chance on someone else. I always knew what I was going to get with Carson, and there was security in that. He was probably right about me being boring."

Link's brow furrows. "No."

"Yeah." I nod. "Carson was wrong about a lot of things, but he had a point about that. My dad was so protective, and I can't blame him. Not after what happened with my mom. The love of his life walked out the door to run an errand and never came back."

"I can't imagine how hard that was."

My nose starts to sting again. "I'm glad I can't remember that time. I mean, I wish I could remember my mom. But I'm also grateful not to have memories of my dad's grief when it was fresh. Is that selfish?"

"You're the least selfish person I know, Hads."

A small shudder sneaks up my spine, a shiver of pleasure when he uses my nickname. He's breaking the rules, but I don't call him on it. I like hearing "Hads" on his lips. It's a reminder we're not just friends.

We're *good* friends.

"Well, I'm being selfish now," I say. "I want to keep going with this fake relationship thing even if you don't. Because of you, I've already climbed *almost* to the top of a clocktower. Sneaked into a pumpkin patch after hours. Broken into a movie theater. And we weren't hurting anyone. In fact, the money you've tossed around has probably been a blessing for strangers."

His eyes cut away, bashfully. "I hope so."

"So help me keep pushing and having fun, okay? And at the end, we'll break up, just like we're supposed to. Nobody gets hurt, and maybe a few more people will find hundred-dollar bills lying around Harvest Hollow."

He runs a hand along the scruff of his beard. "You're absolutely sure you want to keep doing this?"

"I'm sure." I withdraw my hand from his knee and go in for a shake. Even as we're sealing the deal, the warmth of his hand makes me melt a little.

Just friends.

"All right." A smile breaks across his face, brighter than the stars. Excitement ripples behind my ribs. I love seeing that smile. But I could be in big trouble if I don't keep my head squarely in reality.

"So." I tuck a strand of hair behind my ear. "What's next on our fake-dating photo-op agenda?"

"I was kind of hoping you'd have an idea, being the local girl and all."

I give this a few moments of thought. "How about we start with a morning hike? The trails should be pretty empty tomorrow because it's a weekday, and most people will be at work. Boney Mountain's usually the quietest, and the pictures from the top will be gorgeous this time of year."

Link arches a brow. "Boney Mountain? Seriously?"

"Yep." I nod. "The peak looks like a skull, and the parents in town tell their kids he turns into a real skeleton who steals their candy on Halloween if they don't go to sleep."

"A candy-stealing skeleton named Boney?" Link lets loose a string of laughter. "That's so ... cruel."

"But effective," I say.

His brow arcs. "Remind me to never get on your bad side."

We're both silent for a beat, staring at each other. His jaw shifts, which I now know means he's mulling something over. Literally chewing on a subject, teeth clenching, releasing, then tensing again. "And you'll be okay climbing a mountain with me?" he asks. "With the height and all. You're sure ..." His sentences land halfway between a statement and a question, and ends on a hook of vulnerability that's the exact opposite of the hero he plays in the movies.

Magnetron is all raw courage and steel, with enough bravado to vanquish enemies around the world. But Lincoln James—or, rather, James Lincoln—that man is strong, but he also has wounds.

I don't know where they came from, but the cracks in his shell make me want to trust him more than a falsely tough exterior. Opening up to someone else is hard. So is sharing the stuff you keep inside, protected like fruit under a rind or peel. That's the soft sweetness you worry might sour or spoil if you expose it to the air.

If this fake relationship didn't have an expiration date, maybe Link would end up trusting me enough to share, but our time is limited, and then he'll be gone.

Make that gone *again*.

"I'll feel safe if I'm with you," I say because I mean it, or at least I want to. His mouth parts, like he's about to say something, like maybe he's going to tell me how he feels too. My heartbeat picks up, blood racing through my veins. And as the swing gently sways, my body moves toward him, inch by inch, like an invisible string is reeling me in. Link might as well be an actual magnet, because I can't pull away.

I clear my throat. "Can I ask you something now?"

He blinks at me, but he doesn't answer. At least he's not joking that I just used up my one question for the night.

"Who else are you protecting?" I ask. "I mean besides Pippa, Andrew, and Sam?"

"What makes you think I'm protecting someone else?"

I consider the question for a moment. "Because I *did* know you back at school. Not everything about you, but enough to see you put other people first. And I've been with you for days now. That hasn't changed. This is about more than the careers of a few people who'd be fine if you moved on."

"I have a contract," he says, his voice almost a growl. "I'm required to do what Youngblood Studios asks of me to, and if I back out, I'll be in breach of contract. I may owe money back. A *lot* of money."

My mouth curves down. "Surely you have a lawyer."

"I do." His expression is steel. Determined. "She's the one who made sure the contract was rock solid. On both sides."

"So it's about the money then?"

He drops his gaze. "And the studio could send reporters after people I care about in retaliation."

People he cares about.

Does he mean me? My heart flutters thinking about what he's

willing to sacrifice for others. "Don't worry," I say softly. "I'll help you."

He lifts his chin until his eyes find my mouth, lingering there for a moment. Then his gaze snaps up to meet mine again. I draw in a breath and lick my lower lip. My traitorous brain tries to convince me Link and I should practice kissing so our chemistry on camera looks authentic. Sam was there for the barely there kiss in the theater. What would kissing Link be like if we're totally alone?

Another rule broken, Hadley.

I could so easily close the space between us, pressing my lips against his. But just as I'm about to go for it, he reaches out and chucks my shoulder with a gentle fist, catapulting us straight back to the friend zone.

"So, I'll see you tomorrow." He clears his throat, but the words still come out jagged. Then he plants his palms on his knees, and launches his body up. The porch swing jerks and sways. "Say nine o'clock?" he asks. He's standing above me, his eyes dark and hooded.

"Sounds good," I manage to choke out. Just when I think we might be taking the intimacy up a notch, Link does something to reestablish the distance.

"Just you and me and Boney," he says before making a beeline for his rental car.

"Don't forget Sam!" I call out. I say this not to remind Link we'll have company, but to remind myself that none of this is actually real.

Everything we're doing has only one purpose—to convince the public that Lincoln James loves me, so I can turn around and break his heart.

Chapter Twenty-Two

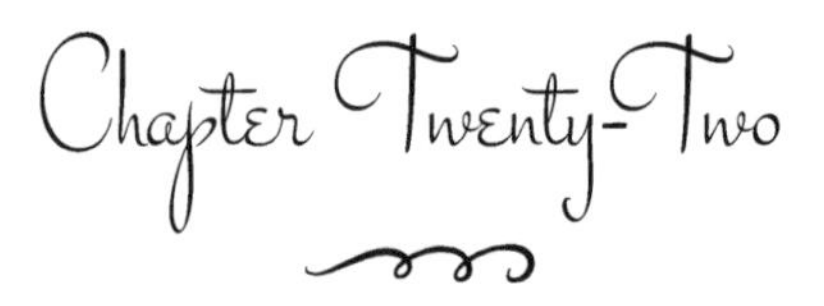

LINK

By the time I get back to the suite, Sam's in his room snoring away like a true blender of wildebeests. So I head back out to the balcony to clear my head. Maybe the cool night air will knock some sense back into me, because *that* was a close call.

I almost kissed Hadley for real. Not like at the movie theater or the clocktower with Sam there filming us. But alone. On her porch swing. And as I drove away—I'm not gonna lie—my heart was banging so hard, I almost drove right over the leaves I just raked and plowed straight into her trees.

But you can't do that, Link. You can't kiss her alone anywhere. Even if you're getting signals from her that she's interested, it's not fair to her.

Hadley's life is here in Harvest Hollow. She's a music teacher with a job she loves, and a roommate best friend, and a two-bedroom house that's cute enough to be in a snow globe. She and her dad have Meatloaf Night every week. EVEN WHEN SHE WAS IN COLLEGE.

Being with me for real would turn her life into a permanent circus. That's not what any of us wants.

Besides.

She has to dump me at the end of this. Our breakup's built

into the deal. So I can't let myself hope for anything more than temporary from her. Not without risking everything. What I need is to get my pulse calmed down so I can stop hyperventilating at the image of her lips moving so close to mine.

So I text my mother.

It's a brilliant plan. Mom's a real quick way to bring my libido back down to earth.

Me: Hey, there. How are you holding up? How are the doggies getting along?

It's three hours earlier back in Malibu—prime time for a single woman to be out with friends or on a date—but she responds immediately. Almost like she was waiting around for a message from me.

Man, I hate thinking that.

Mom: We're good. Plenty of room on the bed.

She follows up the text with a selfie of all three dogs piled around her on the pillows. The comforter's pulled up to her chin, and she's smiling, but the light doesn't quite reach her eyes.

Me: Give those goofballs slurpy kisses from me.
Mom: Will do. Everything good there? How's Hadley?
Me: She's fine. We're hanging in. Doing what we have to do for now.
Mom: Glad to hear it, but you caught me just when I was about to go to sleep. Call tomorrow?
Me: No problem, Mom. Sleep well. I love you. So much.
Mom: Love you too, baby.

A pulse of sadness hits me. I always told myself we're doing what's best for her. That my mom's private home protects her from reliving the past. Thanks to limited exposure to the rest of the world, she never has to explain to new people what she's been through. No loss. No anguish. Just sunshine, surf, and Boo.

Still. It occurs to me for about the millionth time how lonely her life must be.

But this isn't a great moment to second-guess my mom's situation. Not in the middle of a plan to fix things. So I shake off the heaviness and text Pippa that we need to talk. Almost immediately, my phone starts playing "The Imperial March" from *Star Wars*. That's the ringtone I use for Pippa.

As a compliment. Mostly.

"Hey, Pippa," I begin. "I just wanted to let you know Andrew and I have ... parted ways."

"Oh, I'm aware. He already called me. The man couldn't *wait* to break the news." She releases a tsunami of a sigh.

"Whoa. I'm sorry, Pip. I can hear your disappointment all the way in North Carolina."

"Not disappointment, Link. Concern."

"Well, I appreciate that," I say. "You always did have my back."

"The feeling's mutual," she says. "Please don't make me regret that."

I gaze out over the ledge at the mountains in the moonlight. The place where the night sky meets the earth is almost undetectable in the dark, unless you know the skyline. I wish I could spend a whole lot more time out here on this deck staring.

Memorizing.

"Anyway, I really think this is for the best," I say. "And I promise not to let your workload increase."

"That's very sweet. But I'm afraid you can't make that promise."

"Well, I *can* do whatever it takes to make your plan work. I'm done with half measures, Pip. If Hadley and I are going to pretend to be in a relationship, I'm going all in. Doubling down. Upping the ante. I—"

"Link." She guffaws. "Stop the cliche train."

"But you get my point?"

"I do. I'm just surprised by this change of heart. You almost sound ... optimistic."

"I guess I'm just remembering how much I love this place."

"Hmm." She's quiet for a beat. "I didn't think you'd ever been to Harvest Hollow."

"I haven't. But I lived most of my life in North Carolina, and this town is like all the best parts of the state gathered in one spot. I'm telling you, it's out-of-this-world beautiful, Pip. They've got charm up to their eyeballs."

"Sounds delightful." Her voice drips with sarcasm.

"No, I'm serious. Every corner has a sign advertising their upcoming fall festival, and even the streetlamps are wrapped with bows. The shops along the square are all decked out for the season. But they don't skip directly to Christmas around here. It's all fall, all over the place."

"Sounds like you've been out and about quite a bit," Pippa says. "Are you keeping a low enough profile?"

"Yep." I decide not to tell Pippa about running into Hadley's dad. He didn't recognize me, and I don't want to worry her needlessly. "Sam and I have just been driving around town a lot. We've done some people-watching from the car. Everyone here is always smiling. Friendly. It's kind of refreshing."

Pippa snorts. "Just don't ditch Hollywood for Harvest Hollow."

"Of course not."

"Big moves like that aren't unprecedented with you, Link. And if you're falling for Harvest Hollow, or for Hadley—"

"It's not that." My shoulders go slack. "I'm just nostalgic. My mom is, too. She misses this place probably more than I do."

"How's she doing, by the way?"

"I just texted with her. She's hanging in there. Her property's basically a kennel on the beach, though."

"Uh-huh." Pippa pauses. "You know, Andrew's one of the only people who knows who your mother is and where she lives.

And you refused to put anything about her in the NDAs everyone signed."

"I didn't want her name associated with me on any paperwork from the studio."

"Well, let's just hope that's not a mistake."

The cords along my neck tighten. "Maybe I'm a big sucker, but I'm choosing to trust Andrew."

"Why, Lincoln James." Pippa takes a beat. "She's gotten to you, hasn't she?"

"Who?"

"Hadley Morgan's turned you into someone who actually *believes* in other people." Pippa clicks her tongue loud enough for me to hear over the phone. "After only a few days, your girlfriend's already changed you."

"*Fake* girlfriend," I amend.

"Even so. I'm hearing something new in your voice. There's a lightness in your tone. If I didn't know you better, I'd say you might actually be just the tiniest bit ... happy."

"Like I said. It's just this place."

"But once Hadley calls it quits, you're coming back to us here, yes?"

"Of course."

"Good." Her voice is clipped now. "The world will be obsessed with you and your sad, shaken soul."

I force out a laugh. "You're making me sound kind of pathetic."

"Not pathetic. Single and vulnerable. *Available*. Audiences will be so desperate to get more of you, we'll strike box office gold with *Enforcer's Endgame.* And that's all we'll need to convince Youngblood you're their best bet for The Vise-Count. I can practically taste the new franchise, and believe me, Link. It's better than Dom Perignon and filet mignon."

"I don't know. I kinda like meatloaf," I say under my breath.

"What's that?"

"Inside joke, but I'd better go. I've got a big day tomorrow, starting with Hadley taking me on a hike on Boney Mountain."

"Taking you and Sam, you mean."

"Yes. Sam's coming with us. Obviously."

"Good. Now go get your beauty rest, Link. We need you looking fresh for the next round of footage. Sam's really outdone himself so far. You and Hadley actually look like you're in love."

Great. Thanks, Pippa.

Now I won't sleep a wink.

Chapter Twenty-Three

HADLEY

Monday morning already feels strange, even before I remember I'm climbing a mountain. Normally, I'd be going to school and working with the choir on their performance for the fall festival. Instead, I'm dressed in my favorite yoga pants, my favorite long-sleeved workout shirt, and my favorite pink cross trainers.

I'm *not* trying to be adorable for Link. It's just that if pictures and videos of us are going to be splashed all over the internet, I want to look my best. Still, by the time I pull into the dirt lot across from the trailhead, my palms are already sweating and I have to wipe them on my pants.

So much for best or adorable.

I stare up at Boney Mountain, and my heart skips a beat. The tree-lined trails, mossy slopes, and jagged rock formations are beautiful this time of year. But I've always stuck to the lower hills. Until yesterday, when I had to open my big mouth and mention hiking to the top. The craggy peak looms above me like a skull.

Adventure.

Spontaneity.

Skeletons that come to life.

I kind of want to punch my inner voice in the nose.

Before I can change my mind and back out of this whole

hiking idea, Sam and Link drive up and park next to me. They're a couple of prompt men, I'll give them that. From the trunk of my Volkswagen, I grab a backpack with the most important supplies —apple slices, granola bars, string cheese, and a Yeti full of water. I also brought a big box of chocolate-covered peanuts as a nod to my past with Link.

Maybe sharing his favorite vending machine snack can spark some conversation about the good old days. The good old days when I had no idea who James Lincoln really was or who Lincoln James would become.

As Link climbs out of the too-small rental, unfolding himself to his full height, my mouth goes dry, and I fumble for my Yeti. The man sure is heartbreakingly gorgeous. He skipped a hat today, and his finger-combed hair flops in messy waves around his eyes. He's wearing fitted joggers and a long-sleeved shirt stretched across his chest. A soft plaid flannel is tied around his waist. I've never seen Link on the red carpet, but I can't imagine he could look any better than this in a tux.

"We meet again," Sam chirps, his camera equipment in tow. "Today, I'm going to completely hang back and let you two hike together. I'm not going to give any directions. But maybe you could hold hands. Stop and smell the wildflowers. Whisper. Kiss. Whatever."

Kiss. Or whatever.

When I came close to kissing Link last night, he shot off the porch swing like a rocket, which was actually a good thing. I can't want to kiss Link. I can't want Link at all. We have to break up at the end of this, so why would I let myself get too attached now, just because I missed him a little in the past?

I've spent the past five years without James Lincoln in my life. I can do the next seventy or so more without Lincoln James.

Speaking of which, he approaches, nodding at my backpack. "I see you came prepared. You got a snakebite kit in there? Bug repellent?"

"Chocolate-covered peanuts," I blurt, then I begin to blush.

Smooth, Hadley. Smooth.

Instead of smirking at my awkwardness, Link smiles down at me. "You remembered." The dimple creasing his cheek is large enough to fit my whole thumb. My heart swells, making him smile that big, and a shiver runs up my spine.

"Are you cold?" he asks.

"A little," I say. It's safer than admitting he's the source of my tremor.

"Hold on." He heads back to the car, retrieving his green beanie. "Here," he says. "Wear this."

"Thanks." As I tug it on, his delicious scent washes over me. Spice and pine and salt. My pulse accelerates and my body sways.

I'll be lucky not to fall off the top of the mountain.

Together we make our way to the trailhead and start our long hike toward the peak. The path is a stretch of dirt and rocks about ten feet across, with trees and brush on one side, and a drop-off on the other. I just focus on my feet.

Pink cross trainers to the rescue.

The trail winds up the mountain in a series of switchbacks that Link and I conquer one at a time.

After each one, I'm a little out of breath, but mostly I feel strong.

Check me out, world! I'm climbing a mountain with a movie star on a beautiful fall day.

The sky is a clear blue with no clouds in sight. As the cool air fills my lungs, I feel a boost of confidence. Still, every twenty minutes or so, I stop to check our progress. The peak keeps getting closer, which also means we're getting higher. And higher.

Link stays near enough to me that he bumps into some body part whenever we start up a new switchback. But every time, he checks to be sure I'm all right, steadying me if I stumble. His touch is strong and he smells so good, these bumps are dangerous to my heart rate.

When we finally reach the top—panting and triumphant—we find a small grassy clearing with a bench meant for taking in the view. Link turns to me, and I keep my eyes locked on his, trying not to shiver over the steep drop-off on the other side.

He reaches for my hands and gathers them in his. "How are you doing?"

"I'm okay," I say, but it comes out a little breathless. Maybe it's the exertion or the altitude. Maybe it's the gentleness in Link's eyes. Either way, I tell myself I'm safe.

Accidents are just that—something we can't control no matter how hard we try. Tomorrow isn't promised, and nobody knows what the future holds. So I might as well soak up these good moments while I'm in the middle of them.

"You want to sit and rest for awhile?" he asks. "Or would seeing the view from this high be too hard?"

"Let's give it a shot." Slipping out of my backpack straps, I set the pack in the dirt and ease onto the bench. My back is stiff, and my focus is on the ground, but I slowly lift my chin. Up, up, up. Then I look out. From here I can take in all the main streets of downtown along with the neighborhoods surrounding it. The homes look tiny, like the plastic houses and hotels in a Monopoly game.

Another shiver makes me tremble, but this time it feels more like excitement than fear.

Link drops down beside me, putting an arm around my shoulder, and I sink into him, relishing the closeness. My tense muscles slowly relax. Somehow, I trust he won't let anything bad happen. Not because he's Magnetron.

Because he's James Lincoln, and he cares about me.

After a full minute of allowing my pulse to settle, I glance down the trail to where Sam's hiding behind a tree. Link follows my lead. "We can see you, man."

Sam peers out from behind the trunk. "Come on. Let me keep up the pretense. Do some cute stuff already. Be couple-y."

"You make it sound so romantic," Link chuckles.

"He wants cute and couple-y?" I rummage in my backpack, digging out a bag of apple slices. I arch a brow, slowly sliding a slice into my mouth. When it's halfway in, I bite down while Link watches. He sucks in a breath, and I meet his gaze. Then I hold up the other half to feed to him.

His eyes flicker as I slip the remaining apple between his teeth, extra slowly. One millimeter at a time. He finishes the slice and gulps, audibly.

"I was wrong," he gasps. "That was ... pretty romantic."

"Oh, we're just getting started," I say, with the most subtle of winks. Then I pull out the box of chocolate-covered peanuts and tear off the top. "Open up."

He looks confused, but his eyes sparkle. "Huh?"

"You heard me."

He parts his lips.

"Wider."

"Ahhh." His mouth goes slack, and he tries not to laugh as I take aim and toss a peanut at him. It misses, bouncing off the giant dimple in his cheek. It takes six more tries and plenty of giggling on my part for Link to successfully capture a peanut.

He chews and swallows, his eyes bright. "It'll take a month for me to catch all those."

"We don't have a month."

Even as I say it, my stomach twists. His eyes drill into mine, and our laughter fades.

"You're right." His voice is deep. "We're running out of time."

I freeze, completely still, as he slides a calloused hand along the nape of my neck. His touch is tender and tentative as his palm skates along my skin, raising goose bumps as he goes.

I lean into his palm, and his fingers thread through the loose strands of my hair.

"Can I kiss you now?" he asks.

"Yes," I answer. "Please."

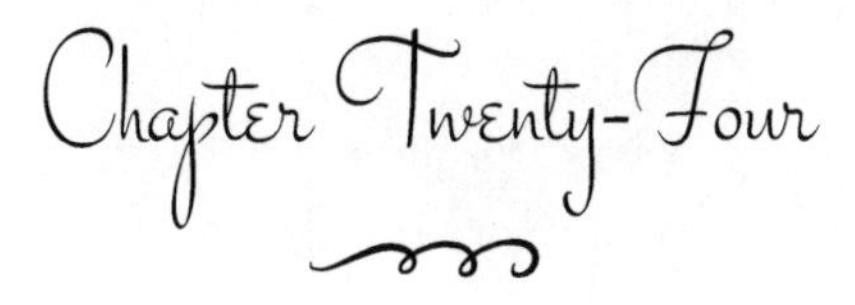

Chapter Twenty-Four

LINK

That's all I needed to hear.

I tug Hadley toward me, but she's already bringing her face to mine, so I let her take the lead. Next thing I know, she's placing soft kisses at the edges of my mouth.

Her lips are so ripe and tempting, I could devour her right here. Desire floods through me, as she fans the flames of a heat that's been dormant all these years. My heart's been asleep, waiting for her.

Now every nerve ending is awake.

She slides up to drop a string of kisses along my forehead, and I use the fresh angle to press my mouth to the smooth skin at her neck. Her pulse quickens under my lips, and when a quiet moan escapes her, I answer with my own low rumble. This moment has been a long time coming.

And no cell in me is pretending. I'm falling hard for this woman.

For real.

To be sure we don't also fall off this bench and tumble off the trail, I gather her to me with both arms, practically pulling her into my lap. She comes willingly, folding her body into mine. Our shapes click into place like they were made to fit together.

Like pieces from a LEGO box.

We don't need the instructions.

"James," she says on a sigh, and sparks shoot straight through me to my core. This woman knows who I am. Hadley sees me—at least the parts I've shown her—like no one else ever has.

The day we met, I was still hiding myself from everyone, still healing, entirely unsure of who I could trust.

I held everything inside.

But I don't want to hold back from Hadley anymore.

She pulls away from me just a few inches, coming up for air. Then our eyes sync up again, and we fall right back into a rhythm that seems like we've been practicing all our lives. Her breath is warm and apple-sweet, and I'm ready to stay on this mountain kissing this woman for the rest of my life when my phone starts buzzing in my pocket. Not a text. A call.

Hadley groans. "Noooo."

"I'm ignoring it," I say into her mouth.

What if it's your mom? What if it's about the dogs?

As if she read my mind, Hadley freezes. "You should answer."

I tear myself away, like the rip of a "pull here" tab, while Hadley slides off my lap. Slipping my phone from my pocket, I see Cal Youngblood's contact on my screen.

Why is he calling?

Usually Pippa runs interference between me and the studio. Or Andrew, although I guess he's out of the picture now. Maybe that's what this call is about.

"Hey," I say, taking the call, struggling not to growl at his unintentional interference. "Happy Monday." The irony in my greeting is clear to me, but hopefully not to Cal.

"Link. Sorry to bug you. Pippa says you're in North Carolina, and I hate to interrupt, but I wanted this news to come from me first."

My blood slows, all five senses on alert. "What news?"

"It seems a few reporters from ZTV and *The Tattler* have

gotten a little overzealous, hunting around for more of a story on you since the whole hospital debacle."

"Yeah. I'm aware. It's why I'm here." Why you're *forcing* me to be here.

"Well, they found something. Or maybe I should say some place."

My body goes rigid. "What?"

"Your house in Malibu."

"How?" Now I'm genuinely growling.

"I've got no idea, but I wanted to give you the heads-up. If they aren't already there, you can expect these guys to be camped out soon. Whoever's living there can obviously ignore them, but that won't make the paps go away. I'm sorry, Link."

Okay. So Cal has no idea I've got my mom set up in the beach house.

Who does he think is there? A secret mistress? I should be insulted, except I'm here with Hadley right now creating evidence of a secret relationship, so I guess I've lost the privilege of righteous indignation. I grit my teeth, heart pounding. This is all my fault.

I've dragged the two women who mean the most to me down this rabbit hole of publicity.

Make that three women, if you count Pippa.

But I don't want Hadley to know I'm upset. Not until I figure out my next steps. So I'm careful about every word I say to Cal, keeping my tone calm and even. "What does the studio recommend I do about this?"

Hadley tilts her head, trying to meet my gaze. Good thing she can't see the ticker tape running through my brain.

"The simplest solution is what we've already planned," Cal says. "Giving them another story to chase." He clears his throat. "Pippa confirmed you're ... working on that exact thing now."

"Right."

That exact thing.

I hate thinking of Hadley as work. She's more like the ultimate pleasure, but I can't argue with the fact that this is our current plan. She's my *only* plan. Unless I call this off. But Hadley wants to keep going. She said so herself last night. And if we quit now, that also leaves my mom vulnerable to being identified. To investigations about her past.

As long as the reporters don't know who lives in the beach house, she might not be subjected to their questions.

"We'd really like you to accelerate the original timeline," Cal says.

We. Great.

"Fine." My hand is fisted around the phone. "I'll talk to Pippa and we'll figure it out."

"Glad to hear it, Link. And good luck moving forward on this. Everyone here at Youngblood Studios really wants this to work out for you."

Oh, do they now? Is that why you're looking for other actors to play The Vise-Count? Why you're dangling threats to my mom's identity?

Cal doesn't know about her, Link. Calm down. Losing your cool is what got you here in the first place.

I step away to the other side of the clearing, out of earshot from Sam and Hadley, and dash off a quick text to Pippa.

Me: I need private security posted outside my mom's place. Now. No one goes to her door.

Response bubbles ripple immediately like Pippa had been waiting for direction. I wonder if she already knows. Either way, relief washes over me when I read her reply.

Pippa: Done.
Me: Thank you.
Pippa: I'm glad you're finally open to the idea of bodyguards.
Me: For now. But this is exactly what I wanted to avoid.

Without waiting for another reply, I call my mom and get sent straight to voicemail. She's probably out on the beach with the dogs, so I leave her a message. I try to keep my voice steady while my therapist's voice plays in my ear.

Focus on what's true, Link. Just the facts. She's safe. You're safe. One step at a time.

"Hey, Mom," I say. "If you see any cars out front or reporters with cameras, there's nothing to worry about, it's just possible some paparazzi are on the scene. We don't want them talking to you, so just stay inside until you hear from me again. I've got security coming, and they'll make sure no one bothers you. You and the dogs are safe. Just don't go out there, okay? And don't answer the door. I'm figuring out a new game plan." I bite back a string of curses that won't help the situation. "Sorry about all this. I love you, Mom."

I end the call with my heart in my gullet and a new determination to make things right. No matter what. When I return to the bench, Hadley's packing the empty box of chocolate-covered peanuts into her bag.

"Is our hike over?" she asks softly.

"Afraid so." I shake my stiff jaw loose. I don't want Hadley to think anything's wrong. Not until I get more information.

Sam heads toward us, wagging his eyebrows. "Man! Whoever called just interrupted the best stream of media I've ever recorded. Was it Pippa?"

"Among others." I stuff my hands in my pockets and paste on a smile.

"Everything okay?" he asks.

"Yeah. We just may need to ramp up our timeline here, or pivot to some other plan."

"Pivot?" Hadley folds her arms across her chest. "What does that mean?"

"I'm not sure." I offer my most nonchalant shrug. "For now, let's get back down the mountain."

Hadley casts a nervous glance at the edge of the trail.

"While we go," I say, "maybe you could tell me about your school. I know you're the Bobcats, but that's about it. I'd love to hear more."

I'm hoping the change of subject will be a distraction.

For Hadley and for me. And it works.

As we retrace our steps, she recounts the history of Harvest High with all the enthusiasm of a former student who came back to be a teacher. She's a natural, drawing me in. No wonder she's decided being an educator is her calling. We're about halfway down when she suddenly stops short at the edge of the trail.

"Argh." She inhales a long breath and winces.

"What's wrong?"

"Something sharp's been rubbing my heel, but now it's gotten bad." She bends down and digs a finger into the top of her cross trainer.

"Blister?" I ask. She glances up, blinking in the sunlight.

"I think it's a rock. Or maybe a burr in my sock. I've gotta get it out, though."

"Hey." Sam passes us on the left, tossing out a grin. He clearly has no idea anything's wrong. "I'll meet you guys down at the bottom. Gotta find a place to pee."

"You and your walnut bladder," I grumble.

"You know you love me," he calls out, waving at us over his shoulder. Hadley's still crouched over, digging in her shoe, when my phone vibrates again. It's another text from Pippa.

Pippa: Security detail en route to your mom's.

I'm tempted to chuck my phone the rest of the way down the mountain. That's how much I want these problems to disappear. Is it too much to ask for a simple life? One where therapy's only for maintaining mental health, not dragging someone back from the brink? Where no one's in debt? Where no one's sick? Where there aren't strangers with cameras and microphones and agendas peeling back the skin of your past?

Yeah, I guess it is too much to ask.

The truth is, I'm not special. I don't get to describe my perfect future and have it handed to me on a silver platter. But if I did, it would look something like this:

A bit of farmland and a bunch of dogs. Space to run and fresh air to breathe. I'd do charity work and found a nonprofit. Raise up a family with a good woman. I'd never leave their sides. Never give them cause to doubt my faithfulness. Never do anything but love them with my whole soul.

This is the reality I'd wish for if I could. Better yet, I'd wish to make this a reality with—

Out of nowhere, Hadley shrieks.

Then she's sliding down the trail.

Chapter Twenty-Five

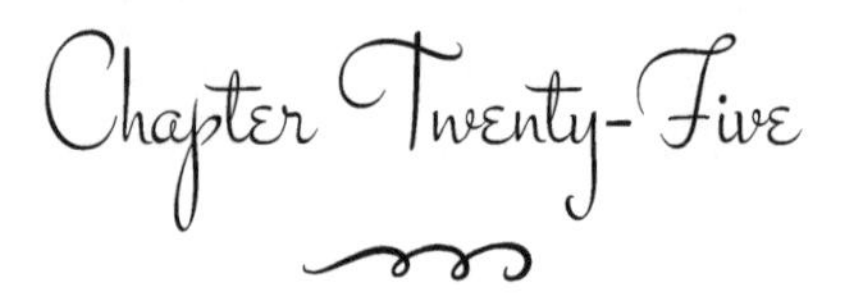

HADLEY

Link crosses the threshold of my house and kicks the door shut behind him. He's still cradling me in his arms like my whole body weighs less than nothing. It's almost like he's a real superhero.

Magnetron to the rescue.

"I'll be fine, I'm just clumsy," I insist for the hundredth time. After losing my footing on a patch of loose rocks, I couldn't catch my balance. The slope was steep, so poor Link had to clamber down and snatch my arm before I tumbled off the edge.

"You're not fine," he says. "You could barely put any weight on your ankle back there. You practically fell over when you tried."

Or maybe I was just dizzy from our kiss.

Either way, Link scooped me up and carried me down the rest of the trail to my car. Now I'm woozy from the warm, salty scent of his skin, and fighting the urge to bury my face in his neck.

How is it possible I'm more dazed by our kiss than by almost falling off the mountain?

Could he be feeling something too?

Am I brave enough to ask him?

What if he's just *that* good an actor?

Oh, he's good all right, Hadley.

That kiss was way better than good.

"I'm going to set you down here," he says, striding over to the smaller of the two couches. It's actually more like a love seat with a coffee table in front of it. My favorite afghan's draped along the back, and there's a throw pillow in each corner.

Link lowers me, slowly and gently, like my body's more fragile than crystal.

"I won't break, you know." I say this with a soft chuckle. My head's still foggy from Link's scent and strength.

Not to mention his lips.

"Tell that to your ankle." He releases me and straightens. "I really hate that this happened to you." His words are rocky, and I'm willing to bet he's blaming himself for this literal twist of fate. If we hadn't been up on the mountain for a photo op, I wouldn't have stumbled. But my clumsiness isn't his fault. And even though I'm pretty sure reminding him he's not responsible won't help, I'm going to give it my best shot.

"You know you can't prevent everything bad that happens in the world." I tip my chin up to meet his gaze. Link towers above me.

His mouth is the grim line he's worn since he picked me up off the dirt.

"I'm still going to try." He shoves the coffee table back with a grunt, making room for his body between it and the couch. Then he kneels in front of me, reaching for the hem of my yoga pants. "Can I take a look under the hood?"

Under the hood? Like under my pants? "Ummm."

"I just want to compare the swelling between your two ankles," he adds.

My throat flushes, but the word "Yes" flies out of my mouth before I can think twice. Link slowly rolls the leg up to just below my knee. When his fingers brush the bare skin of my leg, a ring of fire wraps around my calf.

For the record, this does *not* feel terrible.

"I'm going to remove both your shoes now," he says. "But only if that's all right with you." His voice is soft, and I nod my silent permission. After gently untying the laces, Link slips the cross trainers off of my feet one at a time. A black and blue bruise is already creeping down under the sock on my right foot. Above it, along the edge, a delicate gold chain encircles my ankle.

"Huh." Link huffs out a breath, and his brow furrows, so I feel compelled to explain this wasn't a gift from Carson.

"Nina and I bought matching anklets to celebrate the first day of school."

"Ah." He glides a finger over the chain. "Then we should probably get this off you, in case you start to swell."

"Okay," I manage to choke, but my tongue is a tangle as he reaches for the clasp. He works the hinge, gingerly unhooking the anklet and placing it on the coffee table.

"I want to measure the bruise too, so we can keep track of whether or not it spreads over the next half hour." He tilts his head. "Can I remove your sock?"

"Mmhmm."

Yes, please.

He slips his fingers under the edge, peeling the cotton away. Then, with the tip of one finger, he tenderly traces the edge of the bruise along my ankle and foot. "Does this hurt?" He cups my heel with his palm.

It actually does, but his warm touch is a balm. Still, I don't say this. Instead I shake my head, afraid I may burst into flames if I try to answer. And anyway, I can't formulate words with all the air vacuumed from my lungs. So I just stare at his head while he checks out my feet.

"Well, what do we have here?" he asks over a small trickle of a laugh.

That's when I remember I painted my toenails orange last week, and added bright yellow smiley faces to each one. "They're happy faces."

"They sure are." When he glances up at me, his dark eyes are softening. At least he no longer looks like he wants to punch a wall just because I tripped on the trail. "Is this the latest craze on TikTok or Instagram or something?"

"Nope." I shrug. "Happy faces just make me smile." I'm aiming for nonchalance even as my skin is flaming hot under his touch. "You know how people always warn you to wear clean underwear in case you end up in an ambulance and they have to cut your clothes off?" A chuckle escapes my lips, and Link arches a brow.

"You find unexpected ambulance rides funny?" he asks.

"I guess that does seem a little strange considering what happened with my mom."

Link shakes his head. "I'm not judging."

"It's just how I cope when things get sad, or hard, or uncomfortable. I never want anyone else to feel bad, so I try to keep things lighthearted." I wrinkle my nose. "Does that make sense?"

"Yeah." He readjusts his position on his knees. "My therapist would say humor isn't the worst way to process your emotions. Better than threatening to sock a photographer, anyway."

"Exactly."

"But you don't have to laugh all the time, Hads. Not with me."

Hads. That's against the rules, but I'll let it slide. Again.

"Whatever you're feeling is okay," he says.

At this, my heart squeezes. Link clearly noticed something in me Carson never bothered to recognize—the part where I want to make other people happy, even when this means swallowing my own emotions.

"I'll try to remember that," I say. "But no promises."

He releases my foot. "Anyway, I figure people should always wear clean underwear just because ... you know. Clean underwear."

"Good point." A genuine grin spreads across my face. "But if something terrible did happen to me, and EMTs have to strip off my socks, I want them to know I'm a nice person. Hopefully they'll get that ambulance to the hospital as quickly as possible."

Link puffs out a breath. "As crazy as that sounds, it is very on brand for you."

I prop myself up against the arm of the couch. "Well, luckily, I don't have to go to the ER today."

"To be sure, let's compare these two ankles." Link hauls himself off his knees and onto the cushion beside me. Then he reaches down and guides both my legs over into his lap. My whole body tingles with the proximity of my bare foot to his thigh muscles.

"It's just a mild sprain," I blurt.

"Ah. So you're a doctor now?"

"No."

"You couldn't even walk on the trail."

I arch a brow. "To be fair, you didn't really let me." *And I didn't really mind.* But I nod in the direction of the door. "Any minute now, Sam will be back from The General Store hand-delivering ice packs and ACE bandages. I'm sure I'll be back on my feet by morning."

"What if you're not?"

"We'll figure something out." My stomach fills with butterflies. Link's protectiveness is doing all kinds of fizzy things to my insides. "Unless you're planning to carry me around Harvest Hollow for the rest of the week."

"Maybe I am." One side of his mouth hikes up. Then he grabs a throw pillow to slip under my feet.

"Careful," I warn. "Keep offering this kind of service, and there's no way I'll be able to break up with you." I offer him a slanted smile but he slides his eyes away.

"Then don't get used to it," he says. "The whole point of this is for you to end up humiliating me in public." He runs a hand along the edge of the throw pillow taking pains not to touch me. "An ankle sprain actually helps our cause."

"In what way?"

"You can tell everyone the injury was my fault. Or at least the fault of the paparazzi. Say we were being chased or something, and that's not the kind of life you're prepared to lead."

"But that would be a lie."

"It's happened to plenty of innocent people who were just hanging around celebrities. Everyone will understand if you don't want to subject yourself to the dangers of being my girlfriend." His lids are at half-mast. He must be feeling guilty again. But I refuse to let him blame himself for something he didn't do.

"This could've happened to anyone, Link. Not everything bad in the world is your fault." I reach a hand out and tip his chin up. The scruff of his beard tickles my skin. "I'm serious." I wait until he makes eye contact again. "This is *not* your fault. And I'm not going to say it is. To anyone."

"It doesn't matter if you did." A frown snags his lips. "You dumping me in public isn't my call."

Hold the phone.

Is he saying if it were up to him, he might not want to end things?

"Link."

He breaks eye contact and glances at the door. "Wonder what's taking Sam so long?"

"He's just finding his way around Harvest Hollow," I say. "I'm sure he's fine."

Clearly Link doesn't want to talk about this now, and I don't want to push him. We've still got time for this conversation. No one can *force* me to break up with him. So I prop myself up until I'm straighter on the couch. It's so small, if I reach out, I could probably touch his shoulder. "So." I wiggle my toes until he looks down. I just want to bring some lightheartedness to the conversation. "Now you know about my deepest, darkest secret," I say.

He furrows his brow. He's quiet for a moment. "Secret?"

"My smiley-face feet." I grin. "You're the only one who's seen them besides Nina." I was aiming for a joke, but when Link's gaze slides back up to mine, his eyes are almost haunted, which actually seems kind of appropriate coming from the man I thought ghosted me. Still, he apologized for that already, and I don't want him to suffer anymore.

"Hey." I bob my head as an invitation for him to speak. Lincoln James may want to be a mystery, but for some reason we've got this unspoken connection. I'm sure there's something he wants to share. Or maybe there's something he *needs* to share. Either way, I'll help him get there any way I can.

"Are you all right?" I ask.

He tears his eyes away again. Ugh. Our connection feels severed, which was the opposite of my goal. So I quickly reach for his hand. But rather than a smooth gathering of his hand in mine, all I manage is an awkward fumble.

Strike two, Hadley.

He lets out a long breath, then untangles the mess I've made of our fingers before taking my hand in his. The grip is warm and rough and strong. Calluses at the edge of his palm scratch my skin. Heat pours from him. Link's always smoldering a little on the inside, but the warmth eventually makes its way out.

There's a gentle pulse from him at first, and when I return the pressure, he makes a small noise in the back of his throat. Then his shoulders shudder. A nervous urgency spreads through my chest. I dip my head, looking up until he's forced to make eye contact with me.

When he still doesn't speak, I give one last squeeze of his hand, my focus locked on his.

"Are you still feeling bad about five years ago?" I ask. My voice succumbs to a tremble. I'm afraid of how he might answer—but I keep my eyes steady, my breath even. I can't let Link see my fear if what he needs is my strength.

"Because you don't have to," I add. "Or if you have second thoughts about this whole fake relationship thing, we can call it off whenever you want. I shouldn't have asked you to keep going. Not if you don't want to."

"It's not that." His voice is a rough wave in the night tide. Then he gulps.

"I have to tell you something."

Chapter Twenty-Six

LINK

Hadley's eyes expand just a fraction, but I'm not sure anyone would notice if their faces weren't twelve inches away from each other. We're so close, in fact, I catch the faint scent of apple on her breath. Sweet, tart, delicious. Like a mouthful of fall on her tongue. The deliciousness of her lips is a fact between us, so we probably shouldn't be sitting this close.

At least not until after I've told Hadley the truth.

"Ask me what it is," I say, "so this can count as your question for today. Please."

"Okay. What do you want to tell me?" Her lids dip just a fraction. "I'm ready." She squares her shoulders, which probably means she's not even a little bit ready. Neither am I.

But here we go.

"I had a brother."

Her eyes scrunch up like she's not sure what to make of this. "*Had* a brother?" she says. Then her mouth slips into an *O*, like she's piecing something together.

"Yeah. I mean, he'll always be mine. He's still my brother. But ..." My words falter, and I swallow the lump in my throat.

There's something about saying the words out loud that rattles me, and I don't understand why. It's not like I'm surprised by Tommy. Or his loss. My brother is as real to me as ever. He was never anything but real to me. And yet talking about him to someone other than my mom or my therapist is more difficult than I thought it would be. It's been more than ten years. A whole decade without Tommy. I close my eyes and think about the good stuff; one happy flashback is a start. That's what the therapist says, and it works. Call it up. Focus. Feel it.

Tommy.

Tommy on a swing.

Tommy on a swing in our backyard.

In my memory, the air is cool, and the taste of chocolate and peanuts is fresh in my mouth. Tommy and I had just shared a box of them, and he's got some chocolate smeared on his chin. He's cracking up, head thrown back, as he flies into the sky. His overgrown hair blows out of his eyes as he swoops forward, kicking his legs up and out, pumping hard. From behind us in the house, our mother calls out a warning. "Don't go too high." Her tone is full of worry, even in the recesses of my brain. Mom was always so worried about Tommy.

I lift a hand to my chest now, pressing on my heart.

"His name was Tommy," I say. "*Is* Tommy."

Hadley's lips part, half an inch, like she wants to say something, but she holds back. She's waiting for me to go on. It's too quiet. I have to keep talking.

"He was born with a heart condition. Congenital. The medical term is dilated cardiomyopathy, but I spent the past ten years trying to forget the technical stuff. I just want to remember my kid brother, you know? I want to erase all the hospitals and doctors too. There were so many, we lost count."

"We?"

"My mom and me. And Tommy. It was just the three of us. After we lost him, our family was two. Then my mom pretty much broke. And I'm not talking about money, although we were broke in that way too. When she finally fell apart, I felt like the only one left. That's why I can't let that happen. Ever again."

Hadley nods gently. "And what about your father?" Her question is soft. Tentative. Like she's not sure she should ask. But at this point, I'm done holding things back from her.

"My mom met him the summer after high school. She was a server at a restaurant. He was working there until his deployment. Next thing she knows, he's in the Middle East, and I'm on the way. She had no idea how he'd react. It's not like they'd made promises to each other. So she decided to wait until he was back home to tell him. Except he never came home."

Hadley draws in a breath, but she says nothing, giving me the time and space to share.

"He'd told her he barely had a relationship with his parents," I say. "According to him, they weren't great people. She was afraid of being selfish, not telling them they had a grandkid, but she was more afraid they'd want to be involved." I shrug. "To her, the unknown was too big a risk, so she decided to raise me on her own."

"Pretty brave." Hadley squeezes my hand and keeps her gaze locked on mine. I'm relieved to see no judgment in her expression.

"Ten years later, my mom met Tommy's father. She thought they were in love. Thought they were being careful. She didn't know she was pregnant until she was halfway to her due date. When she called to tell him, his wife answered his phone. Turns out, the guy had a whole other family."

Hadley makes a small noise of sympathy and squeezes my hand.

"My mom grappled with the kind of guilt and self-loathing that can define a person. But when Tommy got sick, she focused everything on him. She could've reached out to the bio dad, asked him for money. Forced his hand to make him contribute." I shake my head, letting the warmth of Hadley's hand encourage me. "Instead she doubled down and took care of him—of me, too—all alone."

I blow out a long breath, wishing once again her fierce mother-love could've been enough to save my little brother. But that's not how it works. "My mom had plenty of regrets, but Tommy wasn't one of them. Raising her two boys—loving us as long as she could—was the one thing she felt like she did right."

"That must've been incredibly hard, though," Hadley says. "For her. For you. For Tommy." Her gaze is direct and clear, and there's no pity in her eyes. Only softness and compassion. Something hitches in my throat, and I feel like I could crawl into her kindness and finally rest. Like I could sleep there forever if I let myself.

If Hadley let me.

"She spent every day shuttling between the hospital and work. She wanted to be with Tommy around the clock, but we needed the health insurance. Even with two jobs, the benefits were never enough. She never complained in front of us, but I'd hear her on the phone with the banks and creditors. We were in debt, but the alternative was unthinkable."

Hadley swallows. "Of course."

"I told her Tommy would be all right. I needed him to be, even though he wasn't. We got four extra years with him thanks to a donor heart. Even now I try to remember that gift and be grateful. Someone else lost a family member so Tommy could live a little longer."

Hadley's eyes are like lasers, drilling into mine. I feel heard. Seen. Understood. Maybe better than I ever have. Better than all the doctors and professional counselors. In this moment, her patience means everything. She doesn't need anything from me, she's just allowing me to need her.

"I've never talked about this with anyone but my mom and my therapist."

Hadley tips her chin. "That's a lot to handle as a kid."

"I was almost eighteen."

"Still a kid, though." Hadley's eyes begin to shine, and something loosens in my chest, like ice cracking across a lake that's been frozen over for years. "You were trying to hold the world on your shoulders," she says.

"I'm sorry I never told you, but I didn't want to be that guy. The one who lost his brother. It was bad enough in high school, with everyone looking at me with sad eyes all the time. So that's not the kind of thing I wanted to bring up at the vending machines in college, you know?"

"I understand," Hadley says, and I believe her. "I don't go around talking about my mother to everyone either. Telling people she died in a car accident when I was a baby is a real conversation stopper."

"You told me about her, though."

"I did, but I don't have actual memories of losing her. It's more the idea of her that I miss. What you went through is ..." Her voice trails off. I could fill in the rest of the sentence with a million words.

"I just wanted to be James," I tell her. "A normal guy without a complicated history. No tragedy. No awkward looks from people who didn't know what to say. I was afraid that could break me like it broke my mom."

"I'm not surprised." Hadley wraps her other hand around mine and the warmth of her somehow makes me feel safer sharing.

"She checked herself into the hospital the day after I turned eighteen. I think she held out as long as she could, but once I was a legal adult, I guess she figured I'd be all right. I *had* to be all right. Didn't really have a choice." My shoulders hitch, an involuntary shrug trying to make what happened okay. "That's about the time I met you," I say. "And honestly, being on that campus—acting like I was a normal student like everyone else—was my only escape. It sounds selfish when I hear myself say it out loud."

"It sounds like self-preservation," Hadley says. Her words are calm and even. "I'm so sorry."

I want to tell her not to feel bad. This is precisely why I don't talk to anyone about Tommy—but somehow, I think she knows that already.

"When Pippa brought me to LA, the first thing she asked

about was my family. She told me questions were inevitable. Interviews. Press junkets. Red carpets. I swore I'd never put my mom in the position to have to relive those losses because of me. The only way to make sure of that was to become someone else. Someone who wasn't Tommy's brother or Pamela's son."

"That's why you got rid of all your social media."

"Yeah."

"And changed your name."

I take a beat to fill my lungs. "I just wanted to give my mom back a piece of her life she'd lost, you know? So as soon as I could, I moved her out to LA. Bought her a house on the beach. Got her a dog to keep her company. The property's secluded. Her life is private. She takes long walks on the sand every morning and watches the sunset every night. A therapist comes directly to her place twice a week. That's how it has to be."

We're both silent for a stretch. Hadley's still grasping my hand.

"I have another question," she says. "Is that all right?"

The fact that she's asking permission means a lot to me. So much of my life is spent avoiding intrusion. But that's not who Hadley is though, I can tell.

"Go for it."

She tips her head. "Do you like being an actor?"

Whoa. Before I can reply, "The Imperial March" sounds on my phone. Pippa's ringtone. "I'd better take this," I say. Saved by the agent, I guess, because I have no idea how to answer Hadley's question.

Do I like being an actor?

I'd better hear what Pippa has to say before I respond.

"Hey, Pip."

"Hold on to your hat, Link. We're jumping to phase two of Operation HadLink. It would've been nice to finish off this week and fly you back to LA, but I talked to Cal and he agrees we should steer attention away from your mysterious beach house and aim the spotlight straight at you and Hadley."

"Spotlight?" My pulse picks up. I like the sound of taking the heat off my mom, but I'm not sure how this will affect Hadley. "What does that look like?"

"It looks like me leaking footage to my contacts today so the HadLink story can spread overnight. In the meantime," she says, "you and Hadley should go out together in town tomorrow. Someplace cozy. Quaint. Maybe try Cataloochee Mountain Coffee. It's on the list I made. Seems like a good spot to be discovered having a romantic moment."

"The locals call it Catty's Coffee," I tell Pippa, glancing at Hadley.

"I love Catty's," she whispers. But she can only hear my end of the conversation. And it was never part of our deal for her to be seen with me in public. Not until the proposal and breakup. And I wanted to keep her life as normal as possible until the end. The literal end. Of us.

"Why do we have to be seen?" I ask Pippa.

"Because that way, when people hear about Lincoln James falling hard for his long-lost love, there will be actual eye witnesses to confirm you've been together in Harvest Hollow. We're adding fuel to the fire, so to speak. Not that our goal is to burn anything down. This is all about building you back up."

"Right." I rake a hand over the top of my hair, trying not to grimace at the idea of exposing her. "The thing is, Hadley twisted her ankle on our hike today, so I'm not sure she'll be ready to go into town tomorrow."

"It's barely a sprain," Hadley hurries to say. "I can ice and elevate overnight. In the morning, I'll wrap up my ankle. And if I need help, you'll let me balance on you, right?"

I release a long breath. She makes it sounds easy enough, but my insides are still in knots. I can't tell what's right or wrong now. Up or down. All I know is I need to protect my mom. But I also want to protect Hadley. Too bad doing both at the same time might not be possible.

Still, if I'm with Hadley, at least I can make sure she's safe. And near.

Which I like a little too much.

"All right." I slide my gaze over to Hadley. "Tomorrow, we start phase two."

Chapter Twenty-Seven

HADLEY

Nina: Hey, friend! Just checking in. You never followed up with info about that LA area code. I'm guessing it was your friend from college trying to reconnect. I'M DYING FOR INTEL. Also, there is basically no wifi or cell service at the cabin. At all. It's like this peaceful little place that's left over from the stone ages. Gavin had to drive me to the mini-mart for these few blessed minutes of technology, so I hope you get my message sooooon ...

Nina: Oh, and I hope you're enjoying your time off from school and NOT developing. Remember you're already the best teacher at Harvest High. Well, tied for first place with me. So how's it going? Have you figured out the arrangement for the fall festival song yet? Wait. That's work. Forget I asked.

Nina: Also, are we still on for meatloaf night? I'm actually looking forward to mystery meat a little bit, but I'll deny admitting that in court if you put me on the witness stand. Delete this thread. (Skull emoji.)

. . .

Nina: Where ARE youuuuu? Don't tell me The Fud talked you into helping Collette with the newspaper after all ... You already said no. If she's got you at school on your days off, I'll murder her.

Nina: jk. I love you girl, but I'm not going to prison over a principal who wears cheerleader bows and waves pom-poms. Plus you'd totally say yes to helping me bury the body, and end up charged as an accomplice. Speaking of which, have you been saying yes to fun stuff while I'm gone? Maybe THAT'S why you aren't responding ...

Nina: Welp I'm headed back to the land of no wifi or phones. But I'll expect a full report as soon as possible. Be good. Or don't be. Either way, I miss you. Love you. Bye.

Nina's texts come in at the same time Sam returns from The General Store. He's got ice packs, ACE bandages, and enough microwave burritos for a blender of wildebeests. While Link wraps my ankle, he fills Sam in on phase two of Operation HadLink.

Sam's excited by the news. Link's busy taking care of me. I myself am aiming for patient and optimistic. Still, the minute they leave, I try calling Nina and get sent straight to voicemail. I don't bother leaving a message. I'm not even sure how to explain my fake relationship with Link.

All I know is I'm running out of time. Because Lincoln James and his girlfriend go public in the morning.

Chapter Twenty-Eight

LINK

Sam eases the rental car into an open spot on Maple, but leaves the engine running. "I'll let you two off here," he says. "Since you don't need me for this couple debut, I'm gonna look for souvenirs for Tanya and the girls."

My mouth slants. "Is that code for grabbing a beer in peace?"

"It's noon on a weekday, and I'm your chauffeur." Sam's face splits into a smirk. "I think I'll stick to shopping." He cuts his gaze to the back seat where Hadley's sitting with her leg stretched out. "Any ideas where I should go?"

She pokes her head between us. "Harvest Farms—the place with the corn maze—has a cute little seasonal store. It's all fall stuff now, obviously. Heavy on pumpkins, scarecrows, and gourds." She points up the street. "If you want to stay closer, we've got a gift shop called An Apple A Day over there. They have apple-themed hoodies, T-shirts, and mugs. Oh, and Book Smart has great things."

Sam's lip twitches. "Like books?"

"Duh." She smacks his arm. "But also journals and stationery and other gifty stuff."

"Great. I'll be back in an hour or so." Sam flashes us a double thumbs-up. "Good luck, HadLink. Just call if you need me sooner."

Climbing from the car, I help Hadley out and over to the curb. For the first time since I came to Harvest Hollow, we're not trying to hide. In fact, folks are strolling on the street around us, window shopping in small groups or pairs. Still, there's no red carpet. No paparazzi.

It's a world apart from the past five years.

The few women I got to know after my *Enforcer* movies rolled out loved nothing more than to be seen with me. They were mostly actors or influencers who wanted evidence of us together to be posted all over social media. I never thought they were villains. They had their own hopes and dreams. I was just a stepping stone across a shallow river. Not that I'm saying we were shallow.

Mostly.

In the end, though, I had to stop looking for someone real to spend time with. Someone who'd understand who I really am. I gave up that search years ago. And nobody could compete with Hadley anyway.

Holding on to my arm now, she hobbles up and stops just outside Cataloochee Mountain Coffee. When she peers through the window, I lean over the top of her to look inside the shop. And I totally don't smell her. Okay. I totally smell her. What can I say?

I love the scent of apples.

The interior of Catty's Coffee appears to be an even mix of modern and cozy. I'm not even in there, and I already feel warm. The walls are brick with exposed ductwork on the ceiling. The edges of the room are lined with permanent booths. Scattered groupings of tables and chairs fill the rest of the space. Toward the front of the shop sit clusters of overstuffed sofas. A woman in an apron is wiping down tables and rearranging stumpy candles and napkin holders.

"Heather's working," Hadley says over her shoulder. "She runs the place now. You'll like her."

"I haven't met anyone in this town I don't like."

"You've only met my dad," she says.

"Point still stands."

"Well, my dad likes you too." Hadley turns away, looking back through the window. "Most of the people in there right now are older regulars. Not exactly the target demographic for *Enforcer* movies. But Heather's got a seven-year-old son. He might be around. Are you ready for him or Heather to recognize you?"

"I'm used to being recognized. The question is, are *you* ready?"

"We don't really have a choice, right? Pippa already leaked the news. We might as well rip off the Band-Aid."

I exhale, surprised by the waves of tension in my gut. Then I'm hit with the overwhelming desire to whisk Hadley away from the spotlight. This kind of possessiveness is new for me. I've never been territorial before. But I feel like she's mine to protect.

Nice try, Link. You're the reason she's about to be exposed.

Hadley reaches for the door, but I grab the handle to open it for her. "So we're really doing it now?" I ask.

Her mouth twitches. "Please don't let anybody hear you say *we're doing it* when we're in there." As she takes my arm, I flash back to her eating apple slices on Boney Mountain. Our kiss at the peak. Her smiley-face toes. What have I gotten myself into?

"Hey, Heather," Hadley chirps as we head inside. "Been busy this afternoon?"

"Actually we've been kind of slow to—" Heather looks up from the table and cuts herself off. I don't miss the double take when she spots Hadley holding on to my arm.

So I smile and bob my head. "Hi."

Heather's mouth opens and shuts. Opens and shuts. Then she quickly recovers, glancing around the shop. "Sit anywhere that's open, as usual," she tells us. "I'll be at the counter when you're ready to order."

She hustles toward the other side of the shop where a barista counter separates the rest of the space from the back wall.

"Come on," Hadley says. "Let's grab this spot in the corner." I help her over to a booth, and she unwraps her scarf, laying it on the table. I take off my baseball hat and set it next to her scarf. Her cheeks glow in the shop's soft lighting.

"We can leave our things here while we order," she says. "I want to save our booth." I guess that's what you get in a town like Harvest Hollow. You can drop your stuff anywhere without worrying anything will be taken.

Hadley uses my arm for balance as we make our way to the barista counter. Heather's waiting for us at the register. "What can I get you?" she asks Hadley.

"Hot chocolate for me, of course." Hadley leans in close to whisper to me. "Heather's got a secret recipe she won't share with anyone. I swear she puts magic in it."

"It's cinnamon," Heather deadpans.

I bite back a laugh. "So, not so secret after all." I peruse the chalkboard menu on the wall. "I think I'll try your hot apple cider."

"Coming right up," Heather says. "Can I get your name, please?"

I blink. "My name?"

"For the to-go cup."

"Goober," Hadley answers for me. "His name is Goober." A smile plays across her lips, and my insides warm. The people who watch my films, read articles about me, and make fan accounts in my honor have absolutely no idea who I am.

But Hadley Morgan does.

"Anyway, we don't need to-go cups," she tells Heather. "Goober and I are staying here, so we'll take mugs and saucers, please."

"I'll have someone bring the drinks to your table." Heather quirks an eyebrow in my direction. "Goober. I like that name. It's a real classic."

When she turns, I quickly stuff the contents of my wallet in the tip jar. Then, I offer Hadley my arm to help her back to our booth.

On the way, moving slowly, I notice an elderly couple across from us. They're sharing the same side of the table, and reading the newspaper together. Neither of them are speaking, but there's a quiet comfort between them. As I watch, I can't help wishing for a future like theirs.

Shortly after Hadley and I take our seats, someone in an apron appears, setting our drinks on the table. Hadley's hot chocolate is topped with an entire can of whipped cream. My cider is steaming, and the scent is succulent. I'm practically drooling, even before Heather drops a plate of warm scones in front of us.

"Apple cinnamon," she says. "On the house."

"Wow, thank you." I didn't realize how hungry I was.

"Enjoy," she says before turning to Hadley. "Your man tips *good*."

"Oh, Heather." Hadley grins. "You have no idea."

My stomach needs these scones. Immediately.

They're a crumble of goodness on my taste buds, and I'm shamelessly stuffing my face, when I look up and spot a small dollop of whipped cream on Hadley's lip. I reach over to wipe it off, and Hadley's tongue darts out—a flash of pink.

Without thinking, I lift my thumb to my mouth and lick it clean.

She meets my gaze, and my insides fill with heat. Which is weird because the rest of me is frozen like a statue. A statue that's absolutely dying to kiss Hadley. She must not feel the same, though, because her eyes go wide, and she starts to choke.

I shove a napkin at her. "I'm sorry." Maybe her hot chocolate is just *that* hot.

"No. It's not you." She points over her shoulder. "It's my dad. He's here with The Fud."

Chapter Twenty-Nine

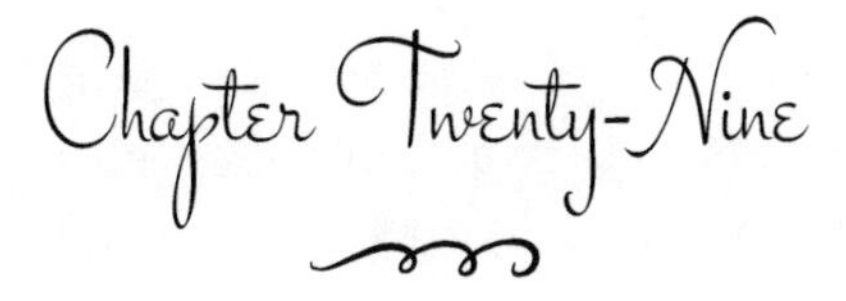

HADLEY

I gulp and sputter, wiping my mouth, then I rub my eyes with the napkin. I *must* be seeing things, right? But no. After blinking a few times, I check my vision, and my dad's still standing there holding the door for the principal of Harvest High.

What the Fudrucker?!

The two of them being in the entrance together at the same time is no coincidence. And I know this, because as soon as they walk through the door, my dad's hand drops to her waist. Then she tips her head up to grin at him. They came here together, and they are touching.

I repeat: My dad is touching my boss, and she is grinning at him.

Grinning!

I absolutely cannot let them see me. More importantly, I can't let them see me seeing them. So before I can think of a better option, I slide under the booth.

"Ouch," I yelp. As it turns out, my twisted ankle hurts when I crouch like this.

"What are you doing?" Link asks. I look up and see that he's ducked below the table.

"Don't look at me!"

"Fine." He frowns. "I won't look at you." He straightens in the booth, hands back up on the table. "But what's a fud?"

"Felicia Fudrucker," I say under my breath. "She's the principal at my high school. And she's here. With. My. Dad."

"So?"

"Shhh!" I grip Link's knee, partly for balance, and partly to signal that we should be quiet. Very, very quiet. My brain is a jumble considering what might happen next. My dad only met Link the one time. I mean sure, they spent all afternoon together. But my dad was talking a lot that day. And eating meatloaf. So maybe he'll just walk past our booth without even recognize—

"James?" Yep. That's my dad. And there's my answer. Definite recognition.

"Hey, there." Link's leg stiffens. "Nice to see you, Mr.—"

"Ray," my dad interrupts. "Nice to see you too! Hey, is Sam here with you?"

"No, he's ... no. Sam? Not here. No," Link stutters. "He's out buying souvenirs for his ... uh, for him."

"Well if you can't treat yourself, who can you treat?" My dad chuckles at his own question. "You know, if Sam's looking for Harvest-Hollow themed stuff, you should tell him to check out the Hollow-Ween store. The place is great. They've got the punniest stuff in there." Another chuckle from my dad. "If you like puns."

"Who doesn't like puns?" Link forces out some laughter. "Heh, heh, heh."

And that's when a female voice I recognize—from countless staff meetings, morning announcements, and requests for me to cover extra adjunct duties—chimes in. "Aren't you going to introduce us, Ray?"

"Ah, yes. Forgive me, Felicia. I just wasn't expecting to see one of Hadley's friends here in the middle of the day. James, this is Felicia Fudrucker. Felicia, this is James ... umm ... You know what? I didn't catch your last name."

"Oh!" Ms. Fudrucker sounds startled. "You're one of

Hadley's friends?" She asks this before Link has a chance to respond, and there's a trill of alarm at the end of her sentence. "Ray." She lowers her volume to a hushed whisper, but I can still hear her since I'm—you know—two feet away from her under the table. "I told you coming here in the middle of the day might not be a good idea."

"It's okay, Felicia," my dad says. "James is cool. You're cool, right, James?" I hear what sounds like the slap of a high five, and imagine how uncomfortable Link must be feeling. When his leg squirms, pressing against my hand, that's all the confirmation I need. The poor guy is probably dying. So I squeeze his knee in a nonverbal thank you, even though he probably has no idea what that squeeze means. Also, how come his knee feels so sexy?

Knees are, like, the second-least-sexy part of the body after the elbow.

"The thing is, James," my dad says, "Felicia and I haven't had a chance to tell Hadley we're dating yet. We just aren't sure how she'll take it. They work together at Harvest High, and Hadley puts her mom on such a pedestal."

My hand on Link's knee becomes a death grip.

"I ... well ... I'm not sure I should be involved in this," Link stammers.

"Oh, don't worry," my dad says. I can practically picture him tossing his hands up in a gesture of surrender. "We're going to come clean with her soon," he says. "In fact, I came close to telling Hadley the other night."

He did?

"When you all wanted to go to the clocktower," my dad says, as if he heard me, "I couldn't go because Felicia and I had plans."

Wait. He said he had poker with the guys!

"I thought you had poker with the guys," Link says.

Exactly, Link! Reading my mind like a good fake boyfriend.

"Ray!" Ms. Fudrucker sounds part disapproving, part bewildered. "You lied?" I imagine her hands on her hips. Unless she's carrying her foam finger and pom-poms.

"I didn't say I had poker," my dad explains. "Hadley *assumed* I had poker, and I decided not to correct her on the matter. The timing just wasn't right to have that kind of conversation. Not in front of her friends."

"Hmm." Link grunts, easing his leg away from my hand. He knows all about letting someone come to the wrong conclusion if it makes things easier in the moment.

"You see," my dad confides, "Felicia's the first woman I've dated since ... well ... since as long as Hadley can remember."

"I understand," Link says, and I'll bet he probably does.

Ms. Fudrucker sighs. "I'm just afraid Hadley might be upset when she finds out about us. I know how the teachers feel about me."

She does? Wait. How do we feel?

Link's leg twitches. "Well, you won't know until you tell her."

"You're very wise, James." Ms. Fudrucker's voice is sweetly sincere. "And as far as the rest of the faculty goes, I'll just have to reassure them that Hadley won't be getting any special attention just because I'm in love with her father."

IN LOVE?!

I squawk like a parrot. Then I cover my mouth, but it's too late.

Ms. Fudrucker gasps. "What was that?"

"Is someone under your table?" my dad asks.

"I ... uhhh ... it's just ..." Link fumbles his words. "Hey. Have you tried the hot cocoa here? I think the secret ingredient is magic."

That's when I remember my mug is sitting across from Link's cider. My dad and Ms. Fudrucker were no doubt too surprised and self-conscious to notice when they first came in. But now Link's drawn attention to our drinks. And my scarf's on the table, too. The one my dad gave me last Christmas.

Busted.

There's a stretch of silence, and I can picture all three of them looking at the mug in front of my empty seat. "Of course, I had to order the cocoa," Link says. "Because I'd heard it was so special. But I also got the apple cider because I was so thirsty."

"Stop!" I say from my hidden squat. I have to put these people out of their misery. Even more importantly, I want to drag myself out of miseryland too. "It's me. I'm under the table." I clamber up onto the booth with a wince as my ankle bears the weight. "I thought I left some gum down here last week."

"Hello, Hadley." Ms. Fudrucker's face goes as red as her Bobcats sweatshirt, which—under different circumstances—would probably make her very happy.

"Gum?" My dad furrows his brow. "Under the table?"

"There wasn't any, after all." I shrug, and it's the worst attempt at nonchalance in history. "I just remembered I would never put gum under a table. Because that would be totally gross and rude. Used gum belongs in a napkin. Or a trashcan. Or worst-case scenario, you should just swallow it when you're done chewing." My father and Ms. Fudrucker both gape at me like I've totally lost my marbles. Maybe I have. "Anyway, what are you two doing here? Were you also looking for some gum?"

"Your father is on his lunch break," Ms. Fudrucker says. "And I'm ..."

"Developing?"

"Hadley Mae Morgan." My dad's brow is furrowed, but his voice is soft.

"Yes, Dad?"

"I guess you heard about me and Felicia," he says. "That we're dating."

Well, The Fud used the words *in love.* But at least we're not talking about the fact that I was hiding under the table claiming to be scoping out chewed gum. "I did hear, and I get it." I glance at Link then back at my dad. "You just needed a new meatloaf partner."

New meatloaf partner? Smooth, Hadley.

Even as the words come out, I realize I sound crazy, but I'm not completely wrong. I think my dad makes meatloaf every week because it's the only recipe my mom felt confident cooking when they first got married. He told me she experimented with different variations of meatloaf every night for more than a month until he finally begged her to stop.

So after she was gone, he started making meatloaf again himself. And I'm pretty sure it was his way of keeping my mother around. We've never really talked about this, but it's so obvious. Dad needs a new meatloaf partner.

I just kind of wish it weren't The Fud.

But we can't always get what we want, right? Case in point, Lincoln James. This is probably the last way he expected phase two of Operation HadLink to go today. I force my gaze back to him, still blushing from Gum-gate. But the kindness in his eyes is an immediate comfort. When his lip tugs up, I flash back to him wiping the cream off my mouth and tasting it.

Yum.

That's when the bell over the door jingles, and Sam hurries inside. He makes a beeline for our table holding an orange bag from Hollow-Ween. "Sam!" my dad hoots. "So glad you're here!" He sweeps an arm in The Fud's direction. "May I introduce you to the lovely Ms. Felicia Fudrucker?"

"It's a pleasure to meet you." Sam shakes Ms. Fudrucker's hand, then turns to us. "I didn't know you had plans to meet family here today. Sorry to interrupt."

"We didn't have plans," I insist. "And you're not interrupting."

"Good." Sam sets his bag of souvenirs on the table. "Because I really need to talk to Link."

The second Sam says "Link", Ms. Fudrucker shrieks. "I KNEW YOU LOOKED FAMILIAR! YOU'RE LINCOLN JAMES!"

"AND YOU'RE IN LOVE WITH MY DAD!" I blurt.

All ambient noise and movement in the coffee house grinds to a halt.

Sam aims a crooked smile at Link and me. "Sounds like we're

making headlines all around," he says, pulling his phone from his pocket. "I thought you two would want to know the story of your relationship is officially out there. In fact, it's exploded. HadLink is all over social media and TV."

In my peripheral vision, I can tell the patrons in the coffee house are starting to whisper. I turn and see an elderly couple across from us staring. A pack of old men frown. Three women at the corner booth scramble for their phones. They're trying to take pictures of Link without anyone noticing.

But I notice.

In fact, I already feel different. Like a goldfish splashing around in her bowl, while everyone on the outside watches her trying to swim. I'm exposed and a little helpless. For the first time, I recognize I wasn't prepared for this kind of spotlight. Yes, I'm on display in front of a classroom of students, five times a day, every school day. But this kind of attention is going to be ... next level.

How did I not realize that?

Heather comes toward us with her head cocked. "You're really enjoying those scones, huh?"

"I'm so sorry, Heather." My face flushes. "Are we causing a scene?"

"Don't worry about that. This is great publicity." A smile stretches across her face. "You're already big news on Harvest Hollow Happenings. Catty's will be packed within the hour."

I gape at her, then address Link. "Harvest Hollow Happenings is an Instagram account," I explain. "It's eerie how quickly stuff gets posted there. And no one's been able to figure out who runs it yet."

"Not for lack of trying," Heather says. "You and Goober are all over fan accounts too. And reels. And TikTok."

"Already?"

"I'm afraid so." She shrugs. "Or congratulations, depending on what your goal is."

Good question. What even *is* my goal? And how come I can't remember a single reason why I thought this was a good idea?

Adventure. Spontaneity.

Yeah. Shut up, Hadley.

Heather hands over her phone. She's got a video playing of Link and me at the corn maze. It starts with the moment I jumped into Link's arms, followed by me knocking him to the ground, and ending as he gently cradles me to his chest. The caption reads "Lincoln James falls hard for college flame Hadley Morgan. #HadLink."

In the clip, I'm glowing, Link is grinning, and we're both covered in hay. This was in the *before* of our fake relationship. All of a sudden, we're in the *after*.

It's a genuine news story now.

"Yeah, that's a good clip," Sam says, looking over my shoulder, "but this meme's even more popular." He shows us a side-by-side mashup of two pictures in one image. In it, Link and I are wearing his green beanie at different times. I'd forgotten I even borrowed that from him on our hike.

Who knew beanie-sharing would make everyone so giddy?

I turn to Link. "Looks like we're a thing," I say. "Officially."

"I don't understand," my dad says. "You two are a couple?"

Oops. This is another thing I hadn't considered. I'm not sure why I thought we could pull off Operation HadLink without my dad finding out. But here we are. "It's a long story," I say, glancing around. "Too long to tell here."

"I've got an idea!" My dad sticks a finger in the air like he's having a real lightbulb moment. "Bring Link over for meatloaf night later. We'll have plenty of time to talk then."

"I don't know, Dad."

"Please." His smile falters. Only half an inch, but still. He must really want this.

"We'd be happy to come," Link says. And the Oscar for Best Fake-Boyfriend-ing goes to him.

"Sam," my dad adds, "you should come too, of course."

Before Sam can respond, the women from the corner booth

make their way over to us. They're all blushing and tittering, with stars in their eyes aimed directly at Link.

"Can we get a selfie with you?" one of them asks. "Our husbands and kids are huge Magnetron fans."

Sam claps Link on the back. "What about you three ladies? No love for my man, Link?"

"Oh, I love him all right," the second woman gushes.

"He's on my hall pass list," the third one says. "And it's laminated."

Ms. Fudrucker frowns. "A *laminated* hall pass list? We don't have those at Harvest High." She turns to my dad. "Ray. Should we have a laminated hall pass list?"

And now I kind of want to crawl back under the booth. Then maybe underground. All the way to the Earth's core. But I don't have time for that because my phone vibrates with a text from Nina.

Nina: BIG NEWS! CALL ME WHEN YOU GET THIS! FINGERS CROSSED I'LL HAVE SERVICE!

My stomach leaps. *Nina knows.* This makes everything more real. I just hope she's not too upset I didn't tell her about Link and me myself.

"Sir Ray," Sam says to my dad. "Thanks for the invite to meatloaf night, but I won't be able to make it." He turns to us. "I came here to tell you I've got to get to the airport. STAT."

Link frowns. "What's wrong?"

"It's Tanya." Sam grimaces. "According to the twins, Mommy broke her butt."

Chapter Thirty

LINK

The good news is Tanya and her butt are going to be okay. The bad news is she fell off a ladder trying to decorate for Halloween. Now she's going to need help getting around while her coccyx heals.

So we're on our way to Asheville to drop Sam at the airport. I'm driving, he sits shotgun, and Hadley's in the back. Meanwhile, we've got Pippa on speaker updating us on Operation HadLink.

"Everyone's absolutely losing their minds over the fact that Link held a torch for his old crush all these years," she says. "We're really leaning into the second-chance nature of your romance."

Second chance, huh? I don't remember getting a first.

"Public opinion is already skyrocketing," she says, "and Cal Youngblood's convinced Link's popularity will only continue to increase. We're talking stratospheric favorability, guys."

Wow. This is a giant word salad. I'm not sure I can digest it.

I check the rearview and Hadley's gazing out the window. Man, I could stare at her profile all day. The dip of her nose. The swell of her lips. She turns and catches me looking.

Say something.

"So ... what do you want us to do next, Pip?"

Real smooth, man.

"You and Hadley should get back to Harvest Hollow as soon as you drop off Sam. Let the civilians see you together and go crazy posting about HadLink."

"We're going to my dad's for dinner tonight," Hadley says. "Is that okay? I can cancel if it's not."

"It's perfect," Pippa says. "Dinner with the family really sells the idea that you're a couple."

I shift my jaw, failing to loosen the tension. I hate that Hadley has to fake this stuff in real time. And now her dad's dragged into the mix? I didn't see that plot twist coming. "And then what?" I ask. "Hadley has to work. She's got a job. A life."

"Of course she does," Pippa says. "She'll stay there in town, and we'll fly you back to LA. You'll do interviews, and in every interaction with the press, you'll tell the world how desperately in love you are with Hadley. How much you can't wait to get back to Harvest Hollow to your one true soulmate. Fans will be swooning all over themselves. You know how to sell it, Link. You're an actor."

Hadley makes a noise behind me. I grip the steering wheel and force myself not to look in the mirror.

"Meanwhile," Pippa continues, "we'll be making all the arrangements for your proposal behind the scenes."

I frown. "You mean my total humiliation?"

"Po-tay-to, po-tah-to," she says. "In any case, it's the culmination of our plan. We already have the ring, and I've been thinking the fall festival would be the perfect place for you to drop to a knee and have Hadley turn you down."

"You bought a ring?"

"Not me. Youngblood arranged for a donation from a sponsor," she says. "And I'll get ZTV there to film you asking her to marry you. Enormous diamond. Giant brush-off. You get the picture."

I blow out a long breath. "Do we still need to televise the proposal? Or could we make things a little less ... public?"

"Youngblood wants to go big with this, Link. Four-carats big, if you know what I mean." She pauses for a beat. "You knew that going in."

"I guess."

"And your cooperation is not only contractual, it also makes you a very tempting option for their new franchise. They'd be foolish to go with anyone else." She takes a beat, and I can just imagine the dollar signs dancing in her eyes. Not that Pippa's only concerned about money. But she's earned her fair share putting up with me.

"The focus at the press junket will be all about your broken heart," she says. "And we're expecting the tone on the red carpet to be off-the-charts supportive of you."

My guts are in a vise now, clamped down and crushing. Of course this is what I signed up for, I just wasn't prepared for how it would feel.

"So you think he'll be offered the role of The Vise-Count?" Hadley asks.

"The studio won't talk about that until after the premier," Pippa says. "But the prospects are good. Women already want to trade places with you, Hadley, and that dream will feel like a potential reality the minute you end things with him."

"What about my mom?" I ask, shifting my focus away from losing Hadley to helping her.

"Everyone knows you're in Harvest Hollow now," Pippa says, "so that helped divert attention. I also had our security team tell reporters they were protecting the home of an old soap opera actress. Not a very juicy story. Once the paps heard that, they lost interest and took off. The world isn't always kind to aging women, you know."

"Understatement," I say under my breath.

"We've still got a couple of guards onsite in case they return," Pippa goes on, "but it looks like we're in the clear for now. But remember, Link. This all started with that photographer at Highland Hospital. You need to be on your best behavior."

"He is," Hadley pipes up. "Always."

"And you're doing a bang-up job too, Hadley. I knew you were the right woman for this role."

Role. Right.

Pippa signs off just in time for Sam to receive a call from a woman at ZTV. She wants to confirm Sam's the one responsible for the viral footage of HadLink. She asks if there are any clips he hasn't sold yet, and tells him she wants to talk "exclusives." By the time we reach the airport, Sam's received half a dozen calls and texts from other media outlets offering money for shots that haven't been earmarked yet.

Hadley claps, as she hugs him goodbye. "Go, Sam! You're famous now!" Her enthusiasm is so high, it's like a helium balloon. I didn't know anyone was this nice without an agenda.

We're halfway back to Harvest Hollow, when Hadley's phone buzzes with a text. She checks the screen and wrinkles her nose. "It's from Pippa."

"I thought we got enough of her already." I frown. "Does she want to congratulate you again for being so good at your role of fake girlfriend?"

"No." Hadley reads the text. "She says the producers at *America's Hidden Talent* want to arrange a Zoom meeting to discuss my spot on the show."

"Makes sense." I return my gaze to the road, but my jaw ticks. "You held up your end of the bargain. Pippa's following through with hers."

"Hmm." Hadley's quiet for a beat. "What if I don't want her to follow through?"

"Don't feel bad about saying yes. Believe me, Pippa's used to this. The producer probably owes her a favor. Her whole life's one big quid pro quo."

"Either way." Hadley's voice is soft. "I'm going to text her back, no thanks."

"Really." I glance at Hadley. She sets her phone down and tips her chin.

"What?" she asks.

"It's just that five years ago, getting on that show was the only thing you could talk about."

"Right. Because I had something to prove then."

I stiffen. "To Carson?"

"No. To myself." She draws in a long breath then slowly exhales on a sigh. "But there *is* something I should probably tell you about those auditions," she says. "Something I should've been honest about a long time ago." She pauses for a moment, and blood starts sprinting through my veins. "I asked you to go with me that day for a reason," she says.

Oh. That.

"Yeah, I know," I say. "Your dad didn't want you hanging out in Asheville alone at the crack of dawn. He's a protective guy. I'm not surprised."

Hadley swallows hard. "That's what I let you think, but my dad had no idea I was auditioning. I didn't tell him until afterward." Her shoulders creep up. "The truth is, he never asked me to bring a friend to those auditions. I just wanted an excuse to spend the whole day with you."

Whoa. My throat goes cotton-ball dry. I feel like I could guzzle a gallon of water and still feel parched. "Me?"

"I just thought ... maybe ... there might've been something happening between us. I was hoping so, at least."

Well, something's definitely happening now. My heart's a sledgehammer in my chest. "I thought you were trying to get Carson back."

"That's what I told you." She tucks a leg up under her. The one without the injured ankle. "I told myself the same thing. But the truth is, I'd been interested in you since the day we met."

I shake my head. "No."

"Yes. But I wasn't brave enough to ask you out. And you didn't ask either. So when Carson pursued me, I felt bad turning him down. You know, I haven't always been *this* good at saying no to people." I glance at her, and her lip quirks. Even now, she's trying to protect herself by making jokes. But I can't find the humor in her relationship with Carson. "Eventually, being his girlfriend just became … who I was," she says. "And being with him felt a whole lot safer than wanting someone I couldn't have."

"I had no idea."

"I did a good job of denying my feelings. But whenever you and I were together, I couldn't help noticing how different you were from Carson. You always tried to make me feel better about myself. Next to Carson, I felt small. But you built me up."

"Yeah. Well." I gulp. "You said it yourself. You didn't know me back then."

"I didn't know *everything* about you." Emphasis on the word everything. "But I knew what mattered. I knew your soul, James."

James.

My pulse is racing so fast now, I'm surprised I don't swerve off the road. I hit the turn signal and take the next exit off the highway. Then I hang a right, and pull the rental car into a gas station on the corner.

Hadley looks at the fuel gauge. "We need gas?"

"No." I find a spot away from the pumps and throw the car in park. Hadley's brow is furrowed. It's a Grand Canyon-level crease. Which is no surprise. My behavior now is coming way out of the blue. "I need to look you in the eye when I say this."

"Say what?"

I glance around the parking lot. Across the street is a grassy park with an old gazebo in the center. That would be a much better place for a meaningful conversation like this. "Hold on." I hop out of the car and run around to the passenger side, throwing open the door. "Let's take a walk. I don't want to do this in a gas station."

Hadley bites her lip, and a prickle of doubt races up my spine. Maybe she isn't feeling what I'm feeling right now. "I don't think extra walking is the smartest move," she says, dropping her gaze to her foot.

"Ah. Your ankle!" Facepalm. "I'm such an idiot." I survey our surroundings, noting that the parking lot is empty, so I crouch down beside the car above the oil-stained pavement. I probably look nuts, but what's more important in this moment is telling Hadley the truth.

"Hadley. From that first time I met you at that vending machine I felt ... changed. Moved. Hopeful. Not because you were beautiful—although you definitely were. But the way you teased me about me hogging the last box of Goobers ... There was a light in your eyes and a warmth to your words. I needed that then more than I even knew."

"I remember that day." Her lip twitches. "You were very cute."

"What *I* saw in the mirror was someone who didn't deserve a woman like you. A guy in debt, and damaged, just digging his way back out. But you made me smile. You made me laugh. You made me believe I could be happy again."

Her nod is slow. Tentative. "We sure did laugh a lot."

"Yeah. And I never let myself consider there could be anything more between us. I didn't want to risk what we had. I figured I'd freak you out if I ever asked you on a date. When you started going out with Carson, I put up a wall. Then I strung up caution tape and barbed wire around the top. I basically tattooed *friend zone* on my forehead."

Spots of pink rise in her cheeks. "Just buddies."

"Exactly. And believe me, I was so grateful for that. For your friendship, I mean. You got me through what would've been an impossible time. Leaving you was the last thing I wanted to do." Heat sears my chest as I remember the pain of cutting her out of my life. "I didn't think I had a choice, so I convinced myself you'd be okay without me. Better, even."

"Ahh, yes." She sighs. "I was *so* good, I got back together with Carson. Again."

"Don't remind me." I groan.

She takes my hand and squeezes it. My heart squeezes along with it. "I thought about you all the time," she says.

"Same. Every day for five years."

"I saw all your movies at least three times." Her thumb rubs slow circles along my palm. Soft, sweet torture.

"I followed you on Instagram," I say. "That's how Pippa found you."

"But you're not on Instagram." Hadley crinkles her nose. "You're not on *any* social media platforms. Not that I checked obsessively … But I did."

"I have a secret account," I tell her. "The handle's nothing anyone could ever connect with me. Nothing to do with me as an actor or even me as James Lincoln." Her thumb stops moving. "And I only followed one person."

Her eyes are big blue ponds. "Me?"

I nod, leaning toward her just as an employee in a ball cap and coveralls exits the quick mart. "Hey there," he calls out, approaching our car.

Great timing, bro.

I never thought I'd be so annoyed by good customer service. I let go of Hadley's hand and rise to my feet. He cocks his head then slows his pace. "Wait. Are you …? You are! Dude." He throws his hands up and hops, pointing at me. "You're Magnetron! No way. Magnetron's at our freakin' gas station. This is so wild!"

Is it all that wild, though? Am I not allowed to need gas?

"I've gotta go tell everyone," he says. "Hold on!" He runs back into the quick mart, then jogs back out with a couple other employees. They've got skeptical looks on their faces. But then they see me and start jostling each other, punching shoulders.

"It *is* him!"

"Told you," the guy with the ball cap says. Then he turns to me. "So what can we do for you, man? Clean windshield? Air in the tires? Check your fluids?" He comes around the front of the car, finally spotting Hadley in the passenger seat. "Ahhhhh." His eyes pore over her. "I see now. You've got a friend." He nods and licks his lips. "Sorry I interrupted whatever you were about to do."

"Eyes off her," I say.

"Dude. I get it." He shoots me a wolfish wink. "When you're famous, it's probably hard to find places to get it on."

"I think you should *get* your mind out of the gutter."

"Whatever you say." He chuckles. "But, hey. Could my guys and me *get* a pic with you?"

"I think you'd better *get* back inside."

"Link." Hadley reaches for my hand again, entwining our fingers. Her eyes lock with mine. "It's okay. I don't mind. A few pictures won't take long. It's the least we could do for your true fans, right?" She arches a brow. A warning.

Your temper's what got us here in the first place.

Yeah. Message received.

She looks up at the man, offering him a bright smile. "And believe me, you didn't interrupt anything. I twisted my ankle and Link was just helping me wrap it."

The man nods and grins. "Nice."

I take a deep breath, letting the calm of Hadley's touch work its way up my arm. Then I let the employee and his friends take selfies with us. But this moment is a clear reminder that I can't promise Hadley the sweet, simple life of a hometown choir teacher.

She deserved better when I first met her, and she still deserves better now. I almost forgot that for a moment. But once HadLink is officially over, she can move on—in or out of the public eye. Either way, that will be her choice.

My mom's identity should remain safe then. And the red carpet can be a love-fest. I'll land that role of The Vise-Count, and Pippa will retain her title as the queen of all agents. Who knows? Sam might even make a killing selling his videos. That's five potential wins. With only one loss.

James Lincoln's heart.

Chapter Thirty-One

HADLEY

After the gas station, for most of the drive back to Harvest Hollow, Link is quiet. Like, extra quiet. I don't think those men meant to be rude back there, or maybe they did. Either way, Link's feeling protective. He cares about me.

He always has.

We probably should've had an adult conversation about our feelings years ago. But in our defense, we were barely adults then. And we were also both convinced the other one wasn't a real option. He thought I wouldn't want a guy like him. I thought he wouldn't want a girl like me. And our actions seemed to prove those two things, neither of which turned out to be true.

Still, we have a chance to set things straight now.

Beginning with me telling him what I want.

"Link," I say into the silence. But his eyes stay fixed on the road. So as we approach a red light, I try again. "James."

His gaze swings to me. "Yes?" His voice is husky and deep, like he's been chewing a mouthful of rocks.

"I've been thinking." I draw in a deep breath.

Spontaneity. Adventure. Be brave, Hadley.

"What if we weren't in such a hurry to break up? Couldn't stretching out our relationship a little longer work in your favor?"

Not to mention mine.

The light turns green, and he averts his eyes. "You heard Pippa. People have short attention spans. And once the initial excitement of HadLink wears off, our breakup will keep everyone invested in the story."

"And that's important?"

"Cal Youngblood thinks so," he says. "And the studio's insisting, so I don't really have a choice. Compliance with their publicity plan is written into my contract." He glances at me, and heat creeps up my throat.

"Maybe they'd change their minds. If you asked."

"There's also my mom," he says, like I didn't just suggest he fight for us. "If the paps are busy following my relationship rollercoaster, they won't have time to dig around and find her."

"I guess," I say, but my heart sinks like a penny tossed in the town square fountain. What he's saying makes sense. I just wish his list of reasons for us not to be together wasn't so long.

"There's one more thing," he says.

Fantastic.

"Once we break up"—he takes a beat—"your life can return to normal. Yours *and* your dad's. That's important." The cords along his neck tighten. "Your safety is everything."

I chew my lip to stop the tremble. He cares about my dad and me, which only makes me want him more. "Thanks," I manage, swallowing against the lump in my throat.

His eyes cut to me, then back to the road. "Are you all right?"

I nod, even though I'm not sure I am. "I just feel kind of dumb now. Maybe I shouldn't have told you how I felt."

How I feel. *Present tense.*

"Well, I'm glad I told you," he says. "Those things needed to be said, Hads."

Hads.

"Now we can move forward," he says. "I hate thinking you didn't know that—"

My phone rings, interrupting him. *I didn't know what?*

His eyes flick to my phone, so I check the screen.

It's Nina.

My head's already spinning, but a rope of guilt coils around my insides. She texted me hours ago when we were still at Catty's Coffee. I was supposed to call her so we could talk about THE BIG NEWS. *My* big news. She thinks Lincoln James is my real-life boyfriend, and I left her hanging. She must be losing it by now.

"I have to take this," I tell Link.

He bobs his head. "Go."

"Hey, Nina. I am so, so sorry."

"HADLEY!" Her shriek practically splits my eardrums.

"I know, I know. I'm the worst." I flinch. "I won't even pretend I didn't totally space on calling you back. It's just been kind of crazy around here, as I'm sure you can imagine. But that's no excuse, and I'm so, so sor—"

"You already said that," she cuts me off. "But it's fine! I've had almost no cell service this whole time. Gavin had to drive me up to the mini-mart again. Did you see my stories?"

"No." I blink, a bit confused. It's like she didn't hear a word I said. Maybe she just feels bad for sharing something in her stories about me and Link without asking first.

"It's okay if you reposted stuff about us already."

"How could I be sharing stuff about you when we haven't even been together?"

"Uhhh." My stomach drops, and goose bumps hopscotch along my neck. "What are you talking about?"

"What are YOU talking about?"

"The big news."

"ME TOO!"

Wait. Does Nina know about my dad and Ms. Fudrucker? No. Her text back at the coffee shop came in only a few minutes after *I* found out that my dad's been dating my boss. "It can't be The Fud," I mutter to myself.

"You're being weird. Take a breath."

I do as Nina tells me. "Okay," I say. "Breath taken."

"I have no idea what's been going on in Harvest Hollow," she says, "but what I posted on my stories happened at the cabin. I can't believe you haven't looked yet."

"Hold on." I open Instagram and search Nina's account. There it is, bright and shiny, on the fourth finger of her left hand.

A diamond solitaire.

"Gavin PROPOSED?" I'm so shocked, I almost drop my phone. "When?"

"A few hours ago, on the lake. He took me out in this tiny rowboat for two, which—when you think about it—was a little bit stupid. What if we'd tipped over and the ring box went into the water? Still, I'm an engaged woman now. And this ring is never coming off. Except to get sized. It's way too big. I'm pretty sure it would fit my thumb."

"That's amazing, Nina. I'm so, so happy for you. I can't wait to celebrate, even though this means I'm going to be losing a roommate."

"Not for a while," she says. "We aren't in any rush. And it takes a long time to plan a wedding." She sounds so giddy, my eyes start to well up. I just want to soak up her joy and forget the only proposal coming my way isn't real.

"When are you going to be home?" I ask.

"We decided not to drive back until the morning. Gavin's going to take me straight to school and drop me off. I'll be back in time for class, but please tell your dad I'm sorry I'm missing meatloaf night."

Yeah. There's a lot of stuff you're missing.

"Well, that ring sure looks worth it," I say. "It's gorgeous. *You're* gorgeous! But I should probably let you get back to your fiancé. Tell Gavin he's the luckiest man alive."

"And that's why I love you," she says. "We've got *so* much to catch up on. BYE-EEE."

We end the call, and I glance at Link, taking in his profile. The waning sun shines on his brow, that perfect nose, and those chiseled cheekbones. Instinctively, I reach out and run a finger along the edge of his beard. At my touch, he turns to face me.

His handsomeness is a fact. But it's the least attractive thing about him, if that makes sense. What I love most is his kindness and strength. His wisdom. Generosity. And this good man is supposed to propose to me soon, but not for real. Not like Nina's engagement. He's going to get down on one knee.

And I'm obligated to turn him down.

"So she's getting married?" he asks. "That's exciting."

"Uh-huh." I blink back tears.

"Are you all right?"

"Yes," I choke out. "I'm just so happy for Nina."

Chapter Thirty-Two

LINK

Can I be honest?

As much as my guts are all twisted up thinking about Hadley, I'm also nervous about dinner with her dad. Not to mention The Fud. Meatloaf night's like a double date. Or like a family eating together.

The thing is, I didn't grow up sharing meals, chatting and laughing at the kitchen table. My mom did her best, but she was at work a lot or at the hospital with Tommy. That meant I scarfed a ton of microwaved meals on my lap watching TV.

James Lincoln. Party of one.

So as we pull up to Hadley's childhood home I exhale, long and slow. Good old nervous-system regulation.

You've got this, man.

Ray Morgan's two-story craftsman is surrounded by a tidy lawn and window boxes bursting with geraniums. He's got his porch ready for autumn, with multicolored gourds stacked by the welcome mat. There's a scarecrow seated on one of two rocking chairs, and a horn of plenty on a side table.

He meets us at the door, throwing open the screen and grabbing my hand. His shake is strong, but not like he's trying to prove anything. A lot of men feel the need to crush Magnetron's grip.

"James!" He claps me on the back. "Welcome to my humble abode."

"Thanks for having me, sir."

"The more the merrier at meatloaf night!" He ushers us into the foyer where the scent of something savory hovers in the air.

"Hey, Dad." Hadley hands over a bag from the market. "We brought you a pumpkin pie."

"With whipped cream," I add.

"My favorite." He beams at me. "I'll just put these in the refrigerator."

As he heads off to the kitchen, Hadley leads me into the great room. The walls are all whitewashed shiplap, and a bay window lets in the beginnings of dusk. An antique roll-top desk sits tucked into one corner, and a console with pictures of Hadley is in the other. For seating, there's a long striped couch, and two cozy armchairs with ottomans. We're about to sit when Felicia Fudrucker comes bustling around the corner.

"You're here!" She rushes toward us waving her arms, but stops short of giving out hugs. "Hello, Hadley. Hello, Link." She lays a hand on her chest. "May I call you Link? Is that too presumptuous?"

"No. Link is great."

"GREAT!" she practically shouts. Then her cheeks go blotchy. "This is all so exciting. Isn't it exciting?"

"You bet." I duck my head.

"I didn't know if I was allowed to tell people I'm having dinner with *the* Lincoln James, so I haven't said a word to anyone. Except Ray. He knows I'm having dinner with you. This being his house and all."

As if on cue, Hadley's dad joins us from the kitchen. "This is Felicia's first meatloaf night, too." A grin hijacks his face.

"Well, lucky us," I say. "And since the news is already out that

I'm in Harvest Hollow, feel free to tell people we had dinner together."

Hadley cocks her head. "Of course, whoever you tell will probably figure out you're dating my dad."

"Now that *you* know," she says, "I'd be happy for the word to spread." A dimple presses into her cheek. "Maybe we'll make it onto Harvest Hollow Happenings. Like HadLink. Wouldn't that be fun, Ray?"

"Guess we'd better come up with our own couple name," he says. "What do you think?" He places a hand at the small of her back. "Should we be FudMor? MorFud?"

Hadley snorts. "I think you should keep working on it." She drops onto the couch, tugging me down beside her. Then her dad and Felicia sit across from us, launching into the story of how they ended up dating.

Apparently, they started talking last year during a big booster club fundraiser. He volunteered to be club treasurer, and they started texting each other. After a month or two of meetings, they went for coffee. Then he asked her out to dinner. Then—

Hadley holds up a hand. "I don't need any more details. Honestly, I'm just happy for you two." She addresses Felicia. "And I'm sorry I didn't take over the newspaper when you asked me to."

"Oh, dear, no." Felicia waves the apology away. "Under the circumstances, I shouldn't have asked you for any favors."

"Well, you would've asked me if you *weren't* dating my dad, so don't go giving me any special treatment."

"I won't, if you won't."

Hadley's smile goes crooked. "So no more apple-crumble cupcakes with cream cheese frosting?"

Felicia chuckles. "On second thought, maybe you *could* treat me a tiny bit special."

"Now what about you?" Ray Morgan directs his question at Hadley. "You've been running around Harvest Hollow with an old friend you introduced to me as James. We spent an entire afternoon together. How come I didn't know you two are involved?"

"If you don't mind, sir," I say, "I'd like to answer that." I really like Ray Morgan. More importantly, I respect the man. And I don't want to put Hadley in a position where she has to decide what's okay to share with him. "It's my fault Hadley couldn't tell you sooner," I admit. "She was just trying to protect my identity."

"Yep." He squints at Hadley. "That sounds like my daughter."

"But we did meet when she was in college," I continue. "And I was James then. I still am."

Hadley squares her shoulders. "James is the one who went with me to the auditions for *America's Hidden Talent.*"

"At that point, I already liked her," I say. "But I thought she was auditioning to try to win back her boyfriend."

Ray Morgan presses his lips together. "You already know how I feel about Carson," he says. "I always thought he was wrong for Hadley."

"And you know I don't disagree," I say. "But that wasn't my choice to make. So out of respect for Hadley—for her relationship—I never made a move."

"By the way," Hadley interjects, "I was *totally* single at the time, and I really liked James too. But since he'd never expressed any interest in me, I thought we were permanently in the friend zone."

"Then I met Pippa at those auditions," I say. "She's my agent. She came to Asheville on a mission, kind of like a talent scout. Except instead of scouting for talent, she just wanted to find a guy who had the right look at the time."

"James *is* talented, though," Hadley insists. "He works hard. He's generous. He's got a good heart. The *best* heart."

"I don't know about that," I say.

"And he just rescued a couple of dogs," she continues. "He had to leave them back home to come see me, but he FaceTimes with them every day."

Wait. Hadley knows this? I thought I did a better job of

hiding the fact that I miss Scout and Jem. Maybe Sam spilled the beans. Or Pippa. Either way, Hadley's been paying attention. More importantly, she doesn't seem like she's pretending.

"I think we've always had feelings for each other," she says. "We just didn't admit them to each other until recently. Right, James?"

I turn to her. "Because you had a boyfriend."

"Because you didn't throw your hat in the ring."

"But then things changed."

She reaches for my hand. "Lots of things changed."

Hadley's dad leans back and crosses his leg. "Can I be real honest with you, son?"

"I'd appreciate that, sir." Even as I say this, my pulse ticks up. Ray Morgan's a protective man. I expect he'll put my feet to the fire, asking about my intentions.

"The truth is"—he exhales a gust of air—"I haven't seen a single one of the *Enforcer* movies. Before today, I had no idea who you were." He keeps his brow furrowed for a moment before breaking into a grin. "I sure hope you can forgive me, son."

"Dad." Hadley rolls her eyes, and I puff out a laugh of relief. He's just trying to put me at ease in the midst of a strange conversation. No wonder his daughter sees the best in others and gives them the benefit of the doubt.

Hadley's apple slices didn't fall far from Ray Morgan's tree.

"On that note." He slaps his thigh, and rises from his chair. "I'd better check on dinner." He looks down at Hadley. "Care to give me a hand, sweetheart?"

"Umm." Hadley glances at me, gauging my comfort level. "Is that all right with you?"

"Of course." I squeeze her hand and send her a smile. "Go help your dad."

Chapter Thirty-Three

HADLEY

I follow my dad into the kitchen where he immediately dons his old apron. This is the same apron he's worn for as long as I can remember. I'm guessing he only took it off to greet us at the door. It says Don't Kick the Cook and has a big boot on the front.

He thinks it's hilarious.

"How can I help?" I ask, crossing to the sink to wash up. There's already a loaf of french bread in a basket and a relish tray with three different kinds of olives.

Meatloaf night's getting fancy.

"Want me to make a salad?" I offer, drying my hands on a dishtowel.

"It's in the fridge. Just needs to be tossed." He grabs a couple of potholders and peeks inside the oven. After a dramatic inhale and a long, drawn-out "mmmmm," he changes the setting from bake to warm. "A fine effort if I do say so myself."

"Smells good," I tell him.

"You think so, huh?" He turns to face me, his mouth lopsided. "You know I'm aware that my meatloaf's not your favorite, but I sure do appreciate you putting up with it all these years."

"Want to know a secret?" I hang the dishtowel back on its

hook. "I kind of like your meatloaf. Except for the one with salmon."

"Sweetheart, nobody likes salmon loaf."

I let out a snort. "Then why on earth did you make it all these years?"

He's quiet for a stretch, his blue eyes softening as he studies my face. "Well, that's quite a question." His voice is slow and gentle. "I kind of assumed you knew."

"I mean, maybe I do?" I try on a shrug, but I don't feel nearly as casual as I did a minute ago. "I just never really thought to ask." I lean back against the counter. "You did it for Mom, right? Meatloaf night's your way of keeping her memory around."

He sets the potholders on the counter. "I did it for you, Hadley."

My heart squeezes, and for a moment it's hard to breathe. "Aww, Dad."

"You were so young when we lost her," he says. "All of a sudden, I had to be both parents. And I didn't know how to be a mother, so I just tried to do the things I thought she would've done."

I pick an olive off the relish tray just to have something to do with my hands. "That makes sense," I say, pausing for a beat. "But you still miss her, though. Don't you?"

"Yeah." He crosses to me and rests a palm on my shoulder. "I always will," he says. "But I've also had a very long time to process those feelings. Now I mostly just wish she could've seen the incredible woman you've become." He inclines his chin, his expression almost hopeful. "And I'm not sad anymore, Hadley." He smiles. "My memories of your mother are all happy ones. They have been for a couple decades now."

Wow.

I had no idea. Truly. I mean, I knew he was a happy guy in general, but I figured the stuff with my mom was still pretty hard for him. It's why I always tried so hard to include the things she loved in my own life.

"Really?" I ask.

He drops his arm, and takes a step back. Then his nod is slow but sure. "At first, I had to work at being happy for your sake. You know the old 'fake it till you make it' theory everyone talks about? Well, eventually I became happy for real. No pretending required."

Warmth spreads through my body. "You did that for me?"

He bobs his head. "And for me."

"That's good." My mouth curves up on one side. "Someone wise once told me, 'If you can't gift yourself ...'"

"Yeah." He chuckles. "That started out strong, but I didn't really know how to finish the sentence."

"Nobody noticed," I say on a small laugh. Then I pop the olive into my mouth.

"You know, you may be all grown up now, Hadley, but you'll always be my little girl. Even though you remind me more and more of your mother every day."

In the great room, Ms. Fudrucker lets out a loud burst of laughter. My dad and I both glance across the kitchen.

"Does she remind you of Mom?" I ask.

"Felicia?" He takes a beat, considering his answer. "She and your mother are two completely different people. Maureen was the first love of my life, and I adored her every single day we spent together. I would've continued to until my last breath, if I'd gone first." He tightens the tie on his apron. "But I'm still here, and I've got a lot of life left."

"You'd *better* live a long time."

"I'll do my best."

I smile at him, my nose tingling with pre-tears. "You know I used to try to be just like Mom," I admit. "Or at least I tried to be what you told me she was like."

He lets my statements sink in a second. Then he asks, "In what way?"

"You always said she was such a gifted singer. That she made up her own songs and played the guitar for me all the time. And that's why you gave me Dolores."

He smiles. "She sure loved that old guitar."

"So I wanted to live out the dream she couldn't. For her sake. And for yours."

"Whoa, whoa, whoa." He shakes his head, running a hand over his hair. "Your mother enjoyed singing, but *you* were her dream, Hadley. *You're* what brought her the most joy. Me too."

I swallow hard, not expecting this shift in the story. "But she loved performing," I say. "You told me that. So many times."

"Yes. She loved singing for you," he says. "For me." He closes his eyes, like he's remembering. "She had the sweetest voice."

"Exactly. That's why I got into music. You always seemed so happy every time I picked up Dolores."

"Honestly?" His lids open. "You looked so much like her, it was a little hard for me at first. Sometimes I wished you just wanted to be a mathematician."

My mouth goes slack, even as my stomach constricts. My goal was always to please my dad. To honor my mom. Who even *am* I if I'm not doing my best for them as a daughter? "You never told me."

His shoulders creep up to his ears. "I thought performing made you feel closer to your mother," he says. "I didn't want to talk you out of it."

"And I didn't want to tell *you* I wasn't cut out to be a professional singer."

"Huh." His arms hang at his side. "So I gave you your mother's old guitar and that made you think I wanted you to be like Mom. I'm sorry."

"No, Dad. No. Don't take that on yourself. Learning to play Dolores was my way of connecting with her since I couldn't actually remember her. I probably would've done it anyway. Same with me wanting to wear her homecoming dress."

"Oof. The chicken pox." He winces, scratching at the dimple on his cheek. "Sweet idea. Unfortunate timing."

"Yeah." I nod. "And you making meatloaf every week is a pretty sweet idea too."

"You know what?" He pushes his hands into the pockets on his apron. "It turns out you're more like your mother than you think. Not the guitar or the performing. In the way you love."

I shift my weight. "What are you talking about?"

"I've seen how you look at that boy in there." My dad nods toward the great room. "And James looks at you the same way. Or Link. Or whatever name he goes by. I'm reasonably certain there's more going on here than either of you told me. But I don't need to know all the details. I can tell you two have something special."

"Dad." I press my lips together, and a ribbon of guilt cinches my stomach. I don't want him to be disappointed. But what's he going to think when I have to turn around and tell him I broke up with Link? "We're just—"

"I don't need any explanations," he says. "I trust you. And him. I'm sure you'll figure things out when you're ready." He winks at me, as another clap of laughter sounds in the great room.

A smile tugs at my lips. "I honestly have no idea what's going to happen with us."

"Sweetheart? Nobody ever does," he says. "So all you can do is try to make the most of the moments when you're in them." He pulls his hands from the apron pockets and claps. "On that note, let's show these newbies how we do meatloaf night."

While he gets the meatloaf served onto plates, I dress the salad and deliver the bowl to the dining room. Then I take in the bread basket and relish tray. The whole time, my mind's unspooling like a one-way yo-yo.

Why hadn't we ever talked about this before? I suppose we were both just trying to please each other. Like our own little *Gift of the Magi*, except instead of New York at Christmas, it's fall in Harvest Hollow.

As we finish prepping the table, we make eye contact and share a small private smile across the dining room. Things feel lighter with him. And you know what?

I'm happy he's found The Fud.

Speaking of which.

When we head to the great room to announce that dinner's served, we come upon a scene I never could've predicted. Felicia Fudrucker is standing on one of the armchairs, and Link is on the ground below, arms out like he's preparing to catch her.

"What on earth?" My dad's eyes go wide, and he wipes his hands on his Don't Kick The Cook apron.

"Ray!" she squeals. "Link and I are reenacting the part in *Enforcer's Return* where Magnetron thinks he's saving Ice-Sis from a cliff. But it turns out Ice-Sis has to save Magnetron because he's about to incinerate from the inside out, so she needs to freeze him from the outside in. It's my favorite moment of the entire franchise, and I'm getting to act it out like I'm Dasha Peet. This is the best night ever!"

"Wow." My dad shakes his head, chuckling. "And I thought you came here for my meatloaf."

Chapter Thirty-Four

HADLEY

Over dinner and then dessert, Link is patient and gracious, answering endless questions about his career, his home, and what Hollywood is like. When talk shifts to his family, he glances at me. Then his Adam's apple travels the length of his throat.

"All I can tell you is my family didn't sign up for this life," he says, "so I do my best to keep them out of the spotlight."

"I understand," my dad says. "Good man."

Yes, Dad. He is.

"But that must be hard," Ms. Fudrucker says. "Do you ever see them?"

He bobs his head. "I do."

That's it. Just *I do*.

I want to ask him more about his mom myself, but I respect his wish for privacy in front of my dad and Ms. Fudrucker. Which reminds me, we have work in the morning.

"As fun as this has been," I say, "we've got school tomorrow." I push back my chair and stand, gathering up the pie plates and forks. "I'll just do these dishes really quickly and—"

"You and Link took the dinner shift at the sink," my dad says. "Felicia and I will handle dessert." Ms. Fudrucker giggles, and I decide not to insist on staying any longer. I really don't need to find out how these two handle dessert or anything else.

So we say our goodbyes including hugs all around, then Link and I head out so he can drop me off at my place. On the drive, I gaze out the window at the star-dotted sky. I'm channeling gratitude for this moment.

For as long as I have it.

"Thanks for tonight," I finally say into the quiet. "You were really great with my dad, not to mention The Fud. That reenactment of Magnetron and Ice-Sis was truly heroic. Not to mention the third degree at dinner. Answering all those questions couldn't have been easy."

"They were fine," he says. "I had fun." He eyes me from the driver's seat, arching a brow. "But I must say ..." His gaze drifts down over my sweater and leggings. "After seeing how much food you Morgans can put away, I'm a little surprised you don't have a pair of designated meatloaf pants."

"Hey!" I pretend to sock his shoulder, and he succumbs to a full-on chuckle. Link's laughter is better than any music my choir ever makes. No wonder audiences adore him. Even as I think this, we turn onto my block, and I'm greeted by an all-too concrete reminder that he's a celebrity.

Reporters with camera crews and microphones are outside my house, standing in the street or on the front porch. Two are peering into the windows of my little orange Volkswagen. There's even a local news van.

"Yikes." I cringe. "Are they all here because of us?"

"They're here because of me," he says. "You're just caught in the crossfire." He switches off the headlights and pulls up to the curb across the street. We're far enough down from my house that nobody notices. At least not yet. "I can handle this," he says. He releases the steering wheel and his hands flex in the dark.

"Are you all right?" I ask.

"As long as the paps cooperate, things will be fine."

"You don't have to—"

"I'll be good," he says. "I promise."

"I trust you." I lay a hand on his knee, and a low rumble sounds in his throat. "Either way, this isn't your fault, you know. You can't control everything, no matter how hard you try. You're not even *supposed* to control everything."

His nod is tight and quick. "That's what Dr. Kwon always says. She's my therapist."

"She sounds smart."

"Yeah," he says. "She is."

He takes a few deep breaths like he's preparing himself. Then he reaches for the handle. "Stay here and lock the doors after I get out. I'll come back to get you after I get rid of them. Okay?"

"But I want to go with you."

"What about your ankle?" He frowns.

"I've been walking on it all day."

"Yes, but it's still fragile. I'd feel better knowing you're safe in the car."

"I'll feel safer with you," I say.

"Hads." Even in the dark, I see his eyes soften.

"Besides. Pippa still wants us to be seen together," I push. "This will be better for the plan."

"The plan. Right."

I hate to think of myself as a burden, but I really do want to get into my house, and I feel like the best and easiest way would be by his side.

At this point, a couple of reporters have noticed our car parked down the street, and they start heading toward us to investigate.

"All right," he says. "Hold on." He hops out and jogs around to my side, with his back to the paparazzi. Throwing open the door, he takes my hand and helps me up. Then he tugs the length of me tight to his body.

"Remember to be nice," I say under my breath, pasting on a smile.

"I *am* nice," he says back. As we walk arm in arm toward my house, the reporters follow, taking pictures, rolling film, and calling out questions.

"Is it true Hadley's pregnant?"

"Did you two elope?"

"What does Dasha Peet think about your relationship?"

"We heard you're just getting back from Vegas. Does Link have a gambling problem?"

"Are you going to sign a prenup?"

"Did you reconnect in rehab?"

"Can we get a pic of HadLink?"

Link stops and we turn to face them. "I understand you all have a lot of questions." He offers a half wave while the cameras flash. "But Hadley was injured on a hike yesterday, and we need to get her inside to ice and elevate her foot. She's good. I'm good. We're both good. And we thank you in advance for respecting our privacy." The whole time he speaks, his voice is low and deep. Superhero voice engaged.

Magnetron.

As we start toward the house again—me with a small limp and him with a strong grasp that makes me feel secure—the crowd follows, asking for more pictures and pushing for more statements. We ignore them until we're finally on the porch. That's when Link and I turn to face everyone once more. "Have a beautiful night," he says to the cameras.

"Enjoy Harvest Hollow," I chirp.

"So you two are staying here together?" one reporter asks.

"Yes," Link says at the same time I say, "No!"

"I mean yes, she's staying here," he adds. "And I'm waiting with her to make sure she's okay. That's what matters to me. After all these years, I just want to be by Hadley's side, making sure she's all right."

He gazes down at me, a tender look of concern in his eyes, and my heart starts spinning like a thousand windmills.

"But if they're still out here in an hour," he whispers under his breath, "I'm staying overnight. I need to know you're safe, and I'm not taking no for an answer."

All right then, Magnetron.

Be still my spinning heart.

Chapter Thirty-Five

LINK

Once we're inside, I move across the house, closing all the curtains and shutters that were left open. Clearly this isn't a house used to worrying about paparazzi. Meanwhile, Hadley locks the front door and turns off the porch lights. When I meet her back in the front room, she's waiting with her hands on her hips.

"You went a little caveman on me out there, Magnetron." She cocks an eyebrow. "You won't take no for an answer. Really?"

"I guess I did do that."

"I hope you know I can take care of myself. *And* my ankle."

This is what she's saying, but she's also a little breathless, so I'm not sure she's being completely honest about her pain. We parked halfway down her block, and she had to walk a decent amount. Still, I know she's strong and capable. And I don't want her to think I underestimate her.

"I'm sorry," I say. "I'll try not to let that happen again. But when it comes to protecting you ... I just want you to be safe."

She quirks her other eyebrow. "I'm not mad. In fact, I kind of liked it, even though I probably shouldn't."

"Well, that's good." I let out a breath of relief. "And for the record, I know you're perfectly capable of taking care of yourself."

I nod at her ankle, but add a wry smile. "Evidence from our hike to Boney Mountain notwithstanding."

She sputters out a laugh. "Point taken. And I appreciate your concern. But given the microscope we're under, I'm not sure your being here all night is a great idea."

"I promise to be a gentleman." I move over to the couch. "And obviously I'd just sleep there."

"*Obviously.*" Her face crinkles with amusement. "But you heard some of the things those reporters were speculating. Their questions weren't exactly flattering. If you stay, we'd only be fanning the flames."

My insides knot up. "That's exactly why I want to be here. To keep them away from you. You're not used to this kind of exposure."

"But I knew there would be media coverage when I agreed to this," she persists. "Maybe I wasn't aware how fast and furious things might get. But that's partly why I said yes in the first place. To push myself. To be brave." She shrugs. "I want to be more than just Ms. Morgan, nerdy choir teacher."

I frown. "You're not nerdy."

"How dare you." In mock protest, she lifts a hand to the rise of her collarbone. "I am a nerd, and totally comfortable with that."

"You just don't see yourself the way others do."

"Others?"

"Okay. The way *I* see you."

"And how is that?"

"You're someone who's brave. And smart and generous. You don't give up. You try new things even when they scare you." I shrug. "And you have happy faces on your toes."

"You're too kind," she says, but a smile tiptoes across her face. "Whether or not you're staying," she says, "I'd better get some ice for my ankle. And some sheets and a spare pillow for the couch. Just in case." She turns toward the kitchen, but I block her. "I'll get the ice and the sheets. Just tell me where they are."

Her mouth goes crooked. "Well, the ice is in the freezer."

I arch a brow. "Very original."

"And we keep spare linens in the hall closet. Pillows, too."

"Got it." I fix her with a stare, not moving.

"What?"

"Sit. I'll do the rest." My lips quirk. "And I'm *not* taking no for an answer."

"So bossy." She flashes me a grin, but she drops onto the couch.

"I could get used to taking care of you, woman."

The truth of this sinks in as I head to the kitchen. I grab a baggie to fill with ice, then return to the front room where Hadley's already unwrapping her ACE bandage. Propping her leg on the coffee table, I position pillows around her ankle for balance, and bring her a hand towel so she doesn't get wet from the bag of ice. "Thank you," she says. Her happy-face toes wink up at me.

"My pleasure," I say.

Yes, I could definitely get used to this.

In the hall closet, she's got a few coats, two pairs of rain boots, and an umbrella. Shoved in the corner is a vacuum, a dust pan, and a broom. There are also tubes of wrapping paper along the back wall. So. This is an all-purpose kind of closet. The fact that it's a little messy makes me smile. This is a side of Hadley she doesn't show the world.

Slightly random and disorganized.

I like it.

"The spare sheets should be on a shelf behind the coats," she calls out from the front room. Shoving the coats aside to collect the sheets, I spy a floor-length dress. It's out of place at the end of a row of hangers. The top is sleeveless, and the fabric is a soft yellow, with a belt made of tiny white flowers.

Man. I could see Hadley wearing this.

Scratch that. I *want* to see Hadley wearing this.

Tucking the sheets under one arm, I unhook the dress to take it with me.

"Look what I found," I say, coming around the corner. "Is this yours or your roommate's? Either way, I'm going to need to see you in it." I wag my eyebrows. "It'll be like I'm back on set, except I'll be your wardrobe guy."

Hadley's lids fly up, and I stop short.

"What's wrong?"

"That's not Nina's." She folds her hands in her lap. "The dress belonged to my mom."

Whoa.

The sheets tumble from my arms, and I almost drop the dress, but I hang on long enough to drape it over the back of the couch. "Oh, Hads. I didn't know. I was just ..." My voice trails off, and my heart pounds hard. All I wanted to do tonight was protect Hadley, but I ended up making jokes about her mother's dress.

Stupid. Idiot. Worse.

Hadley's focus stays on the dress, her eyes going soft. Almost dreamy. "The dress is pretty, though, isn't it?"

I nod, unable to speak.

"I was supposed to wear it to the homecoming dance my senior year," she says. "But I got the chickenpox. How crazy is that?" Instead of sounding heavy and sad, her voice dips and rises like a string of lights. "Who even gets the chickenpox anymore? That's like an old-person thing." A small laugh bubbles out of her, and I come to her side.

"You're not upset about it?"

"About missing the dance? Not at all."

"No. About not being able to wear your mom's dress."

She skims a hand along the fabric. "The truth is, I don't have any real memories of my mom, just the stories my dad told me, and I'm starting to realize even those stories have changed over time. They change because our perceptions of things change, right? For better or worse, we shape them to be what we need. But that dress." Her eyes skate back to me. "Her dress is real, just like her guitar is. They're concrete things I'll always have of hers. So I can make them mean whatever I want." She pauses to swallow. "And I want them to be happy."

We're both quiet for a stretch, but the moment doesn't feel awkward. Just a comfortable silence.

"That's how I feel about Tommy," I say, lowering myself onto the couch next to her. "I don't want to be sad. I don't want my mom to be sad. Ten years is a long time to be sad. He'd want us to remember him smiling."

"I'm sure you're right," she says. Then my chest caves in, realizing how quickly I shifted the conversation from her feelings to my own family.

"I'm so sorry," I say, but Hadley's eyes greet mine with the warmth of understanding. "Is it bad of me to talk about myself?" I ask. "About my family? I'm not being some self-absorbed jerk, am I?"

She takes my hand. "It's the total opposite. You're being honest with me. And vulnerable."

"Huh." A breath puffs out of me. "It's about time, right?"

Hadley extends a finger and runs it along the edge of my jawline, a brush of softness against my beard. On instinct, I press my face into her palm, like I'm a dog nuzzling his companion, trying to soak up Hadley's goodness and grace.

Is this woman for real?

I always knew she was kind, but her compassion seeps through me like a warm tide. Against all odds, I feel comfortable in this moment. Not awkward. Not selfish. Not anything but seen and appreciated for who I am.

While my chin is still cupped in her hand, Hadley kicks the bags of ice off her ankle and drags her feet off the coffee table. Then, in one swift motion, she climbs onto my lap, arranging her legs on either side of my body. With her head above mine, she gazes down at me. Her hair is a cascade around us. A shelter. A shield.

"Hi," she says, drawing her lip under her teeth.

"Hi, yourself," I say back to her. "Is this hurting your ankle?"

She shakes her head. "Am I too heavy?"

"Not at all." This is what I say. What I think is, "We could sit like this forever, and I'd die a happy man."

She traces my lip with the tip of one finger, her eyes searching my face. "Can I ask you my question for tonight?"

"Yes," I manage to croak.

"I know we're not supposed to kiss when we're alone," she says, still chewing her lip, "but is it okay if we maybe break the rules just this once?"

"Maybe. Yes. Break the rules." I'm nodding rapidly now. "Break all the rules. Every one of them."

"Well." Her mouth tugs up on one side. "Maybe not *all*."

"I'll take what I can get," I groan, bending my neck. I'm close enough to capture a kiss, but I duck to the side instead, feathering my lips across the satiny skin just below her earlobe. Then I keep going, my mouth tenderly traveling the length of her chin.

A tiny gasp escapes her, and I lightly dust a kiss on each of her eyelids, then on both corners of her mouth.

I want to kiss every inch of her, but I stay in control. For her sake. Always for her. Everything for Hadley.

Then she gets impatient.

Shifting her face, she brushes her lips against my mouth, and when I taste the warm sweetness she's sharing with me, I'm totally undone. With a low moan, I press my mouth to hers, gently at first, as soft as a whisper. When she tilts her head searching for a better angle, my hands move up from her waist of their own accord. They travel along her collarbone, across the nape of her neck to finally tangle in her hair. And as we kiss (and kiss and kiss some more), my insides begin to unravel. The knots loosen, preparing to re-tie themselves again around the heart of this good woman.

If I could, I'd bind her to me forever.

"James," she says into my mouth, and I consume her breath. My name on her lips is better than air. More necessary than oxygen. My lungs fill with the joy of connecting to someone who knows the real me better than almost anyone.

Whatever I haven't shared yet is all hers.

If she'll have me.

"Hadley," I say back. Those two syllables feel like the only thing tethering me to the earth right now. Or at least to the couch. My insides are on fire, and I know we have to stop. But I don't want to stop.

"I've dreamed of this for so long," she whispers, her breaths coming in jagged sips.

"So have I." Our mouths part just enough so I can speak the words of my heart in the space between us. "I've dreamed of holding you from the moment we met, Hads. All these years. You're the one I always thought about first. The one I always cared for most. The only woman I've ever truly wanted." I'm quiet for a beat, absorbing the truth of my words. "Everything I do, I do for you. You come first, Hadley."

"Yes." She sighs, nipping and biting at my lips. "Yes. Yes."

"I'm all for you." My voice is granite now, a promise stronger than stone. In this moment, I'd give up anything she asked me to, whatever I had to surrender to be with her. "I don't care about anything except—" Before I can finish my sentence, there's a pounding at the door. Hadley startles.

I let out a long low growl. "Noooo. Go away!"

In the heat of the moment, I imagine tossing whoever's interrupting us off of the porch. Better yet, I'd like to melt them like Magnetron would with his microwave eyesight. Not that I'm being dramatic. Much. Still, I can't afford another slip of bad publicity in front of reporters. And it probably *is* a reporter at the door. I have to be on my best behavior, so I force myself to get quiet.

"Maybe they left?" Hadley says after a stretch of silence.

Then the pounding resumes.

"Hadley!" The voice is loud and strident. If the paparazzi are getting this aggressive, who knows what might happen going forward. Hadley locks eyes with me, her shoulders heaving. I wish I could say it was from our kiss.

Pound, pound, pound.

"Your car is out here," the voice calls out. "So I know you're in there. Open up."

"Oh, no." Hadley swallows hard. "It's Carson."

Chapter Thirty-Six

HADLEY

I leap off of Link, landing on my sore ankle with a wince and an, "Ouch!" Link's face is a landslide of emotions, tumbling from passion to frustration to anger.

As I hop on one foot, trying to establish equilibrium, Link hauls himself up from the couch. Then he reaches out, planting his palms on both my shoulders. His touch is steadying. Strong and sure. He makes me feel stable even as my heart's sinking. When I meet his gaze, all I want is to be back in his arms.

"Are you okay?" he asks through gritted teeth.

Before I can answer, Carson bangs on the door again. "Hadley! We need to talk!"

Link's dark eyes flash. "I'll get rid of him."

"No." I lift a hand. "This is my issue to manage."

"Carson's not just an issue," he grumbles. "He's someone who makes you feel small."

"Made," I say, emphasis on the past tense. "I'm not that person anymore." My eyes bounce between the door and Link. "Trust me."

He gives me a quick nod, but his jaw flexes. "I'll be right here behind you the whole time."

I know he will. And although I can handle Carson on my

own, having James Lincoln's support helps me straighten my shoulders and strengthen my backbone.

You've got this, Hadley.

You can say no to the old things you don't want, and yes to the new things you do.

I open the door to Carson standing on the porch. "Are you all right?" he asks. "I was worried about you, angel."

Angel. Ugh.

"I'm great," I say, with zero waver in my voice. "But I'm not your angel." In the background, cameras flash. The reporters who've stuck around yelp out questions. "I'd invite you in," I say, "but it's a little late."

Carson shifts his gaze beyond my shoulder and into the house. His eyes ping-pong back and forth between James and me. "So you *are* with him, huh?" He croaks out a laugh. "I just had to come here to see for myself." His face morphs from concern to contempt. "I've gotta say, it all makes sense now. Why you always held out on me before. I should've known there was another guy all along."

I square my shoulders, refusing to dignify the accusation with a response. I never gave Carson a reason to be jealous. All I ever did was try to turn myself into the person he wanted me to be. "Well, thanks for checking in," I tell him, "but as you can see, I'm perfectly fine. You should go now."

"Not until *he* does." Carson pushes past me through the entryway.

When I stumble, Link moves between us. "You don't get to touch her," he snaps.

"Were you *always* after my girlfriend?" Carson sneers. "Or did you just wait around until I was done with her?"

A grumble erupts from Link's throat, and I lift a hand to his chest. He's doing his best to remain calm, but his heart is thrashing beneath my palm. "I've got this," I tell him, refusing to take the bait. "He can't hurt me anymore."

"Hurt you?" Carson scoffs. "I'm the best thing that ever happened to you, angel."

I round on him. "Do *not* call me angel."

"Come on. You know you love it." His grin is smug, with a side-snarl of jealousy. I don't even recognize this man anymore. Maybe I should've seen the shift coming. But I never would've been with someone like this. His possessiveness isn't protective.

It's petty.

"Now that you mention it," I say, "you *were* good for me."

He snaps his gaze to Link. "See?"

"You showed me what I don't want in a man," I say.

Carson's jaw comes unhinged.

"And for the record, I was *always* faithful," I say, "but no matter how hard I tried, I never felt like I was enough for you." My tone is rock steady now. He can't make me stammer anymore. "And I won't spend another day with someone who thinks I'm less than."

"So you're all evolved now?" Carson harrumphs. "Changed for the better by the movie star?"

"I'm the same woman I always was. I'm just happier about who she is now. And I'm not jumping through hoops worrying about what anyone else thinks."

Link covers my hand with his palm. His deep breaths are a comfort, even as they keep him from exploding on Carson.

"Believe me, I get it." Carson smirks. "It's way easier to feel better about yourself when you're with someone who started out like *him*."

"*Him*?" Link takes a step forward, and Carson flinches, so I increase the pressure against Link's chest. There's a porch full of reporters who'd love to catch him losing his temper again, and it's my turn to make sure Link's all right.

"Hads." His irises laser in on mine. It's a silent question. He wants my permission to deal with Carson, but I told him I had this.

And I do.

"You're absolutely right," I tell Carson. "It is *much* easier to feel better about myself around someone who's loving and caring and generous. Someone who treats people with respect." My mouth angles sharply. "Everyone who deserves it."

Carson rolls his eyes. "Oh, I know all about Lincoln James. The big hero who rescues dogs and donates to children's charities."

"You should try being a human sometime, too," Link grunts. "Feels pretty good."

"Yeah. It must be easy to throw cash around now that you make Hollywood money." Carson glares at Link, one eyebrow cocked, locked, and loaded. "But what about when you had nothing but debt? You know. Back when your mom was in the psych ward?"

Link sucks in a ragged breath.

"That's right." Carson's smile is grim. "I saw the interview."

"What interview?" Link's question comes out hot enough to scorch the air.

"Well, well, well. Look at me finally being the one in the know." His face ripples with amusement. "The lovely Pamela Lincoln—your mother—was on ZTV tonight. But don't worry, the other networks are picking the story up, so the news is spreading fast. Turns out Lincoln James is actually this poor kid from North Carolina whose real name is James Lincoln. That's when it clicked for me. Hadley's old friend at school was named *James* too. I never did get to meet the guy, but they sure used to hang out a lot." Carson turns to me. "I honestly thought you made him up. That's something you would've done, right, angel?"

"She's not your angel," Link growls. "And she's told you twice. You don't get to call her that. Even one more time."

My body shifts into fight, flight, or freeze mode. Not because of what Carson just said about me. Those words run right off my back. It's what he said about the interview.

The reporters found Link's mom?

I can only imagine the volcano about to erupt from the man whose heart is pounding under my palm. He takes a step backward, both hands up in his hair now. He grips his scalp as his eyes go impossibly wide. His breath quickens until he's almost panting.

"They got to my mom," he moans.

"It's going to be all right," I say. "We can do this together. I'm right here with you. You're not alone this time. You never have to be alone again. And *none* of this is your fault. You couldn't have changed anything that happened."

"Whoa." Carson starts a slow clap. "That was quite the speech," he says. "Hadley always was a devoted girlfriend. So self-sacrificing. So eager to please." He sighs. "In the end, I found her earnestness to be a bit boring, myself. But maybe she'll be more adventurous with you, *James.*"

"You don't get to say his name," I blurt. Laying both hands on Carson's chest, I slowly propel him backward. His arms pinwheel as he stutter-steps toward the open door, and I shove him straight through the entryway. As he stumbles, his fall is braced by the pack of paparazzi on my porch.

They shout questions.

Cameras flash and roll.

But I just slam the door.

Chapter Thirty-Seven

LINK

“I’ve got to call my mom,” I tell Hadley in a rush, but I can barely hear the words over the throbbing in my head. “Can I talk to her on speaker?” I want Hadley to hear what’s going on too. For better or worse, she’s in this now with me.

“Of course.” Hadley meets my gaze, her soft eyes full of strength and compassion. I’ve already got my phone out, scrolling my contacts. “Do you want me to leave?” she asks.

“No.” My voice comes out hollow. “Stay. Please.” While I pace the room from one end to the other, Hadley lowers herself onto the couch. Her hands are in her lap, folded. Calm and patient. I draw in a long gust of air and try to center myself too. She can be my anchor, for now at least. Until she has to cut me loose.

I hold the phone out as it rings. My guts are in my throat.

This is my fault. I did this.

“It’s not your fault,” Hadley says from the couch, like she read my mind. Like she knows my heart.

“Andrew must’ve made this happen,” I mutter. “It had to be him. And that *is* on me. If I hadn’t cut ties—”

My mom answers. “Hey, baby.” Her voice echoes in the house. “I was just about to call you.”

“Are you okay?” I rush to ask.

"Ahhh." She takes a beat. "So I'm guessing you already heard."

"Don't worry," I reassure her. "I'm going to find out who sent those reporters to you and make sure they never bother you again."

"James."

"I haven't seen the interview, but it's not too late to distract everyone again. We just have to move up the timeline for the proposal and breakup. But the heat will be off you soon."

Over on the couch, Hadley shifts, and presses a hand to her cheek. Her face is flushed. I hate putting her on the spot like this, but I can't think of another way to fix the mess I've made. "Are you good with that?" I ask her.

Hadley nods. "Of course."

"Oh, James," my mom clucks. "No, no, no. You don't have to do that." She sounds calm, not scared. Maybe she's lapsed into some kind of catatonic state. I was always worried questions about her past might trigger that kind of response.

"What did they do to you?"

"Nothing, James. I'm just fine."

"Did the paps come onto your property?"

"No. You don't understand," she says. "*I* was the one who arranged the interview with ZTV."

Confusion unfurls in my gut, and I have to brace myself, one hand on the wall, one clutching my phone. "What are you talking about?"

"I called Pippa. We made the interview happen." My mother sighs. "We would've told you beforehand, but we thought you might try to stop me."

"You're right. I would've tried."

"I know, baby. I know *you*. And your intentions are always good. But it's time for you to let go now."

"What are you talking about?" I squint, shaking my head. She's right. I don't understand. "Let go?"

"People make their own choices, James. Good or bad, right or wrong. Sometimes they succeed. Sometimes they fail. But dealing with the consequences is what makes them stronger. Don't take that growth away from me now." She pauses. "Or from Hadley."

Whoa.

Hadley cocks her head, and acid rises in my gut. I'd only ever thought in terms of wanting to protect her and my mom. The fact that I might be taking away their agency never occurred to me.

I gulp against the lump in my throat. "Are you saying I'm too controlling?"

"I'm saying some things are *beyond* your control."

"So you went to Pippa."

"Yes," she says. "I convinced her that once I came out of the woodwork and told my story—on my own terms—you'd finally be free of the cloud that's been hanging over your head for the past ten years."

"And she backed you up."

"Pippa wants what's best for you too. She's been watching all the hoops you've jumped through to keep my identity private. She's seen the stress and struggle. The impact on your career. Now we both see it only damaging your future."

"But you're all that matters, Mom."

"No," she says. "You matter. And Hadley matters."

I swallow hard, glancing at Hadley again. Her face is so open and trusting, so totally understanding. The truth seeps through my bones: She'd do anything for me.

And I'd give up everything for her.

"So what do we do now, Mom?" I'm so used to being the one managing things, it feels strange to seek her advice. But she and Hadley need to be a part of any decisions we make going forward.

"Whatever's best for you," she says. "And Hadley. You two need to make your own choices about your future. At least now you don't have to worry about protecting me anymore."

"No, but I *do* have to worry about public opinion, which limits our options."

"Huh." My mom takes a beat. "Are you that concerned about what others think?"

"Not about me and Hadley," I say. "But I'm bound by contract to do whatever Youngblood tells me to."

"And why does he care?"

"The studio's still worried about the press leading up to the release of *Enforcer's Endgame.* They want to control optics on the red carpet and the audience reaction at the premier. Youngblood thinks the best way to get fans rooting for me is for us to go through with the breakup." Even as I say the words, my chest caves in. Hollow to the core. "Pippa's already planning the proposal," I say. "It'll be televised for everyone to watch. And that's when Hadley will end things with me."

"Oh, James," my mother says. "No."

I move to the window and tug the edges of the curtains closer. Zero gaps. "I'm not sure we have a choice, Mom."

"There's always a choice," she says. "You know, Pippa showed me the raw footage of the videos Sam took of you and Hadley. A lot of your conversations were recorded when you had no idea."

"We knew," I say. "It was part of the act."

"Forgive me for saying this, but you're not *that* good an actor. And I don't know about Hadley, but she sure seemed genuine."

Across the room, Hadley rises from the couch and slowly comes toward me.

"You're head over heels for that girl," my mother says. "It's as clear as day."

"Mom."

"And I think she feels the same."

Hadley slips her body up to mine, resting her head against my chest. I reach up to stroke her hair, and my heart beats against her cheek. I haven't said the words out loud to her, but the love is inside there, just the same.

The dogs start barking in the background—a blender of wildebeests—and my mom hushes them, promising treats. Emotion swells up in me, and I feel a prickling at my eyelids.

"How are the goobers?" I manage to ask over the stones in my throat.

"They miss you," she says. "We all do."

"Same here." I blow out a breath. "You know I never would have left if I didn't think I needed to protect you. That's how all this started."

"I believe it started with you losing your temper." She chuckles and I duck my head, sheepish, even though she can't see me.

"I've been working on that," I tell her.

"Glad to hear it. And now I'm even more convinced it was worth coming forward and telling my story."

"What exactly did you say to the reporters?"

She's quiet for a moment. "I just told them the truth. That I've had two great loves of my life—you and Tommy—and everything I've ever done was for my boys."

A new lump forms in my esophagus. "You did good, Mom."

"Well, you've been taking care of me for a while now. And I love you for it. But the truth is, I was starting to feel like an old car, stuck in the past with a stalled engine."

"I just didn't want you to have to relive what you went through with Tommy."

"But I don't want to forget," she says. "I think about Tommy every hour of every day. He's always with me. So it's time I stepped out of the deep freeze and felt things again. Even if the feelings are hard, even if they hurt. I have to walk toward the future, not stay curled up in a ball." She pauses for a beat. "Can you understand that?"

I glance at Hadley. "I can. I do."

My mother lets out a long, audible breath. "Can you also forgive me for blowing up my identity without warning you first?"

Once again I hear the dogs barking—Jem's lower yowl and Scout's high yelp. My heart spreads across the miles, over time zones, and back three hours. "Nothing to forgive, Mom. I love you so much."

"I'm aware," she says with a puff of laughter. "And you're my hero, James Porter Lincoln."

When we end the call, Hadley curls into my body, her head tucked safely under my chin. I wrap my arms around her, and we sway like that for almost a full minute.

We've got some big conversations ahead of us, but in this moment, I just want to be with her in our own magical bubble. Or a Magnetron force field that no one else can penetrate.

In the end, she's the one to break the silence. "Can I ask you an extra question tonight?"

"Always."

"Is any part of you still pretending?" Her voice is quiet, but there's no quiver in it. She's staying strong for me, and my heart swells for her. "It's okay if the answer is yes," she says.

"The truth?"

"Always."

"I was never pretending."

She strengthens her grasp. "Me either."

I want to hold her like this always, but there are things I have to do first. I just hope against all hope that Hadley understands.

"I need to go to LA," I say after another moment of quiet. "To talk to Cal Youngblood. In person. But I don't want to leave you."

She lifts her face, pressing her lips to my neck. "I know you don't."

"Maybe it's not too late to convince him HadLink the couple is just as effective a media story as HadLink the breakup. What do you think?"

She draws in a breath and exhales softly. "I think it's worth a try."

"I know Youngblood's worried the interest in us will die down. But it's possible we've already created enough positive spin to satisfy the studio."

She pulls back just enough to gaze up at me. "I really don't want to go through with some big public breakup."

"Hopefully we won't have to." I tug her back to me, burrowing my face in her hair. She snuggles more deeply into my arms. "Either way, I'll be back," I say. "Soon as I can."

"Yes." She gives me a squeeze. "I know that, too."

Chapter Thirty-Eight

HADLEY

Spoiler alert: James stayed with me overnight.

We slept on the couch in each other's arms, and I gave up worrying what anyone else might think. This whole plan started with the goal of giving the public the wrong idea anyway. And I've never felt more right than nestled on a too-small sofa alongside James. I've never belonged so completely, never let myself dream of waking up in the arms of a man I loved.

A man I *love*. As in currently.

Present tense.

It's probably too soon to say the words, but countless people have already said them for us. And about us. Fans have been commenting in droves on our pictures and videos, noticing the signs we both took longer to admit to ourselves.

In reality, I've known James Lincoln for years, so this seems less like we're rushing things and more like we're finally admitting what's been there all along. Now that I've seen what it feels like to be Lincoln James's fake girlfriend, I want to be his real girlfriend.

At least.

I'm already addicted to his tenderness and protection. To the way he constantly looks to me first, checking in on my wellbeing. And not just my physical comfort, but my interior emotions too.

Being with James feels meant to be, like all the best fairytales come true—minus the wicked stepsisters, a sea witch, or an evil queen.

So at 5:00 a.m., when he presses a last kiss on my forehead, I don't want to say goodbye. Not even a little bit. But I *do* want what's best for James. So if he has unfinished business on the West Coast, I'll let him go and just trust his coming back won't take too long this time.

After spending the last five years convinced we'd never be together again, I want his face to be the first and last thing I see every single day.

Forever.

So I'm stiff-upper-lipping it through my usual before-school routine—trying not to cry—when he texts me from the airport. (The first thing I did after he left was change his contact from Link to James.)

James: I'm on the plane. We're about to take off. But I hope you know I'm a different person than the last time I left.

Despite the pit in my stomach, I can't help jumping to a playful response. I want to keep things light while we're not together. I want to BE his light when we're apart.

Me: I know. You didn't have a beard then.
James: Heh. That's not what I meant.
Me: What did you mean?
James: I mean ... YOU mean a lot to me. More than a publicity stunt. More than just pretending. More than anything. Please believe that.
Me: I do.

I do. I like the sound of those two words together a little too much for my own good.

James: No matter what the future holds, you've changed me for the better, Hads.

I swallow the lump clogging my airway and try not to let the tears in my eyes spill over. What if James can't come back to me right away? What if the team at Youngblood insists we follow through with the original breakup plan?

You can do hard things, Hadley.

Yes. I can. I just really, really don't want to.

Gulp.

Me: Same.

Reply bubbles ripple in our thread, but no new text comes in.

Same?!

That's the best response I could come up with? Then again, maybe "same" is the safest option. I should probably hold back *some* truths to protect my heart until I know what's in store for us. I've already seen what it feels like to miss James for five years, and I'm tempted to crawl into a fetal position and rock in the corner after only an hour.

But I can't do that.

I've got to gather myself and prepare for a day at Harvest High. Soon I'll be facing students who might have plenty to say about Magnetron and me. Not to mention colleagues asking questions in the faculty lounge or lunchroom.

Then there's Felicia Fudrucker. I can't forget the fact that my father's new girlfriend is my boss. For the record, I don't want to forget. After seeing her with my dad last night, I'd love for them to be happy together. But if The Fud and I run into each other in the copy room, will we acknowledge the shift in our relationship or pretend nothing has changed?

And what if the paparazzi trails me to school?

Oh, no.

I almost dry-heave in the bathroom sink.

Why didn't I think this through before? I should've considered that reporters might end up lurking around Harvest High once my "secret relationship" with Lincoln James went public. But I let myself be tempted by the opportunity to do something adventurous and spontaneous. Not to mention the chance to reconnect with James.

The truth is, I have no idea how today will go. Or the next day. Or the day after that one. When will I see James again?

WILL I see him again?

As if he read my mind, my phone buzzes with a new text from him.

Forget protecting your heart, Hadley. It already belongs to James.

James: We're taking off soon, but I'll text you when I land. Don't eat allllll the meatloaf while I'm gone.

Me: I'll save you some. Probably. But you'll owe me.

James: Forget the meatloaf. I already miss the smell of apples and the taste of chocolate and your smile. (Please don't say SAME this time.)

Me: How about DITTO?

Me: Just kidding. I miss you so muchness.

James: Autocorrect again?

Me: No. Correct-correct. Because I miss you more than much. I miss you muchly. With great muchness. All the much. Which is weird, since I haven't had you for five years.

Bubbles. Bubbles. Bubbles.

James: You always had me.

My heart somersaults in a serious case of swoon, and I press a hand to my stomach to steady myself.

Deep breaths, Hadley. It's okay to let yourself feel this, to risk your heart. You and James have spent so much time protecting yourselves and everyone else, trying to avoid pain ...

But you've also avoided love.

To find real joy, you have to trust the fall.

I head to the kitchen where I scarf the breakfast of champions—a leftover apple-crumble cupcake—then I rush to work, hoping if I'm early enough, I can sneak into my classroom before any students or the other teachers arrive.

Luckily, the performing arts wing is at the back of the school with its own separate access road and entrance into the building. But as I rumble onto the small side parking lot, Nina's already there waiting for me, standing in my assigned space. She throws her hands up and lets her mouth drop open in an exaggerated gesture of shock.

Yep. Nina's back in good Wi-Fi range. She must know everything by now.

Well. *Not everything.*

"Hadley!" she squeals as I climb out of my car.

"Congratulations!" I give a little hop of excitement to acknowledge her big news first. "Let me see that gorgeous ring," I gush.

"What? This old rock?" She waves me away. "You already saw it in my stories. Plus Gavin and I decided we're not getting married for at least a year. Maybe more. So enough about us. *You're* the one who's got some explaining to do."

"So you heard?"

"I go away for a few days to get engaged, and you're back here in Harvest Hollow saying hold my beer!"

"It's crazy, isn't it?" I grab my bag from the passenger seat and heft it on my shoulder. My heart's palpitating, and my lungs deflate. The last thing I want is for my best friend to feel like my fake relationship has overshadowed her real one.

Even if what I feel for James isn't fake anymore. Or ever.

"I'm sorry I didn't tell you sooner," I say, "but you were gone, and things got a little insane around here."

"A little insane? That's the understatement of the century. And please, don't be sorry!" She shrugs. "I blame Gavin's family's stupid cabin. I was out of Wi-Fi range and cell coverage most of the time." Her face goes all soft and dreamy. "Except the cabin wasn't stupid. It was incredible and beautiful and Gavin was so romantic, and I'll tell you absolutely every detail later, but only after you fill me in on what's going on with you and Mister LA Area Code."

My shoulders creep up. "So I guess you figured out James from college is Lincoln James."

"Yeah. I'm a regular Nancy Drew, with the entire internet aiding my natural sleuthing abilities. So let me get this straight." She fixes me with a wide-eyed stare. "The guy you *thought* ghosted you after the *America's Hidden Talent* auditions is actually one of the sexiest men alive, and he's been secretly pining away for you the whole time, and now that he's found you and admitted his secret love, you two have been sneaking around town rediscovering your long-lost romance. Do I have that right?"

"Something like that."

"I'm so proud of you." Nina's eyes dance with merriment.

"For what?" I snort. "Losing my mind?"

"No, silly." She pokes the tip of my nose. "You. Said. Yes."

My heart skitters, and a small smile plays across my lips. "Yeah. I guess I did."

Nina starts to laugh, and I am flooded with relief. She's still got my back, and I've got hers. We're still normal.

This is us.

"So." She splays her hands. "Are we planning a double wedding next year, or what?"

That's when my flood of relief shifts into a flood of tears.

"Whoa, whoa, whoa." Nina takes my hand and starts dragging me toward the performing arts building. "Let's get you into the choir room before you turn into a human puddle."

I sniffle, wiping my eyes on the sleeve of my cardigan. "I'm not sad or anything," I garble. "I swear. I'm actually ... happy."

"So what's with all the tears then?"

"It's just a lot, Nina. It's so, so much. So unknown." Sniff. Wipe. Sniff. "I just really, *really* like him. Like a lot."

"Uh-huh." She nods, steering me across the lot. "What's not to like about Lincoln James?"

"Nothing!" I bite back a sob. "That's the scary part. I'm not used to feeling like this, you know?"

"Yeah. Because you weren't ever really scared to lose Carson."

"You're right. And he's a whole other story." Sniff. Wipe. Sniff.

"Well, thank goodness you parked in the back lot," Nina says as we slip into the building. "There are a bunch of reporters hanging around the front of the school looking for you. But don't worry. The Fud's on the scene making sure everyone stays across the street."

"She is?" Sniff. Wipe. Smile.

"Yep. In all her red-and-white Bobcat glory." Nina lifts a pretend foam finger, waving it triumphantly. "No strangers shall be allowed on Harvest High property while Felicia Fudrucker's in charge!"

I choke down laughter as we head past the band room. When we reach my class, I pause to unlock the door. "About The Fud," I say.

"What about her?"

"Hold on to your pom-poms. You're never gonna believe this ..."

Chapter Thirty-Nine

LINK

Me: Just landed safely. Call me if you can, but I assume you're teaching, so I don't want to interrupt. Your principal plays a mean Ice-Sis, and I want to stay on The Fud's good side. (For the record, all your sides are good, Hads.)

My first stop after the airport is my mom's place. It's three hours earlier here, which buys me more time. Of course I'm excited to see the dogs, but more importantly, I want to confirm she's okay for myself. Eyes on her. In person. When I arrive at her place, there isn't a single reporter near the property. No news vans or paparazzi with cameras or microphones. As surprising as this is, I'm even less prepared for what greets me at the door.

My mother is—in a word—luminous.

"James," she says, gathering me in for a warm hug. She's wearing a flowing skirt and sweater, and her hair is in a long, silver-threaded braid. When Jem and Scout bound onto the scene, her face crinkles into a smile. The dogs start snarfing and cavorting and tail-wagging.

It's my own little blender of wildebeests.

"So, no reporters, huh?" I glance over my shoulder as the dogs follow us into the house. We cross to the sliding glass door and head out to the deck.

"Not since my interview," she says. "I guess I took the wind out of their sails. I said my piece and there was nothing left to ask without seeming silly. Or ghoulish. Or cruel."

"The paps can be plenty silly, ghoulish, and cruel."

"Maybe a few of them," she says. "But some of them are just trying to make a living, James."

I arch a brow. "You sound like Hadley."

"There are worse things."

"Good point. Sounding like Hadley might be my favorite."

"Anyway, if any reporters come back, I'll be okay," she says. A breeze off the ocean blows a strand of hair across her face. She wraps her arms around her body. But her eyes are bright, not like she's hurting. More like she's hugging herself.

"Are you sure you're okay?"

She nods, watching the dogs chase each other into the surf. "It felt good to share our story. To say Tommy's name out loud. To answer people's questions. About him and you. I got to honor all three of us."

"I never thought of it like that. I was too busy trying to control everything—like we couldn't with Tommy." I pick up a tennis ball and chuck it to the dogs. "But I'm sorry if I held you back. Or made it hard for you to move forward."

"I gave you plenty of reason to worry." She inclines her head, gazing out at the horizon. "I wasn't well for a long time. I wasn't there for you, either. So don't be sorry. We both just did our best." She turns to face me. "And my love for you boys isn't a part of me I want to hide anymore."

"Mom."

"It's all right. I can own my past," she says. "I made my share of mistakes. But haven't we all? Now every day is a fresh chance to do better. And in the end, I'm the mother of the two best sons in the world. That's a gift no one can take away from me."

I move across the deck to throw an arm around her. We face

the ocean where the dogs frolic along the shore. Before we rescued them, they had their rough patches too. But they know joy now. And they sure embrace those tides.

I whistle as Jem gets too far out, and they all start scampering back up the beach. "Man, I love those dogs."

My mom lays her head on my shoulder. "So do I."

"Do you mind watching them a little longer?"

* * *

My next stop is Sam's house in Burbank. As much as I want to get to Pippa's office so we can figure out our next steps, I owe Sam more than almost anybody. He was by my side, talking me off the cliff through this fake relationship deal. More importantly, he's the one who pushed me to do *romantical, couple-y* stuff with Hadley. And I think it worked.

I hope it worked.

Sam's daughters squeal when they open the door to me. I've known Lyla and Kaitlin their whole lives. They were born right around the time Sam signed on as my personal photographer. But he's more than that now. Much more. He's a trusted friend.

A brother.

"Uncle WINK! Uncle WINK!" Their tandem shouts echo through the foyer. For the record, they can both say the letter *L* now, but to them, I'll always be Uncle Wink.

"Hey there, rug rats!" I gather the girls up, one in each arm, lifting them chest high. "Oh no! You're getting so big! I sure hope I don't drop you!" I let out an exaggerated moan and pretend to stagger under their weight.

"But you're Magnetron," Lyla crows.

"You're super strong," Kaitlin giggles.

"I don't know kids ... I think I'm starting to lose you ..." I zigzag through the house over to the couch in their family room. "Did you two break my forcefield?"

I'm about to toss them onto the cushions, when Tanya

chimes in from an armchair. "Girls. Tell Uncle Wink if he breaks your butts, I'll kill him."

"My apologies." I wince, setting them down gently.

"Ah, you're fine." Tanya just laughs. "It's good to have you home, Link."

Home. Link.

The thing is, LA isn't feeling so much like home to me anymore. If it ever did. And I'm not feeling much like Link, either. Still, I thank Tanya and ask how she's holding up.

"Honestly?" She nods in the direction of the kitchen. "It's not so bad having Sam wait on me hand and foot."

"Hand, foot, and *butt*," he says, coming around the corner. He's holding an enormous green smoothie, and he breaks into a grin when he sees me. "Well, look who's here. If it isn't Harvest Hollow's most famous lover boy."

I cock my head. "Lover boy?"

"I said what I said." He smirks. "I've spent the past two days poring over footage of you and Hadley. Are you gonna deny you're obsessed with that woman?"

I raise my palms. "Guilty as charged."

"I get it." He hands Tanya the smoothie. "Love is pretty much the best, man." He blows exaggerated kisses at her.

Lyla and Kaitlyn groan. "Ewwwww!"

Tanya points at them. "You girls just wait."

"A very long, long time," Sam warns, putting on a fake scowl. Then he swings his gaze back over to me. "So what's the latest with Operation HadLink?"

"Don't know yet." I hitch my shoulders. "I'm heading over to Pippa's office next. But I *can* tell you I won't need to base any of my decisions around my mom anymore. I just came from her place. Apparently, she's gotten real busy taking care of herself."

"I saw her interview," Sam says. "Strong woman. Brave too."

"Like Magnetron?" Kaitlyn pipes up.

I lift my arms and flex my muscles. "Even stronger than Magnetron."

"No way!" Lyla chirps.

Sam produces a straw from his pocket and hands it to Tanya. "So it's just about getting The Vise-Count role now, huh?" he asks me. "Making sure Youngblood signs you for the new franchise?"

"Nope." I splay my hands. "It's about Hadley. Whatever makes her happy. I hope she wants me, but I'm not sure she'd love celebrity life."

Tanya guffaws. "Who wouldn't want to be married to a celebrity?"

"Ahem." Sam smirks. "Plenty of people. *You*, for example."

"Hadley's got a great situation in Harvest Hollow," I say. "I don't want her to give that up for me. I can't ask her to."

Sam snorts. "You need to watch those videos, man. I'm pretty sure she'd do anything for you." He leaves Tanya's side to flop down between his girls. It's a couch full of family now. And my eyes get a little misty.

I clear my throat. "Well, no matter what happens, I won't leave your family hanging. I got you covered. Even if I leave acting."

Sam drapes his arms around the girls. "Appreciate that, man. But I've got options now, thanks to you."

"Oh yeah?"

"Been getting calls from entertainment mags left and right wanting to hire me. Guess word got out I'm pretty good." He splays his hands. "So I'll stick with you as long as you need, but if you decide to take a different road—one off the photo-op grid—we'll be just fine."

The truth is, I already set up accounts for the girls with enough money to cover college tuition pretty much anywhere they'd want to go. *If* they want to go. That's not everybody's path. Either way, I don't want Sam and Tanya to feel like I think they can't provide for their girls. I'm sure they can.

But, hey. A little extra money never hurt anyone.

Sam goes to the kitchen to make a snack for the girls, and I take his place on the couch to read to them. We're three books in when Sam comes back with food to set on the table. I glance at the clock.

"You gotta go, huh?" Tanya says.

"Yeah. I'm dying to talk to Pippa and also dreading it, if that makes sense."

"Sure it does," Sam says. "Your future could be on the line."

I consider his words while I say my goodbyes. "When it comes to my future, I'm less worried about what Pippa and Youngblood have to say than what's on Hadley's mind, honestly."

"Well, good luck." Sam claps me on the back. "And keep me posted, man."

My pulse races and my palms start sweating on the ride over the hill to Pippa's downtown office. The last time I was there, she was scolding me over the debacle at the hospital.

That's when this whole thing was set in motion.

Of course I'll still attend the premier of *Enforcer's Endgame* and all the red-carpet events. I'll do every press conference and talk show appearance. I'll even let Hadley break up with me if that fulfills the compliance clause in my contract.

After that, though, I should be off the hook, right? The only thing still in contention would be the future franchise. Whether or not they'll cast some other actor as The Vise-Count.

Chris. Chris. Chris. Or Flint.

So I clench and unclench my fists, preparing to step into Pippa's office. I'm going to fight for me and Hadley.

No matter what it takes.

Chapter Forty

HADLEY

I try calling James back in between classes, but I get sent straight to voicemail. I figure he must have his phone turned off, probably in a meeting or driving. I'm missing him already, and frustrated. But at least I'm not teary-eyed anymore. And I refuse to give up on James and me. So I spend my lunch hour in the choir room with Nina.

Normally we eat in the faculty lounge, but I'm not ready to face the other teachers and their questions. I don't have any answers for them yet. I don't even have answers for myself. So Nina's the perfect person to keep me company while I work on half a meatloaf sandwich, one honeycrisp apple, and a slice of leftover pumpkin pie.

What can I say? I always eat when I'm nervous.

And I've got next-level nerves working.

"I think the real lesson here," Nina says, "is I should leave Harvest Hollow more often." She's just finished eating a cafeteria burger and telling me all about Gavin's proposal. "Nothing exciting ever happens when I'm in town." She splays her hands. "But I go away for a few days, and suddenly my best friend's in love with Lincoln James, and her father's dating my principal."

I point a fork at her. "Plus you got engaged."

"Oh, yeah. I did do that. But everyone knew Gavin would propose eventually, so it seems a lot less momentous than all this." She waves her hands around me like I'm a whole situation.

"Don't be silly," I protest. "Your future marriage is totally momentous."

"Agreed. But when I told you to start saying yes to things, I had no idea what kind of love monster I'd be creating. Link—or James, or whatever—had better be thanking his lucky stars." She shoves her trash in the paper lunch sack her burger came in. "Anyway, wish me luck with my afternoon classes." She stands, brushing crumbs off her lap. "I had a pretty good Pre-Calc lesson planned, but so far all my Algebra and Geometry students wanted to talk about was Ms. Morgan and Magnetron."

"Ugh. Sorry."

"I don't mind." Nina smirks. "Celebrity gossip is way more fun than math. Just don't tell The Fud I've abandoned my objectives for today."

"I won't."

"Either way, I'm her new boyfriend's beloved daughter's favorite roommate."

"You're my *only* roommate."

"Exactly!" Nina beams at me, then drops her bag in the trashcan by the door. "That ought to afford me some measure of disciplinary leniency, right?"

She waves goodbye just in time for my a cappella class to file in. Some of them are wearing Magnetron masks or fists or carrying Magnetron magnets. The rest of them are humming the Oscar-winning score to the *Enforcer* series.

Shaking my head, I will my stubborn cheeks not to turn too tomatoey. But my face has been like this all day, and if I'm being honest, I don't hate it.

My last student rushes in as the tardy bell rings. That's when Felicia Fudrucker appears in the doorway motioning for me to join her in the hallway.

"Ooooh. Are you in trouble, Ms. Morgan?" one of my students teases.

I flash the whole class a crooked grin. "Wouldn't you like to know?"

My blush turns even hotter, but I'm kind of enjoying this—being playful, and living on the edge. It's not skydiving or bungee jumping.

But it's not *not* fun.

"Hi," I say, stepping into the hall with Ms. Fudrucker. "I'm sorry about the reporters." I grimace. "I didn't really think about what might happen when the town discovered Lincoln James was here."

"Are you kidding?" Ms. Fudrucker's face is glowing. "Your relationship is the most exciting thing to happen to Harvest High since Logan Barnes came back to play hockey with the Appies. And you're not *just* a graduate, like Logan was. You're also a teacher." She fiddles with the Home of the Bobcats button on her collar. "The principal at Stony Peak is positively green with envy."

I stifle a laugh. "I'm not sure inspiring jealousy is the most noble goal."

"Well, I can't help it if we have more newsworthy alumni than he does." She fluffs her hair, which today features a little topknot wrapped in red ribbon. "And on that note, I have a proposal for you."

Proposal? Oof. Too soon.

"I was wondering if you'd be willing to perform at the homecoming football game. During halftime, of course. And we'd want you to sing. Not actually play football."

"Me?" My stomach lurches. I'm definitely regretting my lunch of leftovers.

"You!" She grins, and I'm afraid her face might literally burst at the seams. "Channel 9 reached out this morning, and they're interested in doing some sort of *Where Are They Now* feature on Harvest High's most notable former graduates."

I gape at her, speechless.

"Can you imagine our little Harvest High on cable TV?" She claps her hands. "The Stony Peak principal will absolutely expire from envy!"

I finally find my voice. "Again, I'm not sure how I feel about inspiring envy. But the bigger question is ... why me?"

"Well, unfortunately, no one's interested in putting *me* on television." She blinks. "And you're famous now, Hadley. Being Lincoln James's girlfriend makes you a genuine news story." She pauses, and puts hand to her lips. "And since I'm your father's girlfriend, I suppose that puts us in one of those six degrees of celebrity situations. Except there are only two degrees in our case. But either way, we might as well use your fifteen minutes of fame."

I gulp, and my heart rate speeds up.

My fifteen minutes of fame.

Hmm.

Maybe something like this could keep the story of Link and me as a couple in the spotlight. Enough for Youngblood studios to think we don't need to break up. The only trouble is, I'm not a soloist anymore. I'm not sure I ever was. And I don't love the limelight. But I *do* love singing with my classes.

"What if my students performed too?" I ask. "We could have risers on a stage out on the field, and I could lead them the same way I do every day." I shrug. "That's a more accurate depiction of where I am now than anything else."

"Hmm." Ms. Fudrucker taps her forehead. "Maybe your *advanced* choir class," she says. "Beginning chorus is fine for things like the fall festival and Christmas concerts. But cable TV? Not so much." Her eyes are distant like I'm no longer in the hallway. She's basically talking to herself. "And we'd have to get waivers signed," she continues. "Students aren't allowed to be filmed without permission."

"We should also make the performing optional," I say, drawing her back to the moment. "Just for the members of choir who want to sing."

"*Advanced* choir."

"Right."

"So what do you think, Hadley?" Her eyes sparkle like twin diamonds on her face.

"This means a lot to you, doesn't it?"

She throws up her hands. "Oh, no, no, no. This is totally up to you. Remember. You're not supposed to be doing me any special favors these days." She tilts her head. "But if you *did* want to perform, we could talk more about it after school. No pressure though."

I swallow the lump in my throat, glancing back at my classroom. Forget adventure and spontaneity, although that's certainly a factor. This could be my chance to shift Operation HadLink in a new direction.

Cal Youngblood just needs to see that there are enough ways for Link and me to get positive publicity as a couple. I tip my head, considering my answer. Then I square my shoulders.

"Yes."

Chapter Forty-One

LINK

"We need to talk," I say, pushing into Pippa's office. She peers at me over a pair of cat-eye reading glasses.

"Good afternoon to you, too, Link."

I drop down into a chair opposite hers and ignore the sweat beading at my brow. I almost forgot how hot California is in September. Like I've been gone forever or something. "Please tell me Cal Youngblood changed his mind about the big public breakup."

"As it turns out, I just got off the phone with Cal." Pippa puts on a Mona Lisa smile. "And also TMZ. Plus the *National Tattler* and *People*."

"You've been busy today."

"I always am. And it may interest you to know a decision has been made." She arcs an eyebrow. "You *may* not even hate it."

My pulse ticks up a notch. Hadley and I haven't had a chance to fully discuss what we want to happen next, and there's already a decision? About what? And who made it?

Not me.

"For the record," Pippa continues, "the studio is absolutely thrilled with the way things are playing out with HadLink. You're more popular than ever, trending on every social platform. Their team can't keep up with interview requests, and all the biggest Hollywood VIPs are clamoring for invites to the premier."

I tug at the collar of my shirt. This is good news, but all I want to do is tell Hadley.

Pippa shoves her glasses higher on her nose. "You might also be pleased to hear the other actor being considered for The Vise-Count is refusing to work with Andrew ever since he heard Andrew's the one who leaked the location of your mother's place." She purses her lips. "Apparently your former manager was hoping you'd have a meltdown, and your reputation would implode, sealing The Vise-Count deal for Chris."

"Ah." I exhale. "So it *was* a Chris."

"Too bad Andrew couldn't play fair." Pippa shrugs. "Silly Icarus flew too close to the sun."

I nod, taking all this in. Everything Pippa's said so far works in my favor. "So the reporters are no longer an issue, now that my mom's come forward on her own, right?"

"Correct."

"And Youngblood's happy with me?"

"Completely."

I sit up, my back ramrod straight. "Then maybe Hadley and I don't have to end things after all. Maybe we can wait and gauge audience reactions, see how things go on the red carpet."

"I already proposed the same thing to Cal," she says. "And I'm happy to share that in light of the positive publicity HadLink is generating, the studio has decided you two do *not* have to break up."

"What?" I start in my chair, practically leaping to my feet. "You're serious?"

"I am." She nods slowly.

"This is incredible."

"That's not all, though."

"I don't care. I'm just glad Hadley won't be subjected to dumping me on national TV."

Pippa expels a breath. "That part is true. But the studio *still* wants a TV crew." She takes a beat. "And you *do* still have to propose."

I furrow my brow. "What are you saying?"

"I'm saying they still very much expect you to get down on one knee and ask Hadley to marry you. On camera."

I start tapping my leg. Too much nervous energy. "But wait. She doesn't have to say no?"

"She does not." Pippa leans over her desk. "But are you ready for her to say yes?"

My chest constricts. *Good question, Pip.*

I'm totally against a public breakup, but getting engaged for real is a whole other ballgame. "We need more time," I say, pushing back in my seat.

"I can give you until Friday."

"What?!"

"I'm sorry, but Cal is quite anxious to get the show on the road this weekend."

"I'm not a show."

"You are." Her eyes laser in on mine. "And sweet little Hadley is your costar. Do you think she's cut out to be your fiancée?"

I shift my jaw. "I think she can do anything she sets her mind to."

"I wouldn't disagree. Under *most* circumstances. But the spotlight on you is brighter than ever, Link, and Hadley's a choir teacher from Harvest Hollow. Even if she enjoys this tiny burst of fame, eventually your very different lives will diverge. If you stay together, you could be setting Hadley up for a situation for which she's wholly unprepared."

"What situation?" My eyes flash. "I'm not a situation. I don't want to be a situation."

"Nevertheless. You *are* a celebrity, Link. And dragging Hadley into your complicated world could be ... selfish."

"Or maybe I could give her a better life than any she's ever dreamed of."

"Maybe's a tricky word." Pippa's face creases with sympathy.

"Of course, if you don't want to put Hadley in that position, you could simply insist she refuse your proposal. Letting her go could be the kinder, gentler thing to do."

"I don't know." I spent years controlling everything and everyone in my life in an attempt to avoid negative outcomes. But that didn't work. In some cases I even made things worse. Scary as it is, I need to let Hadley make her own choice.

Pippa sighs. "If you truly care about her ..."

"Stop." My heart feels like it's sinking into my stomach. I don't just care about Hadley.

I love her.

"I'm sure you'll do the right thing." Pippa steeples her fingers above the desk. "In any case, you don't have to propose right now. And Hadley doesn't have to answer today."

"Great." My throat's so tight, the word is a strangled moan.

"You two have until Friday to talk things over," she says. "For the next forty-eight hours, take all the time you need."

* * *

I need to fix this. I need to fix this. That's the thought running through my brain as I stride across the parking lot. What can I say? Old habits die hard. I'm used to being the one who's in control.

But that's not how this works anymore. And it's not how I want things to be. Hadley and I are in this together. I should call her immediately. I'm just not sure what to say.

We need more time to figure things out. A lot more time. I'd suggest forever, but we don't have that luxury. According to Pippa, we've got, like, two days.

This all just snowballed out of control way more quickly than I expected. And by that I don't mean Operation HadLink. I mean my actual feelings for Hadley. I've got to lay them out on the table along with my heart.

So I slip into my car and tell Siri to call Hads.

My hands flex, and I ball them into fists. What time is it in Harvest Hollow? I hate being so disconnected. How's this going to work when we can barely manage to squeeze in a phone call?

"James," she says. "I miss you."

"Me too." My chest constricts. "How are things there?"

"Weird," she says. "Like, really weird."

"Same."

"My last class is starting soon," she says. "I don't have a lot of time."

I blow out a breath. "Tell me about it. I just talked to Pippa. And there's good news and bad news."

"Okay," she says, tentatively. "Good news first."

That's my girl. Of course she'd go with that. "So." I clear my throat. "You don't have to dump me in public after all."

"Ahhhh." Hadley's relief is palpable. "I can't believe it! They're really okay with us being a couple? Like dating for real?"

"Kind of." My insides twist into knots. "They're still expecting ... escalation, one way or another."

"I don't know what that means."

I close my eyes, steeling myself for the rest of the news. "It means I *do* have to propose. You just don't have to say no."

"Wait." I imagine the little furrow on her forehead. "They aren't forcing me to end things?"

"Not unless you want to. But you *do* have to answer me. On camera. By this weekend."

She puffs out a breath. Probably of confusion. "So the only thing that's changed is I'm not required to turn you down."

"Exactly. They've offered an alternative to our fake breakup. A real engagement."

"So ... you want me to say yes."

"If I'm being honest, I don't know, Hads." I swallow hard, heart banging in my chest. "I think you should be the one to decide."

"What if I can't?"

I start nodding at no one. "This is a lot, and I get it. We've known each other for years, and yeah, I've had feelings for you the whole time. But this is all so new. And you're being put on the spot because of me. I'll understand if it's too much."

She's quiet for several moments and I taste my pulse in my throat. "This changes everything, James."

"Maybe. But it's still a proposal," I offer. "I was always supposed to propose."

"Yes. But before I didn't feel like I had a choice. I knew we had an expiration date, and I was just following the plan. But now..." She sighs. "It's all up to me."

"I'm sorry."

The last thing I want is for Hadley to default to doing what she thinks I want.

Like I said. Old habits die hard.

"You don't have to decide right now," I tell her. "But they're also not giving us a ton of time, either."

"I just need to think."

"Of course." I run a hand through my hair as the sun beats down on my scalp. Why is LA still so hot in the middle of fall? I just want to be back in Harvest Hollow with the cool, crisp air on my skin. I want to smell apples and hear the sound of a crackling fire. I want to taste Hadley's sweet cinnamon kiss. I want to look into her blue eyes, always.

Is that too much to ask?

"James."

"I'm here." My name on her lips makes my heart swell so big I feel like it just might crack my ribs. The thought of her choosing to walk away shatters my heart. But if Hadley decides not being with me is best for her, I'll let her go. I'd do anything for her, no matter the pain.

If that's what she wants.

After a long stretch of silence, she finally speaks. "You know, we still have rules in place. And I haven't gotten to ask you my question for today. So. Do you trust me?"

"With my life," I say.

"Good. I have an idea."

Chapter Forty-Two

HADLEY

It's almost halftime, and I haven't been this nervous since I auditioned for *America's Hidden Talent.* The butterflies swooping in me that day have morphed into giant birds. I feel like every bald eagle in North Carolina is currently nesting in my stomach.

Taking a deep breath, I check myself in the full-length mirror one more time. Half my hair is up in a twist, and the rest is draped along my shoulders. My cheeks match the pink of my lip gloss, and there's an extra coat of mascara on my lashes.

"You look beautiful," Nina says.

She's hiding out with me in the quote unquote *nice* bathroom directly behind the concession stands. Besides the two private stalls, this space boasts a vanity and a small couch. It's usually reserved for teachers and volunteers, but Nina put an OUT OF ORDER sign on the door so no one would bother us for the first two quarters.

I feel a twinge of guilt that parents selling snacks and drinks at tonight's game will have to use the student restrooms. But I need to stay tucked away from inquiring minds to preserve my sanity tonight.

For days, I've faced a barrage of questions from pretty much everyone in Harvest Hollow, not to mention requests for interviews from reporters, and countless posts and hashtags from strangers across the internet. All anyone wants to talk about is Lincoln James and his long-lost love. That's why I'm stuck in the bathroom listening to cheers from the stands.

Hashtag glamorous.

The throb of excitement echoes inside my chest. Not to mention the marching band's songs, and the announcer calling plays from his booth above the bleachers. I pick up Dolores and strum a couple of chords, just to loosen up.

Nina grins at me. "You look so gorgeous holding that guitar, Link's going to pass out when he sees you. He won't even be able to propose."

Nervous laughter bubbles out of me. "Oh, he is definitely going to propose. That's been the plan from the beginning."

"I wonder what kind of ring he picked out," Nina says. "Or did the studio find a sponsor? Is some jeweler getting free advertising for contributing a ginormous diamond to HadLink's cause?"

"I don't know," I say. "James and I have spent every spare minute over the past two days talking on the phone, FaceTiming, or texting. We've been trying to cram in an entire relationship's worth of communication in the time we had. And probably the only thing we haven't discussed is the actual proposal."

"How come?"

"He didn't want to pressure me," I say. "He wants the answer to be my choice."

"Very cool," Nina says. "Either way, I'll bet it's going to be a flawless rock. You're one lucky woman, my friend."

"Yeah. Lucky. If a forced proposal is romantic."

"I'm talking about how much he adores you."

"He does," I say. "But this is all a little nuts, don't you think? I'm still not sure I can handle this lifestyle. The fact that we're actually going through with a mandatory proposal? Bizarre."

"True story."

In fact this is brand-new territory for me, and way more

adventure and spontaneity than I ever imagined. Tonight's bigger than jumping off a hay bale or sneaking into the movies or climbing the clocktower or hiking Boney Mountain. I'm leaping off a cliff with my heart on the line and no safety net below me.

Except for James.

Meanwhile, Nina said my dad's in the bleachers sitting next to Ms. Fudrucker in the first row, front and center. They're both decked out from head to toe in every piece of red and white spiritwear ever made. My dad even bought a matching seat cushion for her, so right now, both their butts are crushing the Home of the Bobcats. I'm so happy for them.

And also so, so nervous.

I haven't seen James since Wednesday—unless you count FaceTime. Which I definitely don't. Still, we've been talking about the future, sharing our dreams, and learning everything we don't already know about one another. We acted like we had all the time in the world.

Like forever.

But if I can't smell the man, it's just not the same, right?

An anxious giggle escapes me, and I imagine being close enough to catch his scent again.

Soon, Hadley, soon.

Meanwhile, I'm trusting Pippa got everything right.

She's the one who arranged for a helicopter to deliver James to the stadium. He's scheduled to arrive after the homecoming court makes its way around the track in their limos. The king and queen won't be announced until the dance tomorrow, so I don't feel *too* terrible about stealing some of their thunder.

Besides, Ms. Fudrucker convinced me they'll be thrilled to end up on Channel 9 with Lincoln James. I didn't have the heart to tell her local cable isn't quite as exciting as ZTV. But we got their crew here too. Well, Pippa did.

After the helicopter lands in the fields behind the stadium, James is supposed to jog over to the track. Then he'll follow a red carpet to the platform where I'll be waiting with the choir. That's when we're going to sing to him. Well, we're going to sing in front of pretty much everyone in Harvest Hollow. Not to mention the entire television viewing audience.

This is all totally normal, right?

I just hope Pippa doesn't force him to show up in his Magnetron costume.

Nina's phone buzzes, and she checks the message. "Eek! It's The Fud." She lets out another little squeal of excitement. "She says it's showtime!"

My hands are shaking as Nina leads me by the elbow out toward the field. The stands are packed, and the sidelines are standing room only with reporters and television crews on standby. Nina squeezes my arm. "Go get 'em, Hadley."

What have I gotten myself into?

The crowd's already going nuts for the homecoming court, who all are hanging out of the sky roofs of their respective vehicles. As the limousines complete their circle around the track, and the marching band finishes its performance in centerfield, I make my way toward the platform that's set up underneath the scoreboard.

The advanced choir's already gathered there on portable bleachers. The microphones across the stage will play through the stadium speakers once they're switched on. Okay. The eagles inside me now are flapping their wings and laying eggs and doing whatever else birds might do.

"Adventure and spontaneity," I whisper to myself.

You can do this, Hadley. You love James Lincoln, right?

With all my heart.

And I can't wait to tell him.

If I thought the crowd was going wild for the football game and the homecoming court and the marching band, that's nothing compared to the roar that erupts when the jet-black helicopter appears. The blades whir overhead before making a slow, breezy descent. I hold my breath—not on purpose, I'm just physically incapable of normal lung function right now.

Behind me, the choir begins to sing "In My Life," by the Beatles. We have a different song prepared for when James is onstage, but my students will be our soundtrack until he reaches me.

Before the choir is halfway through their song, my prince charming bursts onto the scene at the edge of the stadium. A crew from ZTV travels alongside him as he makes his way down the red carpet. His sculpted body fills out the tailored suit like a fictional superhero come to life. Those broad shoulders and the muscled legs make my own knees go weak. His black hair is a swoop over his forehead, and his beard is the perfect shadow around a wide smile. I can practically see his lashes from here.

I can *definitely* see the long-stem red roses he's cradling.

We lock eyes, and my heart skips a beat. All other sounds in the stadium fade into silence, and I exhale. This is it. We're the only two people on the planet right now, and I'm about to face the question of a lifetime.

In less than a minute, he'll be up here by my side, holding my hand, asking me to marry him.

Chapter Forty-Three

LINK

She's wearing her mother's dress.

That's the first thing I notice.

The butter-yellow material with a belt made of daisies looks like it was made for Hadley. My eyes begin to burn, not only with the beauty of the gesture, but with Hadley's beauty in general. I've never seen her glowing this brightly. When she spots me, she practically sparkles, and her lips curve up on both sides. Her soft, smooth skin almost looks like it's vibrating. Like her bones might break free from her body any minute and dance off the stage into my arms.

As she meets my gaze, I duck my head in a half bow and accidentally poke myself with a thorn. Lifting my finger to suck the blood, I remember there are cameras on me.

The stadium lights are blinding, and the hum of the helicopter still buzzes in my ears. Not to mention the roar of the crowd. Cheers and chanting blast us from all sides.

HadLink. HadLink. HadLink. HadLink.

There's an entire choir behind Hadley, swaying and singing a Beatles song. The melody floats above the stadium, competing with the din of the crowd, and man, those lyrics are amazing.

The idea of someone loving you more than any other person, place, or thing in their lifetime?

That's incredible.

The choir's song draws to an end just as I climb the platform to meet Hadley. Perfect timing, I'll give them that. I come toward her holding out the roses, but say under my breath, "Watch out for thorns." She takes the flowers from me carefully. She leans into the microphone and says, "Thank you."

The audience goes wild.

Who knew the words "thank you" could induce such pandemonium? Setting the flowers down at the foot of the stage, she picks up something in exchange.

Dolores. Her mom's guitar. Oh, wow. Wow.

WOW.

I can't help noticing the tremble in her legs as she steps to the microphone, but she's not limping anymore, so I'm glad she's had the chance to heal. The crowd quiets—as much as a stadium full of football fans at a homecoming game can—and Hadley says, "James, this one's for you."

She steps back, strums a few chords, then she and the choir launch into an acoustic version of Taylor Swift's "Today Was a Fairytale."

My heart's officially in my throat now.

I must've heard Hadley practice this song a hundred times on the drive to her audition. It's been five years, but I still remember every word. As the cameras roll, she leads her choir, letting her students share the spotlight. She's in her element. Singing along with them. But all I hear is Hadley's voice.

I know that's not possible. Not really. The kids are closer to the microphones than she is. But every note she sings is an arrow straight to my heart. It's that same intoxicating blend of sweetness and edge that's always been all hers.

I'm all hers.

As I move toward her across the stage, she turns to me, and time slows down. Just like the song lyrics say. In fact, the words couldn't be more perfect for us. Hadley's in a dress, and I'm wearing dark gray —not a T-shirt, but a suit. And I want to be her prince telling her she's pretty every day for the rest of our lives. I want my kiss to make her feel like today is a fairytale. Most of all, as Hadley's standing there singing her heart out to me—*for* me—I'm in love with her.

I sure hope she's fallen for me too.

As the song comes to an end, it feels like the whole world's stopped spinning just for us, and there's a fleeting moment when I swear I could hear a pin drop in the stadium. Then the applause is a clap of thunder, everyone on their feet hooting and hollering for Hadley.

She tips her chin, her eyes warm and wonderful, as they bore into mine. I pat my jacket pocket where a four-carat diamond is waiting for me to declare my love for her in front of everyone. We're both expecting this. It's been the plan all along. Me putting my whole heart on the line.

Here's the thing, though. This moment might be fake, but the stone is genuine, and so are my feelings for Hadley. And no matter what her answer is, this is not how I want to propose.

Hadley Morgan deserves a real man down on one knee, not a movie character on display. She needs to know she's adored even when the nearest spotlight is miles away. I don't want our story to be about hashtags and news reports. Confirming or denying rumors. Staged publicity stunts. All I want is to rescue Hadley from this crazy fishbowl.

And that's exactly what I'm going to do.

As I close the last bit of distance between us, one of Hadley's students steps forward to take the guitar from her. Now it's just her standing there—open and vulnerable—the woman who taught me I can't protect everybody from everything, no matter how hard I try.

Hard things will happen in life, but there's always room for more joy. So maybe I can't control what the future might bring, but I know I want Hadley by my side for whatever comes.

No matter what.

I take the microphone from her, and another round of cheering erupts. Squaring my shoulders, I take a deep breath, and speak directly into the mic.

"Hey, Hadley Mae Morgan."

"Yes?"

"Do you wanna get out of here?"

Her eyes pop wide, and she glances around at the reporters, the TV crew, and the choir. We're in a stadium full of people, and she was expecting me to propose. But a few days ago, Hadley asked me to trust her, and I sure hope she's willing to trust me now.

When her head bobs, just a quick dip, I drop the mic to grab her hand. "Yes," she tells me. "YES!"

Then Hadley and I are running.

After only a few steps, she stumbles. She might not be limping anymore, but her ankle's not up for a race. So I move in front of her and say, "Hop on." She kicks off her shoes, hikes up her dress, and jumps onto my back. This is starting to feel an awful lot like a real Magnetron moment.

And I'm not mad about it.

As I hop off the platform with Hadley wrapped around me, the cameras move with us, trying to keep up. But I've got love on my side and Hadley on my back. She's like a pair of wings to spur me on, so I bob and weave through a crowd of spectators holding up their phones. They're taking pictures and videos of us fleeing, but they're also a barrier that lets us separate from the ZTV crew and paparazzi.

As we approach the packed parking lot, Hadley cinches in her arms and legs, and I feel like I could launch right into orbit with her on my back. "Are you all right?" I call over my shoulder.

"Never better," she chirps.

"Where's your car?"

She gives me directions, her breath warm and sweet in my ear, and I carry her past the rest of the school to a large brick building labeled Performing Arts. Around the back of the building is her little orange Volkswagen. Behind us, fireworks start going off over the stadium.

What a halftime show this turned out to be.

I hope nobody's disappointed. Especially Hadley.

I'm breathing hard now—practically hyperventilating—not just from running with a person on my back, but from the thrill of abandoning the plan and veering off course. As I set Hadley down and turn to face her, her eyes meet mine, so bright and trusting. I reach for one of her hands, entwining our fingers.

"What are we doing?" she asks.

I duck my head, gazing down at her. "Improvising."

"Ah." She tips her chin, arching a brow. "So this is just an acting exercise?"

"Far from it." Lifting my free hand, I softly trace the outline of her lips with a finger. "Do you know how much I missed you since I've been gone?" A tiny gasp escapes her, and I move an inch closer. "You're the most beautiful thing I've ever seen, and I just couldn't say what I needed to say to you in front of those cameras. I know there's a lot we still have to talk about, and so much to figure out, but I also know I want to make this work. With you." My mouth's gone dry as a hay bale, so I swallow hard. "I see a future for us, Hads. And all I want is to—"

"Goober, wait."

Whoa. My heart starts to pound. "I can't," I say. "I won't. I mean every word I'm—"

"Just kiss me."

"What?" A laugh puffs across my lips.

"Please," she whimpers, and I suck in a breath so hot, it's like I'm inhaling a waterfall of lava.

As I gather Hadley to me, my eyes pin hers. "If I kiss you now, it's for real. Forever."

I pause, giving her a chance to back out if this is all just a fantasy. If I'm only dreaming.

Instead she nods.

Hadley Morgan wants this too.

My lungs are close to exploding, and my insides are about to join them. In slow motion we move together, and I press one featherlight kiss on her honeyed lips. Then we breathe into each other. Sweetness. Heat. Desire. Everything I've been holding inside since I first came to Harvest Hollow. Since she told Pippa no, and I realized how strong she's become.

And all I want is to be the one she wants to be strong alongside. The one she wants to give herself to. The one she'll be linked with for eternity.

From around the other side of the building, we hear a group of people approaching. They're cackling and jostling and loud.

"We need to go," Hadley says under her breath, but it occurs to me we have a problem.

"You don't have your keys."

She reaches down and makes a jingly set of keys appear from her dress like magic. "Pockets," she whispers, and a soft laugh spills out of her.

"You're incredible."

"I know," she says. "Don't forget it."

We scramble into the car, me in the driver's seat, her sitting next to me. Hadley buckles her seat belt. "This was not how I saw tonight going, but you're definitely bringing adventure and spontaneity to my life."

As I start up the car and drive away from Harvest High, we both start laughing, and we keep on laughing all the way across town. I don't know exactly what I'm going to say to Hadley when we stop.

But I do know exactly where I'm taking her.

Chapter Forty-Four

HADLEY

James drives us to Harvest Farms, the place where Sam took the very first pictures and videos of HadLink. He parks in the same spot as before, and we grab hands again, silently creeping along the edge of the farm. This part of the property is dark now, except for the moon and the stars and some scattered lights coming from inside the corn maze.

They have things set up for a haunted maze tonight, but they won't start selling tickets or letting anyone in until after the football game.

James and I sneak in through the back entrance like we did last time, and it seems like we've lived a lifetime since them. But when we get to the stack of hay bales where I jumped on top of him, the way I felt that day comes rushing back.

James comes from behind to give me a boost, lifting me up high enough to sit on the top of the hay. As I turn and settle in, his hands still grip my waist. His grasp is firm, and his strength stirs something in me. All I want is to be what he desires.

To be his.

"Hadley. I—" His voice catches, and I'm helpless against the hitch in his breath. It's the most irresistible thing, seeing a man the whole world adores looking at you like you're the only one he wants.

"We've got a weird road ahead of us, don't we?" I glance at a giant fake spider hanging from a corn stalk. "Like ... even weirder than this haunted maze."

My perch on the bale puts me slightly above him, and he moves into me, burying his face in my neck. "I don't care," he murmurs. "I'm past caring about anything but you."

My throat's on fire now, and I'd probably agree to live in this corn maze permanently if I could be with him. "James."

He pulls back to gaze into my eyes. "Hadley. I'm in love with—"

"Wait," I interrupt, my heart doing backflips like an Olympic gymnast. Once I hear those words, I'll never be able to unhear them, or return to a time when I wasn't loved by the best man I've ever known. It's a precious moment I want to savor.

But the truth is, I love James back. With every fiber of my being, every wisp of my soul. The part of me that is here on earth, and the part that's eternal. Beyond this body.

It's all for him.

Without another word, I swoop down to capture his mouth with mine. Our kiss is hot and urgent, and his lips are greedy, erasing all thoughts of logic and reason or resistance I might've had. I'm nothing but a bundle of nerve endings sitting on a hay bale in a haunted corn maze at Harvest Farms.

He shifts just an inch, and we both suck in air, a sweet surrender to something as normal as breathing. I feel like I've been shot out of a submarine, submerged and sinking. Drowning in his arms.

I run my fingers through his hair, stroking his beard, and soaking up the feeling of being cherished. After a moment of quiet, he fixes his eyes on mine.

"I love you, Hadley."

He said it.

"I love you, too."

He raises one thick brow. "So what are we going to do about this, then?"

"Hmm." I tap my chin, considering the best answer. "I guess we could start with me meeting your dogs."

His eyes dance. "They're going to love you," he says. "My mom will too. But not as much as I do."

A grin splits my face. "It's kind of hard to compete with this kind of muchness."

His eyes go wide. "That reminds me." He hauls off his jacket laying it across the hay bale, and begins to unbutton his dress shirt. I haven't seen his bare chest in more than five years. Not since we got in a water fight in the quad at CU and I tossed a bucket over his head. He'd stripped off his T-shirt and I just about fainted at the sight of his abs. But this is different now. This is the man I love.

"What are you doing?"

"Showing you something," he says, shrugging free of one sleeve. Half his torso is exposed now, a ripple of moon-drenched muscle from stomach to chest to shoulder.

"This isn't fair," I moan. "I can't fully appreciate you like this while I'm sitting next to a spooky spider."

He chuckles. "I'll put my shirt back on soon enough. I just want you to see this." He turns, and I gasp at the sight of the spread of angel wings tattooed across his back. "For Tommy," he says.

"Oh, James." My heart swells at the deep, brotherly love etched onto his body.

"I used to be so worried people would ask about the story behind the tattoo," he says. "I never let my back face the camera when my shirt was off. I told myself the caution was necessary. But I always felt a little like I was hiding Tommy. So I'm done with all that now. Everything's out in the open. The freedom feels amazing. Almost as amazing as you."

"Does it hurt?"

"Not anymore." His smile slips sideways. "I got this a while ago. But even when the ink was fresh … it was a good kind of hurt. If that makes sense."

"I think it's beautiful." I reach out and press a palm to the smooth skin of his shoulder.

"Then I hope you'll like this one too." He slides all the way out of his other sleeve to reveal a fresh bandage on the swell of his bicep. Peeling the bandage back slowly, he shows me a second tattoo. It's slick and shiny with some kind of ointment. An artist's abstract rendering of an apple. Across the center is the word *muchness*.

I gasp.

"I got this Wednesday night. For you," he says, turning to face me again. "Like an apple for the teacher. And also because you always smell like apples. And maybe because I'll never forget the look on your face when you fed me that apple slice on Boney Mountain."

For a moment, I'm too overwhelmed with emotion to speak. Then I finally find my voice. "It's perfect," I say. "You're perfect."

"No, not by a long shot. But I *am* James Lincoln. Thanks to you." As he gently reattaches the bandage and slips back into his shirt, my eyes fill with tears from the sweetness of his statement, not because I'm going to miss his bare abs.

Mostly.

"Come here." I pull him toward me so I can help him with his buttons. When the last one's done, I tip my head. "Can I ask you my question for tonight now?"

He bobs his head. "Shoot."

"And you promise to be honest?"

His Adam's apple dips. "Always."

"Good." I flash him a smile. "Will you go to homecoming with me?"

Epilogue

JAMES

The streetlights are on and the moon is full, and I'm pacing inside the atrium next to the Harvest Hollow post office. Both my hands are stuffed inside my pockets. Only one of them is holding a ring.

It's a brilliant-cut solitaire with two baguettes I had designed just for Hadley. Not the four-carat diamond the sponsors wanted me to give her a year ago. Luckily three hundred sixty-five days never flew so fast.

It's been one wild ride.

As it turns out, the footage of Hadley's choir serenading me at halftime went viral. Quick. After Taylor Swift shared the video, Pippa got in touch with her people and arranged for Hadley to meet Taylor. Then I surprised them both by having my friend Violet join them. Violet's the little girl I met at Highland Hospital.

Magnetron's biggest fan.

Inviting her whole family to meet T-Swift was a no-brainer. And I think playing the guitar alongside Taylor and Violet in a private room with zero cameras almost made my real girlfriend explode with happiness.

By *real girlfriend*, I mean Hadley, because there's nothing fake about that woman. And our relationship's as genuine as they get.

Since last fall, we've had to juggle plenty of distance, annoying tabloids, and two dogs who don't like airplanes. Still, we're committed to sharing and talking and working things out. We care enough to trust and learn from one another. With Hadley by my side, I've grown more in the past twelve months than I have in a long time.

Maybe ever.

And make no mistake—Hadley Morgan has blossomed too.

Since she opted not to compete on *America's Hidden Talent,* the producers invited her to be a vocal coach for contestants. She said she'd participate for any seasons filmed during the summer. That way she can help the singers on the show and still teach her classes at Harvest High.

I don't think the principal at Stony Creek will ever get over it.

As for my mom, she's found a whole new gig of her own now too. She runs a sprawling ranch for rescue dogs just outside of Asheville. She and her team travel the country finding the least adoptable dogs to bring to the ranch for a stretch of rehabilitation before they go to their forever homes.

She claims to understand exactly what the dogs need—a little time and patience, plus a whole lot of grace and love. Since that was the recipe for my mother's comeback, I'm not inclined to disagree.

Good old Pippa is opening her own talent agency with a little help from yours truly. In light of her tenacity, my investment is sure to pay off. The woman managed to bring Hadley and me together against all odds, so finding other diamonds in the rough to polish up should be an easier challenge than we were.

Speaking of diamonds.

I see Hadley through the window. Her dad's escorting her to the building. It's after hours, just like the first time his daughter brought me here. Only now he's bringing her to me. I was aiming for a surprise, but Hadley probably knows something's up.

She's smart, and she knows me so well.

When they come through the entrance, she's already scanning the place. They find me waiting in front of the hall that leads to the clocktower. When our eyes finally meet, her whole face breaks into a smile.

My favorite smile of all time.

"Hey there, Vise-Count." She dips into a curtsey. "Fancy meeting you here."

I tip a pretend hat. "Oh. Haven't you heard? All the cool Regency-era superheroes hang out next to the post office."

"*Do* they now?"

"Indeed." I nod. "But most of them aren't allowed to climb the clocktower."

Hadley's father chuckles. "Just the ones who have special permission from the postmaster."

That's right. After a wildly successful premier of *Enforcer's Endgame*, Youngblood Studios offered me the role of The Vise-Count. Hadley and I talked, and we decided I could do a whole lot of good with the money I'd earn. So I signed a three-movie deal. And when those are over, we'll reevaluate. But I'd be fine hanging up my cravat.

As it turns out, the only thing audiences love more than a truly brokenhearted hero is a man who's truly, madly, deeply obsessed with his soulmate. That's me. I'm that man.

So much for Andrew's test groups.

I may not see myself as a hero, but I'm still playing one, at least for now. Part of my contract includes approval of filming times and locations, so we can plan around Hadley's work schedule. That way she'll be able to join me on set when she's free, and I'll be in Harvest Hollow between shoots.

In the meantime, I'm building a new house just outside of town, another step closer to my dream.

A bit of farmland and a bunch of dogs. Space to run and fresh air to breathe. Raising up a family with a good woman. I'll never leave their sides. Never give them cause to doubt my faithfulness.

Never do anything but love them with my whole soul.

Hadley approaches with her father now, and I offer her my arm. "Shall we?"

Ray Morgan pats me on the back. "I still can't believe you got my daughter to go all the way up there."

He's talking about the clocktower.

Hadley and I climbed to the top last year right after the homecoming dance. It was the only place in town we could escape the paparazzi.

Fortunately, things have died down since then. When you're a couple without much drama, reporters lose interest. And that's just the way we like it.

Together, Hadley and I make our way up the stairs now, step by step to the clockface and bells. She must be expecting a proposal at this point. But I've still got one surprise up my sleeve.

As part of my preparation for the role of The Vise-Count, I've been learning to play an English guitar. I'm absolutely terrible, but I like to think it's the thought that counts.

When Hadley spies Dolores leaning up against the wall, she draws in a deep breath.

I let go of her hand and pick up the guitar. Then I perform the world's worst version of "In My Life."

While my voice cracks and the guitar moans under some truly awful strumming, Hadley bites back laughter. Her eyes sparkle at me until I reach the final chord.

"I'm sorry," she blurts, swallowing a grin. "But that was the sweetest thing ever."

"I know." I offer her a crooked smile.

Then I drop to a knee.

Pulling the ring from my pocket, I feel my hands begin to shake. Not because I'm afraid of Hadley's answer. But because I'm gazing at my forever.

"I may be the worst at singing," I begin, "but I promise to be the best at cherishing you. And like the song says, I've loved other people and places—"

“And dogs,” she interjects.

“Yes, and dogs.” I smile up at her. “But above all else, in this life, I love you more, Hadley Mae Morgan. In fact, I love you muchness.”

“So muchness!” she blurts. Then she takes a giddy little hop when I clasp her hand.

“And tonight, with all of Harvest Hollow below us, I’m finally the one with the question.” We lock eyes. “Will you be my wife?”

Hadley nods and laughs through her tears. I stand to slip the ring on her finger.

“James Porter Lincoln,” she says, “I thought you’d never ask.”

The End.

***

Now don’t miss the rest of the Sweater Weather series!

You can find all seven cozy fall-themed books on Amazon!

Emma St. Clair — Just Don’t Fall

Melanie Jacobson — The Fall Back Plan

Courtney Walsh — Can’t Help Falling

Julie Christianson — Faking the Fall

Carina Taylor — Easy as Pie

Savannah Scott — A Not So Fictional Fall

Jenny Proctor — Absolutely Not in Love

Bonus Scene!

Want to read a bonus epilogue following HadLink's happily ever after?

Grab it FREE when you sign up for my email list.

(This super-swoony scene contains spoilers from the book, so definitely read Faking the fall first!)

You can also find me on Instagram—I hang out there every day—or email me at julie@juliechristianson.com.

Let's have some fun!

Also by Julie Christianson

The Time of Your (Love) Life Series:

That Time I Kissed My Brother's Best Friend:

A Sweet Romantic Comedy

That Time I Kissed The Groomsman Grump:

A Sweet Romantic Comedy

That Time I Kissed My Beachfront Boss:

A Sweet Romantic Comedy

That Time We Kissed Under the Mistletoe

A Sweet Romantic Comedy

The Apple Valley Love Stories Series:

The Mostly Real McCoy: A Sweet Romantic Comedy (Apple Valley Love Stories Book 1)

My Own Best Enemy: A Sweet Romantic Comedy (Apple Valley Love Stories Book 2)

Pretending I Love Lucy: A Sweet Romantic Comedy (Apple Valley Love Stories Book 3)

The Even Odder Couple: A Sweet Romantic Comedy (Apple Valley Love Stories Book 4)

Jill Came Tumbling: A Sweet Romantic Comedy

(An Apple Valley Love Stories Novella)

His Third Second Chance

(An Apple Valley Love Stories Novelette)

The Apple Valley Love Stories Collection:

A Complete Sweet Romantic Comedy Series

Acknowledgments

My first heart-felt thank you goes to my beloved family for mustering up the requisite patience to love me all these years. You're smart, kind, hilarious, and also the reason I write romcoms.

(*Sizzle Kiss? Name of my band.*)

To the incredible indie author community: When I started this journey, I had no idea how supportive a group of humans could be, and I'm grateful every day that this job allows me to work among you good people. You are all the best.

To anyone who just finished *Faking the Fall*: I've dreamed about book-lovers reading my words since I was a little girl. I also dreamed about showing up to school in my underwear. So I'm very glad YOU won this round of "Julie's Dreams Do Come True!"

To those of you who've been reading my books for a while now (some of whom have already become dear friends IRL and on Bookstagram) please know you are the reason I do this every day. We laugh. We smile. We get teary-eyed. We laugh some more. Let's keep doing that. Deal? Deal.

To the amazing Sweater Weather team: I adore you guys so much. I don't know how I got lucky enough to be a part of your crew, but this entire collaboration was a joy. Kiki, Courtney, Melanie,

Carina, Patty, and Jenny — you are marvelous, and I'm in awe of your storytelling.

And finally, to Julie of the Past: You didn't give up. Thank you, thank you, thank you.

Love,
Julie of the Now

About the Author

Julie Christianson is a former high school English teacher and current romcom addict living in the suburbs of Los Angeles.

A lapsed marathon runner, Julie loves her hilarious family, her two crazy rescue dogs, and cracking up at her own jokes. Her goal is to write stories that make you laugh out loud, fall in love, and live happily ever after.

Learn more about her books at juliechristianson.com

Made in United States
Orlando, FL
19 September 2023